WIDOW'S TALE

Maureen A. Miller

PROLOGUE

Serena Murphy squinted into the wind, searching cliffs lashed by angry surf. Maine's autumn freeze wrapped her in its clutch and whipped her hair over her face.

Serena was looking for a body.

The maelstrom assaulting the deck of O'Flanagans Tavern did not deter her. She leaned forward and gripped the rail.

A month had passed already, and each day before the dinnertime rush, Serena came out to search the cliffs for any trace of her husband, Alan, who'd been pronounced lost at sea.

Alan was dead. She was sure of that. Even the sea spoke to her, weaving a tale of his demise in the fishing boat she had urged him to repair. She was certain he was dead because he haunted her. Not as a physical ghost, but there were signs—small, intimate signals that could only be executed by Alan's malevolent spirit.

"Serena! Get in here before you catch your death of cold!"

Tempted to ignore the intrusion, Serena caught a glimpse of her part-time waitress, Rebecca, with her head stuck out the back door.

What an image she must portray to the young woman. Every night Serena stood out here, perched atop these cliffs, searching for a body. *Searching for ghosts.*

But that's not what her waitress saw. She saw a distraught widow anguished over the loss of her husband. She did not see *her*. She did not see the woman who feared Alan even after death.

It took effort, but Serena called across the wind, "I'll be right there."

Alone with the waves that crashed against the rocks below, Serena waited for pain to envelop her. She waited for heart-wrenching sobs or any raw emotion that might signal despair over the loss of her husband.

Only the bleak whistle of the wind and the somber ring of a buoy answered.

CHAPTER I

O'Flanagans was as much a tradition in the small Maine coastal village of Victory Cove as were the lobster boats and sailors that kept the establishment thriving over fifty years, and through three generations. This colonial institution was the home of Serena's childhood. It was also her legacy now that her parents had retired and moved to Florida.

Serena talked the O'Flanagans out of flying north after Alan's disappearance. Instead, she was grateful to have the pub to keep her busy. Its patrons were family in their own right, protective and loyal to the last O'Flanagan.

The heavy oak door drew shut behind Serena, locking out the bad weather with a finality that almost made her feel safe. She leaned back against it and eyed the overhead wooden beams—timber rafters permeated with the aroma of beer and lobster bisque. The scent stabilized her. She drew in another deep breath and held it until the trembling in her limbs subsided.

"Yo, Rena, are you going to keep a thirsty man waiting, just hanging around here like a long-haired dog on a hot summer day?"

In this place, there was no time for emotion. Alan was dead. He would not hurt her anymore.

But finding his body would have made it seem real.

One last breath and Serena hoisted forward. "Thirsty my ass, Coop," she chastised Cooper Littlefield with affection as she ducked under the service panel to emerge behind the oak bar.

Serena eyed the empty mug with an arched brow. "Seems to me I just filled this about five minutes ago."

"Fast and plentiful, honey."

"Yeah, yeah," she fit the glass beneath the lager tap, "just like your women."

Serena's smile prompted Cooper's worn old face to crack a grin, revealing a prominent gold-capped tooth. White hair was buried beneath a knitted black cap and gray stubble framed a congenial face. Eyes set in a permanent squint studied her.

"Well, that woman out there—" he flung a gnarled hand towards a window overlooking the Atlantic, "was a bitch today." Coop's hand snapped back and wound over his mouth.

Serena shook her head.

"You can't be afraid of everything you say around here. I'm okay, and you're right, she's a bitch every day. I know."

"Any news?"

"No." She clenched her trembling fingers. "No news."

Serena turned and caught a glimpse of her reflection in the mirror behind the bar. Haunted eyes stared back at her. She shook her head against the image, and before twisting back, dredged up a smile for Coop to ease his worry.

The old sailor lifted the beer to his chapped lips as she could swear that he murmured, "You're a lot better off."

Every day, Serena prayed for news. But nothing had changed since yesterday, or the day before that, or last week. The police made their judgment based on Alan Murphy's boat washing up on shore, soon followed by other personal effects found scattered along Victory Cove's rugged coast.

There was one hell of a storm the afternoon Alan set out to sea. Most questioned why he went out at all. But the folk of Victory Cove had never taken to Alan Murphy. His slick, educated, condescending mannerisms were unwelcome in this small blue-collar town. Still, they kept their aversion to themselves because they loved Serena. She belonged to them.

Serena reached across the bar to swipe under Coop's mug, throwing a fresh napkin down beneath it.

"Rena, honey, can you get me anothah?" Harriet Morgan's voice boomed from the far end of the L-shaped bar.

Harriet exhaled into her clenched fist, wriggling her fingers to entice circulation. As she approached, the woman nodded at Cooper and then unwound her scarf to reveal a hefty secondary chin. "You didn't pick up those extra traps, Coop."

"So you closed your tackle shop," he muttered, "and came down to O'Flanagans to bring 'em to me?" Coop's narrowed eye caught the twenty-ounce mug sitting before the robust woman. "And the thought never occurred to you that you might tip back a few while waiting here."

"I don't need your sorry ass as an excuse. You know damn well I got me a keg undah the counter at the shop." Harriet's cheeks were unnaturally rosy, and in just the right light, her gray hair appeared blond.

"Weather's hell out there today," Harriet rambled on. "I got no business, so why not come down and drink in good company." She tipped her head at Serena.

Coop snorted as some of the white froth caught on his mustache. "Well, I'm flattered, Harriet, I really am, but the missus has been good to me." A quick grin flashed a golden tooth. "I'll die a loyal man."

"I ain't talking about you, Bittyfield, so shut that mouth before I come over there and shut if for you."

Serena laughed. It felt good to watch Cooper and Harriet in their verbal volley.

The door to the tavern opened. Wind penetrated the bar, propelling napkins off the polished surface to spiral in erratic bundles on the floor. For a suspended moment a shadowy stranger stood eclipsed by the harsh sky outside. The door slammed shut and left the brooding figure to glare at the proprietor of O'Flanagans.

"Well, if it isn't the grieving widow."

Serena's chuckle died on her lips. She stared at the tall visitor with his windswept dark hair and eyes the color of a turbulent gale. It was as if the Atlantic had come to life in the form of a man and then surged into her tavern to rein its force upon her. Her breath caught when he stepped forward.

"Hello, Sis."

The stranger slanted a glimpse at Coop's scowl and Harriet's combative pose, but the intense gray eyes swiftly returned to their target. The force of that stare made Serena swallow and clutch the counter.

"Brett?" Her voice was a hoarse whisper.

"You remember me?"

Was there amusement to Brett's tone? His slight grin beguiled Serena with memories.

"Is there something we can do for you, sir?" Coop bristled, his chest puffing up on a wheeze.

Brett Murphy acknowledged the question with a flicker of his glance and then approached the oak bar, splaying his hands on it.

"I'm looking for my brother."

"Alan—he's…"

"He's what, Mrs. Murphy? Are you going to tell me that he's dead?"

Serena recoiled, and were it not for the shelf behind her she would have stumbled backwards to flee the judgmental gaze. Instead, her Irish temper surfaced.

"That's what they tell me."

All the pain of the month-long search for Alan's body–all the despair by the lack of effort on behalf of the police–all the nights of phantom sounds whispering to her, each shadow holding the promise or threat that he might reappear, poured into her retort.

An unnamed emotion flickered through Brett's eyes. Was it regret? God help her, was it still desire? The storm settled again as black eyebrows sank into a frown.

"Can I get a beer?"

Serena hesitated and drew from the spout Brett indicated with a pitch of his head.

Undaunted by the stranger, Harriet rounded the corner and approached him with hands on hips.

"So you're Alan Murphy's brother." Harriet's gaze scoured up and down his frame and finally narrowed into a scowl. "You don't much look like him."

Serena silently concurred. Alan had dark hair and eyes that were black. His build had been lankier, not revealing the raw strength that stood before her now.

Brett tipped back his mug for a hearty swallow and then set it down with an embittered smirk.

"Why do I feel like this pack is going to drag me out back and lynch me?"

"They don't take kindly to strangers." Serena challenged.

If her brother in-law had an issue to take up with her that was fine, but if he decided to drag in those closest to her, he had a hell of a battle on his hands.

Brett must have heard the aggression in her voice. He nearly smiled, or was it a trick of the light against those silver eyes?

"Do you have a moment to talk in private?" he asked. "I just met with the police. I feel like I'm getting the run-around." His eyebrow inched up. "Or maybe they just don't want to talk to a city boy."

The spoonful of cereal Serena had for lunch churned in her stomach. She settled a hand over it and wished she could flee out the back door to her apartment upstairs.

Instead, Serena attempted a reassuring nod at Coop and then sent a wary glance at Harriet.

"It's okay," she soothed them both.

But by no means did she feel confident that everything would be okay.

Aware of Brett's eyes on her back, Serena had trouble breathing. She managed courteous smiles and nods to her patrons as she moved through the dining room, but as soon as she reached a secluded booth in the back corner and watched Brett's long body tuck in across from her, a gasp dusted her lips.

"I'm sorry, Brett," she rushed out.

The sincerity of that statement ripped through her. But what was it that she was sorry for? Having to talk to Brett about his brother's death? Having to face Alan's death herself? Or was she sorry that in her deepest thoughts, she felt safer now that Alan was gone?

"Sorry?" Brett's voice was husky.

"When Alan—when Alan—" Even now, Serena struggled with the word that followed. It all seemed so surreal.

"When it happened, I couldn't find any of you. Your parents are in Europe somewhere," her eyes locked with his, "and you," she wavered, "well I haven't seen you since the wedding."

Ten years ago.

Brett hadn't changed much. He must be what, thirty-six now? His hair was still a rich, dark shade and his olive complexion made those gray eyes appear striking. *Exotic.* Her gaze dropped to the sharp slash of his jaw, framing a mouth that frowned more often than it smiled.

"The wedding was a long time ago, Serena." Brett's voice hadn't changed either—nor its affect on her. "You haven't tried to find me," he hesitated, "you haven't once tried to talk to me."

Was Brett referring to her attempts to reach him about his brother, or about the past decade in general?

"You are not an easy man to trace." She sought composure. "I called some of the major broker houses in Boston, but—are you still a broker?"

In the absence of his response, her fingers began to tremble. What didn't help was Brett's long look—an encompassing stare. Time had done nothing to diminish the impact of Brett Murphy.

Serena withdrew her fingers beneath the table and onto her lap, and then she scrambled for something more to add.

"I worked in London for awhile," he spared her. "Paid my dues there." An amused twitch tugged on his lip. "You know, they don't call us stock brokers anymore. We're FC's. Financial consultants." The twitch was gone.

"I came back to New York last year." Brett continued. "About two months ago, Alan's calls just suddenly stopped. That might not seem odd to you, but he used to phone me constantly. Always woke me up with the damn time change." A muscle in his jaw tensed. "So, the fact that they just stopped—it wasn't like him."

A glass fell over on a nearby table and Serena's body jerked.

"Two months ago—" *how could she even guess what Alan had been up to?* "He—he was busy—"

"Two months ago, Alan was alive." Brett injected.

The detached words hit her in the stomach.

"Brett, I—I still don't want to believe it happened," she whispered. "I still look for him, even though the police say it's over, I still look."

Because until she found Alan's body, he would continue to haunt her.

"Well, now you're not looking alone, Serena."

If the statement was meant to comfort her, the steely set of Brett's eyes didn't express it.

"Look," he began. "It's been ten years. You seem awkward around me. There's nothing to feel awkward about. Nothing happened. It was just—"

The inability to finish that sentence proved Brett wrong, because it was indeed awkward.

Brett hastened on. "I'm here for one reason, and once I find out what happened to Alan, I'll be gone."

Caught off guard by the warmth that momentarily infused his words, Serena swallowed, "Brett, I wish I knew more. You have no idea how much I wish I knew more. He was so young, he was—"

"I know what Alan was. I won't portray him as a saint, but character flaws aren't an excuse to be dead. I'm not going anywhere, Serena." Brett's tone was resolved. "Not until I find out what happened to Alan. I don't know what you've done so far. I don't know what efforts the police have put out, but I won't let it go. I can't."

Brett reached across the table, and had her hands been resting there, she wondered if he would have splayed his atop them.

"I have to know what happened to my brother."

It was well past midnight when Serena sat alone at the bar, frowning at her reflection in the mirror. Pictures of friends and patrons were taped along its frame just below the row of freshly cleaned glasses hung upside down. Some still dripped water onto the antique cash register, its brass face tarnished from years of such abuse.

Brett had not stayed long, but it was long enough to contemplate the grim resolve in his eyes. Had he convicted her as his brother's murderer?

Serena cupped her forehead in her palms and wondered if Brett had grown that cynical. From Alan she had come to expect that look of aversion. But Brett, even though it had been ten years, she could still feel the heated glance he'd given her just five minutes before she married his brother. Such was the intensity in his eyes—she'd nearly tossed her fate to whim—nearly given it all up, just for the chance that he might touch her.

Nearly.

Fearful of the night, Serena hastened up the external staircase. Lately she had taken to leaving the living room light on so as not to come home to complete darkness.

The brass lamp cast a soft glow over the mantle of a stone fireplace, its innards charred from years of use. A patchwork throw rug covered the wood floor in front of twin loveseats positioned L-shaped before the fireplace. Reluctant to enter the shadows of the kitchen, Serena was drawn towards the lamp. She settled down on the loveseat and focused on the blushing shade.

Drifting into a restless sleep, as was the case every night for the past month, she woke to the sound of footsteps treading across the floorboards.

Fingernails digging into the sofa, she sprang up and stared into the shadows.

"Who's there?"

The steps resumed, heavy and deliberate, seeming to resonate from directly behind her, yet when she spun about, nothing was there but a wedge of moonlight from the window.

Talking to the entity had done little to dissuade it in the past. Serena drew herself up into the corner of the loveseat and grabbed a throw pillow against her chest to muffle her wild heartbeat.

The next assault on her senses came with the same frequency. It was the anxious sound of a child crying. The nocturnal ghost who paced around her bore little impact compared to this agonizing peal.

No. Please, no.

She pressed her face into the pillow and listened to the infant's wails. Mournful and persistent, they echoed around her in a cyclone of despair, spinning her till she lost her balance and felt reality mercifully slip away.

CHAPTER II

A tentative rap on the front door broke Serena from her tormented slumber and into the morning light. She rubbed at raw eyes and tried to focus on the silhouette behind lacey yellow curtains.

The shadow was a short one, not very intimidating. Encouraged, Serena unfolded her legs and hastened towards the door.

"I'm coming, Rebecca."

Rebecca Sorenson stood drumming her fingertips against her crossed arms. "It's about time-"

Taking stock of Serena's appearance, Rebecca shooed her back inside. "Wow, another bad night? You look like shit."

Serena ran a hand through her hair, hoisting loose the ends that had tucked into the collar of her sweater. She glanced at the short woman who evoked life with vibrant red curls, sizzling amber eyes, and a constant need to be in motion. *Firecracker* was the word that came to mind when she looked at Rebecca Sorrenson.

Conversely, Serena felt old and drained. She sank back onto the loveseat.

"I didn't get much sleep."

Rebecca was already in the kitchen, slamming cabinet doors in a loud effort to make coffee.

"Well that much is obvious. Have you considered seeing someone?"

Seeing someone. A shrink. The final confirmation that she was losing her mind.

"No."

The rich aroma of coffee wafted through the loft as Rebecca vaulted up onto the counter and swung her legs around to face the dining room. "You can't go on like this," she scolded.

Serena closed her eyes. The wraithlike sounds never attacked during daylight. She felt safe enough for now.

"I'll be fine, just let me take a shower and then I'll head downstairs."

"Simon's down there prancing around like a wounded peacock," Rebecca said. "Squawking about the lack of respect he gets, and the fact that we should start putting some—what did he call them—*nuveau* dishes on the menu." The redhead launched off the counter with two mugs in hand.

"So that was Brett Murphy?" she continued. "How long did he stay? Too long, huh? He's not bad on the eye, but temperament-wise he seems like a real pisser."

Serena hoisted herself up and accepted the fact that there would be no rest this morning. She reached for the coffee.

"He's understandably concerned about his brother."

Ever the voice of reason.

So why was she losing her mind?

"Hmmmph, he looked like he just wanted to pick a fight."

"Like his brother?" The words slipped before Serena could check them. She caught Rebecca's brow wrinkle.

"Alan never struck me as the hostile type." As if to confirm this, Rebecca glanced around the room for a picture of the man.

Serena followed her gaze until it landed on the silver-framed photo of their wedding. Alan Murphy's smile was handsome, his grip around her waist, possessive.

Serena clutched the mug with both hands and stared at the picture. To women in general, Alan Murphy could hide his dark side—so much so, that he was quite the charmer. It was only natural that Rebecca would succumb, but it still felt like a tiny stab of betrayal.

"I have to talk to Simon." Serena changed the subject. "I don't know if he's started ordering the food for Thanksgiving."

"You better. He mentioned something about serving Dove in grape sauce."

"Uggh," Serena smiled with disgust, grateful to her cheery friend for helping her to retain a small fragment of sanity. "Thanks Becky."

Rebecca reached forward for a brief hug. "You'll be okay. It's all going to be okay. It'll just take time."

Perhaps what Rebecca said was true. Perhaps in time she might begin to feel normal again.

But having Brett Murphy here was not going to make the healing process go any quicker.

"Order turkeys, potatoes, green beans, and carrots. We'll make the gravy and rolls from scratch. That's it. Everything else we have here."

"But everybody can have that meal at home on Thanksgiving." Simon Turner whined. "They come here for something different."

Serena shook her head at the lanky man and then rifled through her list of suppliers.

Not to be undaunted, Simon persisted. "I'll compromise. We'll have turkey as an entrée, but let me offer another dish as an alternative."

With a quick nudge of her hip, Serena closed the drawer and glanced up at Simon. He was in his late- twenties, tall, with pale blond hair that was thin enough to hint he would be bald by the time he hit thirty. The blue eyes of a wannabe businessman pleaded with her as she staged reluctant compliance for her maitre de.

"One dish." She held a single finger up for reinforcement.

Simon gripped her forearms. "Great!" His enthusiasm vanished as his near invisible eyebrows furrowed together. "My God, that's only a week and a half away—I've *got* to get going."

What have I been saying all along?

Simon Turner was not from Victory Cove, he was from Portland. He was also gay.

Sometimes, she wondered with a twitch of the lips, which of the two bothered Cooper Littlefield more.

It was ten thirty. When the door to the tavern swung open, Serena assumed it would be Rebecca back from her morning job at the Day Care Center. Instead, the dominant silhouette of Brett Murphy filled the frame. For the span of a breath, their eyes locked.

Blood pumped in her ears. She cleared her throat and reached for a coffee mug, holding it up.

"Coffee?"

Brett crossed over to one of the barstools. He nodded at the offer and twisted to study the tavern.

"So where are you staying?" Serena inquired.

"The Vacation Inn down by the Interstate," he said.

She bit back the offer to one of several rooms upstairs. Judging from the grim look on Brett's face, he probably would not have accepted.

"Have the police been any more helpful with you?" *Than with me?*

"Not particularly." Brett fiddled with the handle of the mug, dark eyebrows furrowing in anger—or anxiety.

She couldn't tell which.

Ten years. Ten years, and Serena was still like a fist to the gut.

Brett saw everything. He saw the patches of blue skin beneath her eyes, and the fatigue in her stance. He caught the furtive motion of slim fingers as they toyed with the hem of her sweater, and he glimpsed the dark hue of fear in her stare.

Was it mourning he saw there?

He detected tiny wrinkles of pain at the corners of Serena's eyes, and maturity in her expression he had not seen the last time he was with her. She was no longer the innocent little girl he'd wanted to steal away from his brother. She was a woman now.

Christ, he thought it had been a fluke. He was still young then. He could have written off the affect Serena had on him as plain old lust. But, lust was for the youth, and he was *no* youth.

A desire that transpired a decade ago would not overrule his senses, though. He was here for a reason. His brother was dead. It could have been an innocent boating accident as everyone else claimed, but he doubted it.

"Why did it take you a month to reach me?" Brett sought stability by going on the offense. "You couldn't have been trying that hard."

Serena's lips trembled as he tried not to stare at them.

"Except for the few scraps of information Alan would share with me about you over the years," she said, "I had no idea where you were, Brett. No address, no phone number. A friend of Alan's in Boston finally looked up your name and located you in New York.

"Okay, look," Brett's hands splayed on the rim of the bar, real close to her fingers. "You're going to have to help me out here. I need to know what happened, Serena. I need to find out what happened to Alan."

Brett tried not to notice Serena shudder, or the way her eyes were riveted on him, unblinking.

Was it possible that his troubled sister in-law had finally been pushed too far? Could she have been pushed enough to kill?

He couldn't afford to let Serena get under his skin. He had to stay subjective. He had to find the truth. No matter their differences, no matter his opinion of Alan, Alan was family.

"Look," Brett said. "Forget the police report. Why don't *you* tell me what happened?"

He waited for Serena's response, but she remained mute.

"Serena," he paused until her eyes jumped back to his, "tell me what happened."

What happened with what?

My relationship with Alan? The demise of that relationship? Or the demise of Alan himself?

Serena felt cold again.

"That day?"

"Yes." Brett's expression was unreadable.

That day.

It was no different than any other day in October. Alan had been away for almost two months. His long absences, no matter the legitimacy of the latest excuse, were growing more and more suspicious. Sadly, she had stopped caring whether he was around or not. Each time Alan returned to Victory Cove, his attitude was abrasive, his mannerisms secretive, and any probing into his whereabouts was met with open hostility.

That day.

Serena was in the kitchen upstairs washing the dishes when the familiar heavy tread of Alan's boots ascended the staircase. She glanced at the calendar, calculating the length of time he had been gone. He walked in and did not even venture a glance in her direction.

Two individual souls they were. Children who had rushed into a marriage Alan soon grew tired of. Serena often wondered what prevented him from asking for a divorce.

For her, it was a product of upbringing, growing up in the idyllic warmth of her parents' marriage. Anything less than what her parents shared, Serena would have considered a failure. *For better or for worse.* Yet, the fact that Alan chose to stay away from her for months at a time, carrying on a business that was clandestine at best, threatened her resolve.

Serena gazed onto the deck and the silver, choppy Atlantic beyond it. The breakers were rough, but not like that day.

"Alan came home around two in the afternoon." Her voice was distant. "He said he was taking our boat out."

Serena felt no need to let Brett know that it had been two months since she last saw her husband.

"I reminded him that the *Stew* needed repairs," she attested. "I had been trying to get him to work on it for awhile, but he never seemed to have the time." *Never seemed to be around.* "And then there was the weather. A storm was coming in. The tavern was packed because the lobstermen were staying inland. Alan said he'd be back before it hit." She flinched. "That was the last I saw of him."

Her gaze fell and her throat constricted. It was the closest she came to grief.

She *did* grieve for Alan Murphy. She never wished for it to end like this, to see someone so young lose his life.

But her grief began long before Alan died.

"Actually, Harriet was one of the last people to see him," Serena added. "Even she tried talking him out of taking the *Stew* out, but Alan didn't want to hear about it."

Brett's gaze revealed nothing.

"What was so damn important that it had to be done that moment?" he asked.

"Alan wasn't big on sharing his business practices." Serena's voice faltered. "I don't know."

Okay, Brett believed her on that account. His brother was very secretive.

But he shouldn't be dead.

Brett had to look away from her. He stared at the nicks on the bar, scars that had been glossed over with replenished lacquer, and tried to get the memory of Serena in her wedding dress out of his head.

They had met several times leading up to that day, with nothing more than civil pleasantries exchanged. But for some reason that day was the catalyst. As ill-timed as it was, Brett chose that event to make his statement. Perhaps it was the champagne-colored dress, or the cascade of shimmering cinnamon hair across freckled shoulders–but the sight of Serena took his breath and his ethics away.

They ran into each other in the hall prior to the ceremony. Serena grabbed his hand with the spontaneity of genuine delight. "I'm so glad you could make it here for this, Brett."

Brett's gaze dropped to her hand. He stared until he noticed her fingers start to tremble. He saw the diamond and cursed.

"Are you sure about this?"

Either the question itself or his husky tone must have startled her. Serena snapped her fingers back.

"Sure about what?"

"Alan." He felt tension creep into his neck. "Are you sure about this marriage?" *How to ask this of someone you barely knew?*

Her mouth opened, but it took a moment for sound to come out. "I'm not sure what you're asking?"

"I'm not sure either, Serena. But I know how my brother is, and I just, I just—" he struggled. "You should just know that maybe there are others who have feelings for you. Maybe you shouldn't rush into this."

Serena did not blink.

"Others?" she whispered.

Brett took that final step. He touched her arms and felt her breath dust his lips as he lowered his head. He hesitated with a thousand alarms going off inside his head, and then he brushed her mouth with his.

For one moment there was shock, followed by the sharp pang of pleasure. They both jumped back, staring at each other.

"Serena, I—"

"Aaah, I see you've found my brother."

Alan Murphy appeared, his fingers descending on Serena's shoulder, their grip reddening the pale flesh.

Brett almost groaned aloud at the recollection.

"Brett," Serena's voice jerked him back to the present. "When was the last time you talked to Alan? Did he say anything," she floundered, "anything at all?"

And now, Serena, the woman, was asking him to recall the last conversation he had with his brother. Brett recalled it. Every single word. Alan's declaration that he and Serena had been expecting a child. Alan's horror that Serena didn't want that child——that it would interfere with O'Flanagans. Even now, Brett could hear his brother's bitter voice as he chronicled Serena's visit to the clinic to have it *taken care of.*

Looking at this beautiful, haunted creature, Brett found the story inconceivable. The harsh fact remained, though. He didn't really know his sister in-law well enough to dispute Alan.

"He told me what happened." Brett's voice was hoarse. "Why, Serena?"

Serena grabbed a dishrag to conceal her shaking hands.

Oh God, now Brett's behavior made sense. It would be brutal to say that Alan hated her. She didn't believe her husband was capable of such an ardent emotion—but he had grown tired of her. When he was not inflicting that rage towards her, he would weave tales to anyone that would listen. Tales of her frigidity, her infidelity, anything Alan's malicious mind could conjure. Fortunately, in Victory Cove there were very few to listen or give credence to his tirades. But Brett was fresh bait, and his *brother*. Alan would cash in on the allegiance of family.

"I don't know what Alan said to you. It's hard to deny something when you have no idea what you were accused of," she hesitated. "I understand if you have an issue with me. It seems to be a Murphy family tradition."

Serena stepped out of the sanctity of her domain and drew to a halt two stools away from Brett.

"But know this," she met Brett's eyes. "I had nothing to do with Alan's death if that's what you're thinking."

Before Brett could respond, Serena walked out the door and crossed the deck, her head ducked into the wind. Its roar pulsed in her ears as she clutched the rail and leaned over to gulp in air laced with salt and brine.

Alan's ghost was out there. Each night he came ashore, summoning her to find him.

Would it be today?
Would they find the body today?

The Christmas-like jingle of the bells strung to the front door of Morgan's Bait and Tackle Shop sounded over Brett's head as he entered the cramped quarters of Harriet Morgan's store. He located Harriet behind the cash register, hastily clamping down the lid of a Tupperware container filled with chocolate chip cookies. A quick brush of the back of her hand across her lips left traces of chocolate.

Gray eyebrows narrowed at his approach as Harriet rose to her feet and plopped her chocolate-stained hands on the counter.

"Lookin' to do some fishing, are ya?"

Her voice oozed enough sarcasm to make Brett smirk.

So, Serena Murphy had the entire village of Victory Cove wrapped around her finger. But he was not from this town, and he was trying to stay immune to Serena's allure. And he could not be bullied by the likes of this daunting shop owner who had within her reach several large utility knives and other menacing tools that belonged in a torture chamber.

"Yes, I'm fishing."

Brett stopped adjacent to a meshed net affixed to a metal rod. He liked knowing it was there, *just in case.*

"I'm looking for answers," he added.

Harriet roosted herself on the bench behind the counter, crossing her arms and giving him such a once-over, Brett felt like he was up on an auction block.

"What are the questions?"

Acknowledging that he was on foreign turf, Brett was nonetheless undaunted by Harriet's tactics.

"Let's not waste each other's time," he began. "I want to know what happened to Alan, and you seem to want me out of your town. It's obvious how protective you are of my sister in-law. I doubt you think her capable of murdering her husband, so what other theories do you have?"

Harriet gasped, clutching her sheepskin vest. "Serena? Rena has a tough time killing spiders."

Alan had led him to believe otherwise.

"It had to be obvious to all of you that there were problems between the two of them." Brett persisted. "Alan may not have treated her very well. Don't you think over the years that anger was building up inside her, enough so to—"

"I don't know who the hell you think you are," Harriet roared. "You showed up here a month too late to be judgmental. Heck, before Alan went out on the boat that day, we hadn't seen him for months. We have no idea what happened. For all I know, he was with *you* out there. Maybe *you* pushed him ovah."

What the hell was going on in Alan's life?

Most of Brett's anger was defensive. Harriet was right. He was too late. The last time they spoke, Alan had been tense, disinterested in the *shop talk* of the stock market that normally riveted him so. For over a month Brett tried to reach him, only to find that Alan had disappeared from everyone's life. But Brett felt he should have tried harder.

Bottom line, he should have called Serena.

All that he knew now was that Alan returned to Victory Cove to take his fishing boat out in the middle of a storm, and was never seen again.

He just didn't buy it.

"Harriet," Brett reached up to rub a pain in his forehead. "May I call you Harriet?"

"No."

"*Ms*. Morgan," he corrected. "He was my brother. I'm being told I will never see him again. No matter what he's done to hurt you, to hurt Serena, to hurt himself—he's still my brother. Please, can you remember anything about the afternoon he got on his boat?"

Harriett fidgeted in her seat, brushing lint off her corduroys.

"It was a shock to see him stroll into the shop," she started. "Serena told me he was away on business, but we all had our doubts."

In other words you all sat around and gossiped over beer at O'Flanagans.

"He wanted netting which was odd," Harriet continued, "and he bought a Gorilla Big Game hook, which was very odd. Alan wasn't really an angler. He had that boat for sport, more for show."

"Whoa, you're losing me here," Brett interrupted. "Gorilla hook?"

Harriet's chapped hand motioned towards a series of black chrome hooks mounted on the wall behind the counter, out of the consumer's reach. "Those are for catching the meanest fish you can find—usually used for shaahks."

"Sharks?" Brett echoed. "So my brother shows up after disappearing for two months and decides he wants to go fishing for sharks right in the middle of a raging storm?"

"When he set off, the storm wasn't here yet. Maybe he thought he was going to beat it?"

It was odd that she didn't even react to his synopsis of that fateful afternoon. "And the police don't find any of this suspicious?"

"No offense, Mr. Murphy, but your brother was a bit eccentric. He was very cagey about his work." Harriet arched a graying brow. "I mean he was into landholdings or something like that, right?"

"Something like that." Brett's ambiguous answer stemmed from his ignorance. "Where did he keep his boat?"

Harriet hefted off the bench to approach a large bay window dissected by wooden grids. It overlooked the marina where tarpaulin-swathed vessels bobbed up and down in the surf.

"On the end theah. Serena saw him pulling out that day and ran after him down the pier. She was yelling, trying to wave him back, but I don't think Alan even looked at her. He knew she was there, though."

Shaking her head, Harriet withdrew from the window and glanced at Brett.

"If you're looking for answers, Mr. Murphy, *that's* where you're going to find them."

Riveted by the sea, Brett did not answer.

"But," Harriet added, "*She's* less apt to give up information than I am."

He slanted a look at the woman. "Somehow I find that hard to believe."

He reached for the door and heard the merriment of the overhead bells.

"Thank you for your time, Ms. Morgan."

CHAPTER III

Rooted outside the door to the loft, Serena steamed the glass with her breath. Inside, the solitary lamp held the dark at bay. It was cold—in the twenties, with a wind chill considerably lower. She couldn't stand out here any longer. Unlocking the door she watched as the drapes billowed from the invasion.

Across the floor, the bedroom was dark. Light from the dining room penetrated enough that she could discern the foot of her quilted bed—but after that, a barrier of shadows concealed all the horrors of night. Sprinting into that abyss, Serena clipped her knee against the wooden footboard and tumbled across the bed. With an unsteady hand she reached for the brass lamp as her childish behavior was suddenly mocked by the light.

Weary to the point of being comatose, the comfort of the plush quilt and feathered pillows lulled her eyes shut. As if not allowed this simple indulgence, clamoring footsteps began to resonate from the living room.

Jolted up onto her elbows, Serena cast an anxious glance through her open door and found it impossible that the sinister stride should return when confronted by this battalion of lamps. Yet, the sound was undeniable. Steady, persistent, doleful steps that progressed across the floor.

Crawling to the foot of her bed and then sliding off to clutch the doorframe, she peered into the living room.

It was empty.

The footfalls paced back and forth, recalling times when Alan would be deep in thought, plotting some job he would inevitably choose to keep private.

Despite all rational thought, Serena called out.

"Alan?"

The footfalls stopped.

Had they ever really been there, or were they simply echoes of her beating heart? Muddled thoughts were curtailed by the muffled cries of a child, a baby whose mournful peals now resonated all around her.

"No," Serena moaned, holding her hands to her ears. "Go away."

The child's cries persisted until Serena slid down the jamb onto her knees. She clutched her stomach and crooned to the infant.

"Shhh," she whispered, rocking back and forth.

Someone was at the door again. On trembling arms, Serena propped herself up off the floor.

Blazing sunlight streamed through the kitchen windows. Disoriented, Serena used a three-foot tall statue of a fisherman to assist her off hardwood planks. The Grandfather clock read eight-thirty. She blinked several times and then recalled what had woken her in the first place.

Someone was at the door.

The shadow outside was not the familiar petite silhouette of Rebecca. It was tall, formidable, and Serena instinctively shied away from it.

"Serena, I know you're in there."

Brett.

She couldn't tell if he was any less threatening than a ghost.

Brett pounded the door again. This was a stupid idea, he thought as he turned away, but a click behind him made him stop.

The weary figure inside the doorway staggered him. Serena's silky, fawn hair was tousled around her face. Soft bruises circled beneath her eyes and her eyelids were swollen as if she had been crying.

Wary, she watched him. "What do you want, Brett?"

My God, his first thought was that he wanted to hold her. She looked so desperate, so forlorn, and still with a beauty that tugged at something inside him.

"You look like hell," he said.

Serena grunted and stepped back from the door, not so much to let him in, but to get away from the sun. "I've been hearing a lot of that lately."

Brett followed Serena into the living room where she flung an arm towards the loveseat, motioning him to sit.

"Coffee?" She didn't seem to care about his response as she hastened into the kitchen.

"Yes, please."

Brett studied the quaint abode, all wood and windows, with a flare of maritime.

Outside, the Atlantic glowed with innocence—but inside, Brett frowned when he noticed that all the lights in the loft were on. His observations were interrupted when a mug was thrust in his face. He watched Serena retreat to a wooden chair and fold her leg beneath her before she sat.

"Having trouble sleeping?" he remarked.

Serena reached up to run her fingers through her hair. She sat up straighter and sipped at her steaming coffee. "You might say that."

"Maybe you'd sleep better if you didn't keep so many lights on."

Uneasy, she glanced at all the lamps still illuminated. "Maybe you should mind your own business."

"Cranky this morning, Serena?"

In an odd way, Brett was pleased to see some life in the inert figure slumped in her seat, clutching her coffee like a shield of the Order of Knights.

"What do you want, Brett?"

"Did Alan like to fish for sharks?"

"What?" Serena rubbed her shoulder, taken aback by the question.

Serena continued to massage her shoulder, which ached from the night on the floor. She flinched when she heard Brett call her name.

"Serena, are you okay?"

Her head snapped up because she swore she detected a note of concern in his husky voice. But when she looked, his gaze was still set in a cynical frown.

"I'm fine," she stated. "No. No, Alan did not like to fish for sharks. Alan didn't like fishing period."

"Then why the boat?"

It was a question Serena had addressed with her husband several years ago, only to be met with a rhetorical reply that concluded the discussion. The truth was that she had no idea what Alan did while he was out on that boat. Her only endeavor with Alan out to sea had turned into a disaster. Just the recollection made her clasp her stomach.

To conceal her pain from Brett, she continued. "Escape? An excuse to get away from it all."

Whatever *it all* was.

Brett's scowl was skeptical. He crossed his arms and Serena tried not to focus on how the motion evidenced the strength in his biceps. Surrendering any discipline, her eyes dusted across the sculpted outline beneath Brett's flannel shirt. The masculine terrain tempted her to recall what it had felt like to be in his embrace. Daring her gaze to climb higher, Serena found herself trapped by gray storm clouds.

"I just don't buy it." Brett challenged.

"I don't know, Brett," she blinked. "I've tried to think of what might be going through his head, why he would go off like that—"

"Did you two have a fight?"

"No," Serena sighed. "After awhile, I didn't have the energy to fight with him anymore."

Brett watched Serena's profile. Eclipsed by the sun, her hair shimmered. A graceful neck emerged from the thick knit sweater, her petite nose red from the repeated motion of wiping her sleeve against it. Feathery eyelashes glistened in the sunlight as she lifted a knee to hug it close to her chest.

Every troubled nuance of Serena tugged at Brett.

What had Alan done to her?

Brett massaged a hand over his face to channel his thoughts. Alan was family. This enchanting creature was a virtual stranger. His brother's death was a mystery no one seemed intent on solving, and Brett wanted to know why. As dejected as his stunning sister in-law may appear, he believed that she was the key to unlocking the truth.

"Do you have access to a boat?"

Serena's head shifted as she gaped at him. "Why?"

"I want to go out there."

Skeptical, she said, "You know the police have already searched. Again and again."

Brett stood up. "I want to see where Alan, where he—"

Frustrated with lack of expression, Brett paced back and forth. He listened to the protesting squeak of the floorboards, which revealed the age of this establishment.

Lost in his mechanical stride, Brett drew to a halt, surprised by the sudden stiffening of Serena's body. In slow motion, her hands released her knee as her leg sank to the floor and her head cocked to the side, listening to—*him.*

Serena's eyes were locked on Brett's boots as he resumed his gait. Puzzled by the desolation in her glance, he halted directly before her and stooped down to look into her vacant gaze.

"Are you okay?"

Eyes flecked with gold starbursts blinked twice, then focused. "Uh huh."

He scowled at the unconvincing reply. "Do you want some more coffee?"

"I'm fine, thank you." She smiled as though she found his question droll. "Harriet can get us a boat."

"Can you operate it?"

Her look of affront amused him.

"Of course," she said. "My father taught me. Lately though," any semblance of color drained from her face, "lately the ocean hasn't been too kind."

Still forcing himself to be cynical, Brett was convinced that Serena was playing him, looking for sympathy he was not about to extend. He had learned to suppress his attraction to his sister in-law ten years ago, and he damn well would do it again.

"Great," he stated with forced enthusiasm, "then I'll be back around one. Is that enough time?"

"Yes."

"You should try to get some rest before then, you look like you need it."

Serena's eyes flicked over Brett. Judging from her suspicious glance, she probably thought he was only interested in keeping her lucid when she commandeered the boat.

Maybe she was right.

"I don't like this idea one bit.

"I'll be fine, Harriet."

Serena stood on the pier, eyeing the thirty-foot hull of the *Mighty Morgan.* "You know I've done this before."

Harriet looked like a puffed up bird, expressing its indignation. Her short grayish-blonde hair was ruffled by the wind and her cheeks were bright red from the sun and the sea, and perhaps a little too much beer. She glanced at the burgundy and white striped hull, then towards Serena.

"It's been awhile," Harriet pointed out. "And besides, it's not you I'm worried about—I don't trust *him.*"

Serena smiled in resignation. "Why, because he's a Murphy? Brett's different, Harriet. Don't ask me why, but I believe I can trust him."

With an eyebrow arched in disapproval, the tackle shop owner reminded her, "You trusted Alan at one point too."

No. Not really. I might have loved him once. But I never trusted him.

"Regardless, I'll be fine. I need to do this. I haven't been out there since," Serena hesitated, "since it all happened. I think this will be good for me."

Their attention shifted from the bobbing vessel to the tall figure advancing down the pier with a stride that held no moderation—a stride that was focused on its destination, and not the picturesque pier. Serena drew in a quick breath as she watched the dark intensity on Brett's face.

"Oh, Rena honey, what have you gotten yourself into?"

"Shhh, I can handle him."

"I don't think you can." Harriet drew upon her most menacing expression as Brett joined them.

"Ladies." Brett acknowledged the blatant hostility, and just grinned.

Harriet ignored him and stooped to unwind the heavy coiled rope. She addressed Serena. "You'll radio in?"

"Every half hour. Seriously Harriet, we won't be out that long."

Serena glanced at the pervasive black line along the horizon, a grim reminder of what loomed far out on the Atlantic. It caused neither Harriet nor her alarm. The coast was enjoying rare sunshine today, with minimal winds.

"I'll have her back soon." Brett assured prying the rope from Harriet's calloused hands.

With his free arm, Brett assisted Serena on the short jump to the deck, although she did not rely on his grip. Tossing the sodden cord onto the vessel, Brett leaped across the increasing gap as the gentle waves lulled the craft out to sea.

Harriet raised her wrist in the air, pointing at her watch.

"A half hour, Rena."

With a smile and a salute, Serena turned around to make her way into the hutch. She seized the controls with the familiarity of bike handlebars.

Brett stood by Serena's side, gripping the frame of the cabin, watching her hands maneuver. He marveled at the adept moves and his gaze drifted up to catch vitality in her features that he had not witnessed on land. Wind from the increasing pace of the boat whipped through her hair, adding a flush to her cheeks and a spark in her eyes, making her appear more spirited than the despondent vision that greeted him this morning.

In time, Brett drew away from that absorbing sight to search the green-gray ocean through the water-streaked windshield.

"Do you know where you're going?" he asked.

"No."

As it picked up speed, the hull thrust against a series of choppy waves. Brett reached up with both hands to clutch the rim of the roof for support. Over his shoulder he located O'Flanagans, a small silhouette on top of the craggy coast. The only other discernable outline was that of a solitary lighthouse projecting into the cove from its lofty perch above the cliffs.

A lone sentry. This head light was a spectator during the events of the fateful storm that claimed his brother.

"I mean, I have no idea which way he set out that afternoon." Serena explained. "No one really leaves word. Only Coop tells Harriet which direction he's going before he sets out in the morning. He was lost out there once before, drifted for days before they found him."

"Was he okay?"

"Came back more ornery than ever."

Brett grinned, but his face was averted from her, so she didn't notice. His glance did skew in her direction when he sensed their speed decreasing.

"If I was taking someone out fishing," Serena answered his silent inquiry, "this is the area I'd throw the anchor."

How she determined that, Brett could not tell. The ocean was docile, milky green in the spots touched by the sun. The *Mighty Morgan* rolled gently enough that he could release the frame and stand on balance alone.

"Could you catch sharks here?"

Serena seemed surprised by the question, but mulled it over. "I'd go a bit further out."

Brett tipped his head. "Then let's go a bit further out."

Curious, Serena obliged and urged the lever forward, kicking up the *Morgan's* speed. They traveled in silence, each scouring the water for signs of debris until Brett's hand settled on her arm.

"Slow down, I think I saw something."

The clamor of the motor diminished to a drone. Above this, Serena could perceive only the wind brushing against her ears, and the seagulls that circled above, scavenging the boat as a potential source of food. She craned her neck to look around Brett's soaring frame, trying to catch a glimpse of what he had discovered, but the ocean was vacant.

"What did you see?"

Dejected, he turned to her. "Nothing, I guess."

She recognized that helpless expression.

"I want answers as much as you do." she empathized. "This past month, all I've managed to do is go through the motions of my life, uncertain what news the next day will hold," she glanced at the sea. "Every time a police car pulls up in front of the tavern, my body goes cold and I think, *today*, they'll tell me today. But no one tells me, Brett. They—they just shelter me. I don't want to be sheltered. I want answers. I want to know what happened."

I want the ghosts go away.

In the bright sun, Brett detected the dusting of freckles across Serena's nose and cheeks, and noticed that her eyes vividly mirrored the ocean. She looked haunted. Beautiful and haunted. Brett fought that tortured image. Serena was the only potential antagonist in his brother's life…at least that Alan had made him aware of.

"That makes two of us. Why would Alan be fishing for sharks in the middle of a storm?"

"Sharks? You keep asking about sharks? Why?" Serena seemed genuinely perplexed, or an incredible actress.

"Harriet said he purchased a Gorilla hook or something like that. She said that these hooks were used for catching sharks."

"He wouldn't be going after sharks. That would have been too ferocious a prey for him." She shook her head. "He had to be after something else."

Brett searched the ocean. When he turned back his eyes were narrowed.

"I don't think my brother died in an accident, Serena. You have to know more than you're letting on."

Serena reached for the frame of the cabin. Brett could tell his comment hurt her, but she lifted her chin.

"I know Alan talked to you," she said quietly, "but did he *really* talk to you? Do you really know what your brother has been doing all these years, or has he lied to you all along? I mean, I didn't see you bailing him out of jail the last time, so I'm going to assume he didn't share that little excursion with you. He probably didn't tell you about the other times either, did he?"

Serena tried to glare, but the fatigue overpowered her. "If you're so concerned about your brother, Brett, find out where he was the past two months. Find out where he was, and maybe that will explain what motivated him that afternoon."

Jail?

Serena was certainly not the only one Alan had lied to. Brett knew his relationship with Alan wasn't the best, but he never anticipated that his brother would secret a jail sentence.

Subdued, Brett asked, "Why was he in jail?"

Serena sighed and dropped down onto the vinyl holding container. "It was brief, but he tested the limits too much. He'd sell land that wasn't his to sell. Sometimes he'd get away with it; other times they'd toss him in jail until I came along with the bail money."

"What do you mean he'd sell land that wasn't his to sell?"

"He would make an offer to a landowner for $10,000 an acre, and because their land had not sold in so many years, they would accept it. Meanwhile, he didn't have that sort of cash, so he would turn around and find a buyer that was willing to give him $25,000 an acre for the property." Serena gave a feeble shrug, "He'd take their money, pay the other guy his ten thousand, and hope that he could close the deal before either was the wiser. Sometimes it worked, other times—" she looked away, "well, let's just say our lawyer got tired of the act."

Alan had boasted to Brett in the past about what a game the real estate market could be, and Brett knew enough about his brother to be skeptical, but he never suspected Alan would end up in jail. What other schemes had Alan engaged in that he was not aware of?

Serena's accusations stung because of their precision. Retaliation became Brett's only defense.

"Maybe he kept doing it because you kept showing up with the bail. Did you try any discipline? Did you explain that it was a strain on the relationship?" His eyebrow cocked and his fingers clenched around the balustrade. "Or was it?"

Busying herself with the controls to buy enough time to consider her response, Serena felt there was some validity to Brett's charge. Initially she thought that Alan could be reformed. His schemes were usually harmless, and after each scandal he doused her with words of love and affection. As a young girl she reveled in Alan's attention. But she grew old quickly. Eventually his false words no longer incited her devotion.

Still, she was married to Alan, a sanctity that she had to maintain if only to save face amidst a town that disapproved of the union.

"It was a strain," she conceded. "Every time he promised it would be the last. I grew out of believing his promises, but he was still my husband. He needed help and his family never seemed to be around—"

"I was around." Brett snapped. "He called me all the time, and never let on that any of this was happening. Tell me Serena, who am I inclined to believe, the brother I grew up with, or you?"

Sad eyes gripped Brett as Serena turned around and whispered, "You should believe your brother. You don't even know me."

Dammit. She looked so tragic with her hands tucked into the pockets of her jeans. If she were any other woman, he would reach for her and comfort her. But this was his brother's wife and the only person Alan had cast in a negative light.

"Maybe you consider it a blessing that he's gone?"

Serena blinked against the salty air that made her eyes brim with tears. In a husky voice she uttered, "We better start heading back. We're not going to find anything out here."

Frustrated, Brett slammed his fist down on the wooden hull and watched as she turned away.

How dare she make him feel guilty? Even Serena had said to trust his brother and not a woman he barely knew. Yet when Brett looked into her soulful gaze, he felt like he had known Serena for an eternity. A decade made no difference. Brett still wanted her. But the situation was as impossible now as it had been then.

Serena was Alan's wife.

Brett shook his head and reached up to massage a pain at the base of his skull. Despite himself, his eyes trailed the slim dip of her back, and he opened his lips to apologize, but the words never sounded. Instead, he tried for innocuous conversation to ease some of the tension.

"You said you hadn't been out on the water in a long time," he hesitated, "when were you out here last?"

Brett swore he saw Serena's shoulders flinch and her fingers clutch the helm. Other than her body's brief signal of distress, Serena remained mute, and no amount of goading on his part could draw any more out of her.

"We really needed to do this, Alan. We needed to get out here and talk."

"About what?" Alan's gruff reply was not about to dissuade Serena.

Alan had been gone for two months, and when he returned, had not even noticed that Serena now dressed in oversized flannel shirts and favored her back.

Spring touched Maine and the day was sunny, warm and inspiring. Serena would not be deterred by Alan's somber attitude. Instinctively, her fingers settled on the slight swell of her abdomen and she smiled a private smile that only incited a glare from her husband.

"What are you up to, Serena? I don't trust that shit-eating grin."

Don't frown, Serena reminded herself. It was going to be okay.

Just four months ago she had thought of contacting a lawyer and severing their painful union, but that same day brought the news of her pregnancy. Suddenly Serena felt strong enough to mend their failing relationship. Her enthusiasm faltered during the two-month span that Alan was away, but when he returned, she proposed this excursion on the boat as a time to announce their impending arrival.

"Can't we just have a good time today, Al? I haven't seen you for such a long time. I miss you." Was that really true?

O'Flanagans Stew *slid through the water as she felt Alan's black eyes bore into her before he turned away.*

"This boat is a mess. Did you bring someone aboard while I was gone?" The dark gaze condemned. "If I find out that you had a man here, I'll kill both of you."

It was just a figure of speech, Serena reminded herself. Nonetheless, the sun suddenly seemed less brilliant and the ocean less docile, as clouds materialized where just moments ago blue skies lingered. In mortal acceptance, she

*acknowledged that the damage to their relationship was
irreparable.*

"We're going to have a baby."

*Conscious of the whistle of the wind and the shrieks of the
gulls above, Serena focused on Alan's silence. His back was
still to her, tall and thin as he stooped over a holding tank.
The only sign that she had spoken was in the stiffness of his
posture.*

"Al?"

*Alan whirled around and crossed three steps till he was in
Serena's face, his pointer finger jabbing painfully through a
sweater and a sweatshirt to bruise her upper arm.*

*"What do you want me to say? That's great, dear?
Another mouth for me to feed with what little money we have
left?"*

*Last time Serena had checked the bank account she was
unaware of any financial problems, but she'd be sure to check
again as soon as they returned to land.*

*Serena gauged the proximity of the cove almost two miles
away and suddenly felt vulnerable.*

*"Hell, you don't need my money anyway." Alan
continued. "Everything comes from your parents. Our house,
the Inn, even this goddamn boat." Alan kicked the storage bin
as he slammed the lid shut. "How do I even know it's mine?
You constantly throw it in my face that I'm not around much,
so the damn kid must not be mine!" Again his eyes leered close
enough to make her shrink away.*

*"I'm almost five months pregnant. You remember when
you came home for the holidays—"*

*Under Alan's menacing stare Serena began to shiver. She
took a step of retreat as her foot connected with a coiled rope.*

*"Why the hell would I have slept with you, you're a
goddamn icicle in bed." Alan said, apparently remembering*

the occasion. "You should be on the pill, dammit. You're going to get rid of it, and that's it."

"No!" Serena's hand shot out, holding both Alan and his words at bay.

"What do you mean, no*?" Alan advanced, his eyes black slits on a face scarred by hatred.*

Serena wondered fleetingly where the man was that she had fallen in love with. Was this monster hidden beneath all along?

Anger and defense drew a chilled voice from Serena's lips. "I will not give up this baby, Alan. I will leave you if that's what it takes, but I'm keeping this baby."

"Leave?" His harsh laugh caused a daring seagull to rethink its flight pattern. "That's supposed to be a threat? I keep leaving you whenever I damn well feel like it. Every time my parents send a check—I leave you. When that runs out, I'm back. But you're a fool who still believes that love—not money ties this relationship together. Get rid of the kid," Alan ordered.

Serena was desperate, heedless of the impact of her words. "I'm keeping the baby, Alan. That's the bottom line."

Alan straightened his back. "Oh it is?"

Alan's hand shot out before Serena could avoid it. It cracked against her cheek and ear. Aside from a resonant buzzing in that region, she would have been okay. But the motion set her off balance, and to compensate, her foot sought stability, landing within the twist of rope. Gravity hoisted her over the edge.

Before Serena had time to acknowledge what happened, she found herself gulping for air amidst swells that crashed against the hull of O'Flanagans Stew. *Her palms landed on the barnacled surface, seeking a handhold as she spit out enough water to manage a scream.*

"Alan!"

Backlash from an errant wave cascaded over her as she gulped in air deluged with seawater. Through the salty curtain, she distinguished her husband's profile above and anxiously held her hand up towards him. Alan stooped down and she was conscious of his grip, forceful and piercing on her shoulders—only he wasn't pulling her out of the water.

In retaliation to the sudden pressure, Serena kicked her legs, which grew burdensome in the ice-cold Atlantic. Flailing arms ineffectively battered his grasp as she began to feel faint. The freezing water and lack of oxygen numbed her efforts.

When the resistance left her body and darkness descended, she was aware of being lifted. Squinting against the sun, she noticed Alan's silhouette hunched over her, his lips moving. The sound was a hollow echo that matched the blood pounding in her ears.

"Come on, you'll live."

Serena coughed with such severity that her entire body racked in spasm. Pain vaulted her swiftly to consciousness.

"No," she cried.

Serena curled up on the soaked deck and clutched her stomach.

"No," she repeated.

CHAPTER IV

"Serena?"

Serena jolted at the invasion of Brett's voice.

Her hand seized the throttle with white knuckles.

"What happened the last time you were out here?" Brett asked.

Momentarily locked in the past, Serena tried to find traces of her husband in the man before her, but there were none. Even Alan's brown hair, which she thought was a common denominator between the two brothers, on Brett was much richer, a shade shy of black.

And then there were Brett's eyes. Silver. The color of Maine's autumn sky. Instead of just looking at those eyes, Serena delved into them, wondering if the demon that possessed Alan lurked inside Brett too. She trembled at the intensity concealed there, but found no monsters.

Brett stood paralyzed. It was as if Serena possessed him, entering through his eyes and penetrating his soul for answers. Never before had he felt so vulnerable. Was she a witch? Had she cast a spell on Alan and now had her sights on him?

Detecting the tremor of Serena's bottom lip, Brett felt the nagging signs of doubt. He had wanted to convict her, to exorcize her from his mind. But could he be wrong? Could she possibly be a victim herself?

"Do you want to talk about what happened?" he asked.

Serena shook her head.

Brett squatted down onto the holding container. Elbows on knees, he avoided staring at her, but in his periphery, he found that she had returned her attention to the *Mighty Morgan*.

The remainder of the journey inland was spent in silence. Brett welcomed the jarring thud of the pier, and reacted by tossing the coiled rope towards Harriet, who stood rooted in the very same spot he left her.

"Anything?" Harriet asked Serena.

Brett hurdled onto the dock and took the rope from the shopkeeper's hands to channel the boat into submission.

"Serena?" Harriet repeated.

"No."

Serena's subdued response elicited a grunt from Harriet. Harriet then looked at Brett. Disregarding the intrusive stare, Brett reached for Serena's hand to assist her off the boat. His outstretched fingers remained empty as Serena leapt onto the wooden planks. Without a look back, she hurried down the pier and hiked up the hill towards O'Flanagans.

"What did you do to her?" Harriet's accusation lashed out as soon as Serena was out of range.

"I didn't do a damn thing. She—"

Brett's glance followed the distant silhouette, "she remembered—something."

The pain in Serena's eyes. The distrustful signals of her body. Brett was certain that she had recalled something traumatic.

But would she ever share it with him?

"No good. You damn Murphy brothahs are no good."

"Now just a minute," Brett crossed his arms and loomed over the stately merchant.

"I don't know what Alan has done to make you so bitter. I'm not about to argue with you about my brother," Brett sighed. "I will admit that he was prone to some trouble in the past. Regardless, don't label people you have just met, *Ms.* Morgan."

Snorting her contempt, Harriet placed her hands on her hips.

"You just go fix that girl," she ordered. "Fix whatever damage you've done. Make her smile again. She had nothing to do with her husband's death and I think you know it. That man brought everything on himself."

Harriett dipped her head in a knowing nod. "Earn my respect, Brett Murphy."

"Rena, honey, where ya been?"

Sliding under the service panel, feeling instantly protected within the barricade of polished wood, Serena wiped her eyes, ran her fingers through her hair, and turned to face Cooper.

"I was out on the *Morgan.*"

Coop set his beer down with enough force to spill some over the rim. Mechanically, Serena reached for a towel to sop up the mess.

"That's—great. I mean you haven't been out on the water in a long time." His craggy face was one big question mark, but Serena ignored it.

"Rena, thank god!" Simon hastened from his post at the door. "Something disastrous has happened."

"Your subscription to *Muscle Man* ran out?" Coop quipped, earning a look of disdain from the thin-haired maitre de.

Ignoring Coop, Simon straightened the knot of his necktie and continued. "We've booked two parties of eight for the same window-front table and both are standing in the foyer screaming at each other!"

Serena propped her hands on the counter and stooped forward to crane around Simon. The commotion up front sounded like the rowdy cries of adults in verbal combat.

"That they are." Serena declared with a smirk.

"We have to do something!"

Simon's whine made Coop cringe. He turned his attention to the thirteen-inch color TV mounted in the corner.

"Simon," Serena began patiently, "you told me that you had aspirations of running a bistro in New York, right?"

With a sigh, Simon seemed to read where she was going. He pursed his lips. "Yes."

"Well you're going to have to face much graver situations than this."

Serena continued with sincerity. "I need you, Simon. You know I haven't been myself, I—I sometimes feel like I'm losing my mind, and I depend on you so much, and you have been there for me. For that I will always be grateful," she smiled. "I know I have put a lot of burden on you, but it's only because I trust your judgment—and someday I'm going to be the first patron in that bistro of yours, and I'm going to order the most expensive dish on the menu."

Simon cleared his throat. "Dammit, Serena. How am I supposed to manage a comeback to that?"

Without waiting for her response, he tightened the knot of his necktie and tugged at the cuffs of his crisp white shirt. "Don't worry, I can handle them."

Coop's back was still to Serena, though his snort and brief utterance "*sap*," triggered a weary smile from her lips.

That was how Brett found her.

Used to the reproachful stares by now, Brett didn't care. The only set of eyes he was intent on lost their smile when they landed on him.

"Bar's closed." Coop challenged.

"Cooper!" Serena admonished.

There was no doubt in Brett's mind that Serena was unsettled by his presence. She avoided looking at him.

"You be polite, Coop," she admonished. "Remember that everyone is allowed into O'Flanagan's for some food and spirits."

On the last word, Brett caught Serena hasten a glance towards the ceiling. She wrapped her arms about her and reached for the thermostat, snapping back when Coop bellowed, "Woman, it's already about eighty degrees in here!"

Brett noticed a tremor quake through Serena's limbs.

"Actually," he argued, "it's getting real cold out. You probably should turn that up."

With a mute nod of gratitude, Serena upped the thermostat.

She hoisted a glass under a nozzle and said to Coop, "To cool you down. It's on me."

"Well in that case, little Rena…" Clearly mollified, Coop grinned, "—you can turn up the heat any time."

Reluctant to move away from Coop's congenial smile, Serena flicked a nervous glance in Brett's direction. Aware of his eyes on her, her heart drummed faster under the perusal. When Brett straddled a bar stool and put his elbow on the counter her nerves wrought havoc on her hands. She tried to keep herself busy, but there was no way to keep from staring. Brett Murphy seemed larger than life. God, she wondered if his strong arms could warm the chill that stole through her body.

"A Sam Adams, please."

Serena immersed her trembling hands into the vat of chopped ice and withdrew a dark bottle. Uncooperative fingers fumbled with the twist cap as she extended the drink to him.

"Thanks."

Brett watched Serena's unnerved gestures and wondered what tale she had recalled this afternoon. She hadn't been the same since then. He was curious enough to want to stay and confront her after closing.

"And thanks for the trip today." He saluted with the bottle.

Beside him, Coop's black cap spun about. Brett found himself stared down by a pair of jaundiced eyes.

"You went out on the *Morgan*?" Coop gaped. "With him?"

Serena dodged the question by waiting on another customer. Her absence allowed Coop to sneer at Brett. "What are you up to, Murphy? What do you want from her?"

Brett set his beer down and stared at the wooden Cuckoo clock, willing it to move faster.

"You know," Brett said. "I'm getting tired of everyone asking me what I'm doing here, and accusing me of having less than savory intentions for their little *Rena.* You know why I'm here. I want answers. I believe she has some." His eyebrow hefted. "As a matter of fact, your resentment makes me even more convinced than ever."

Coop was silent for a minute. "Maybe you'll find those answers you're looking for," he ducked his head. "But I don't think you're going to like 'em."

As Serena returned, she flicked her gaze from Brett to Coop and back again.

"Are you playing nice, Coop?" she asked.

Coop swiveled in his seat so that his attention was rooted to the hockey game on the overhead television. He slid his empty glass towards Serena and declared, "Just sitting here watching TV and minding my own business."

She looked to Brett for confirmation, but he just shrugged.

Alone. Brett wanted to talk to Serena alone.

Studying her, Brett watched her tremulous effort to maintain a cordial smile. She nodded graciously to departing customers and executed timely jokes to the ones who remained. Yet, beneath, he sensed fatigue and despair slowly breaking her down. Gradually, the crowd thinned, and Brett waited out Coop whose head dipped forward. Several times the man emitted a hearty snore before the sound jarred him awake.

"Coop," Serena called, "come on, it's time to go home. Martha'll be worried."

"I ain't going home and leaving you here alone with him." His neck lolled in Brett's direction as Brett caught the heavy stench of beer.

"*Both* of you are leaving. It's closing time." Exhaustion added just the right dose of irritation to Serena's voice to prompt the old man out of his seat. Ambling towards the door, Coop hesitated to see if Brett followed. The motion caused him to sway and reach for the wall.

"Is he driving?" Brett murmured.

"No," Serena scowled. "You really do have a low opinion of me if you think I'd let him do this and drive. Coop lives down the hill, and if he doesn't get home by eleven, Martha will be up here pulling him by his ear."

Before Brett could act contrite, Coop's voice rang unnaturally loud in the empty tavern. "Come on, Murphy. I'm not letting you stay here with her."

Slanting a final look at Serena, trying to interpret her gaze, Brett reluctantly rose and pursued Cooper into the night.

With the absence of customers, the silence engulfed Serena. Reaching for the remote beside the register, she aimed it at the TV, reducing the blond reporter to a horizontal line before she was obliterated. With three twists of her wrist, Serena flicked the switches to swathe O'Flanagans in darkness.

Apprehension settled in with the shadows. Reluctant to make the trek upstairs, she eyed the door to O'Flanagans deck.

Wasn't it a better option than the terror waiting in her loft?

Assaulted by the bone-chilling wind, Serena embraced the cold—its effect a reminder that she was still alive. She crossed the rutted planks and rested her elbows on the balustrade, listening to the waves below. Luminous under a full moon, the black cliffs still held their secrets with a tenacity that she could never resolve.

"Serena?"

Serena spun around, afraid that the ghost had chosen to assail her here in the wake of the moon.

Chilled in his old suede jacket, Brett could only imagine how cold Serena was in her insubstantial fleece. Her shiver was apparent, but as he approached, he had the uneasy feeling that he was the culprit.

"What do you want, Brett?"

Brett moved into the ring of moonlight. He nearly succumbed to the need to touch her. To warm her.

Frustrated by the affect she had on him, Brett again sought balance in accusation.

"What are you doing out here? Are you looking for his body again?" Brett plunged on despite the impact of his words.

"It's quite the show," he said, "everyone seeing you out here every night, the grieving widow searching the cliffs for her husband who hasn't returned from sea."

Dammit, Brett wanted Serena to fight. He wanted her to defend herself so that he could sanction his emotions. It was crazy, but he wanted her to just come right out and say, "It's okay, Brett. It's okay for you to feel this attraction, because I feel it too."

But no. When Brett's mouth opened, it was to pose a desperate question.

"Why did you do it, Serena?"

Serena hugged her arms and tucked her chin against her collarbone to ward off the wind. She closed her eyes. If only she could be immune to Brett's accusatory tone. If only his judgment wasn't so important to her.

It was cold out. And Brett was near. Irrationally, she wanted to lean into him and soak up his warmth. Instead, she cleared her throat.

"I have nothing to defend, Brett. But if you want to condemn me, if it sets you at peace so that you can go home with a villain in your mind," she breathed, "so be it."

"Dammit, Serena. What happened? How did you grow to hate him so much? Why did you do it?"

Serena's head came up. "I didn't kill him if that's what you think!"

Brett cursed. "I'm not talking about you killing Alan!"

With a quick gasp, Serena's hand latched onto the rail. She ignored the bite of ice against her fingers. "What—what *are* you talking about?"

Even in the dark she could see Brett's jaw clench.

"The baby," he whispered in torment. "Alan told me what you did to the baby. *How could you*?"

Conscious of the air stealing from her body, Serena felt a bout of vertigo that threatened to pitch her off the ledge. Echoes from her pounding heart muted Brett's words, but she saw his lips move. She couldn't stop to listen. She just wanted to run. Run fast and far from her ghosts.

On a strangled cry she took flight.

"Serena!"

With each mounting stride, Brett's appeal grew more remote. Serena raced up the grassy hill, increasing the distance between them. All that was discernable now were her brief puffs of breath as she blindly climbed the sea cliff.

Instinct.

Serena ran on instinct. Clouds of moisture billowed from her lips into her eyes, while muscles pumped and groaned against mistreatment. Unconsciously, she aimed towards the soaring silhouette of Victory Cove's unmanned lighthouse. Racking sobs prevented her from advancing any further, though. Her knees folded and she fell headlong into the frozen pasture.

The ground was hard and cold. Unforgiving.

Serena's body writhed in pain across the brittle grass. She came to rest in a fetal position, her sobs hollow echoes. Agony tore through her, though little had to do with the fall.

All at once, the tears stopped. Serena heard the distant sound of broken waves, and the roar of arctic winds. She felt so tired—so utterly drained.

Were it not for the cloudless sky and the near full moon, Brett might never have found Serena. She had charged the craggy knolls with a familiarity bred by a lifetime, while Brett stumbled over loose rock and slick grass, trying to gain ground on the ghostly specter outlined by a luminous ocean. He almost passed her. She was so silent, so still, that he felt his heart neglect a beat. Lying on her side, Serena's knees were tucked up against her chest, her breath casting shallow clouds against the dirt.

"Serena."

No response.

Brett stooped and hoisted Serena into his arms. Negotiating the trail with caution, he used the floodlights of O'Flanagans as a homing beacon, ever conscious of Serena's soft breath against his throat.

With his elbow, Brett nudged the door to her loft aside and crossed the wooden floorboards. Gently, he set her down on one of the loveseats and reached for a quilt to secure around her.

The fireplace was heaped with half-used kindling. Brett stoked the mass into a roaring blaze that cast flickering shadows across Serena's pale face. Heedless of the door he left askew, Brett sat on the edge of the sofa and leaned over the inert figure, his finger tracing the arc of her throat, feeling the pulse beating there.

"Serena?" he whispered.

Fawn-like lashes fluttered. Her eyes opened, taking several seconds to focus on him.

"Are you okay?" he whispered.

With a feeble smile, she managed, "Do I look it?"

No, she didn't. Her lips were blue, her skin pallid, and her breathing seemed too shallow to suit him, but she resisted his hold and attempted to sit up.

"Lay down," he ordered. "You have nowhere you need to be right now. Just rest."

Anxious, her glance searched the living room. "How do you know what needs to be done?" she argued. "I have plenty of things that have to be addressed right now. I need to turn on more lights."

"They can wait," Brett challenged, but released his grip on her arm.

"Please," Serena sat up fully, facing off with him.

Her eyes dropped to his lips for a split second before she continued in hushed urgency. "Please, Brett, let me get up, I have to—I have to—" she stammered, "it's dark in here."

Brett stayed fixed, his arm across the back of the loveseat, a physical barricade that prevented Serena from rising. He studied the warm glow of the antique lantern, and the blaze of the fireplace. The lighting was nearly intimate.

Perhaps she was right. Maybe they needed more lights.
Brett's eyes returned to her face.

"There's enough." His voice was husky.

"*No.*"

Serena touched his arm as if to cast it aside, and froze when a footfall sounded behind her.

Brett's head snapped. He searched the shadows beyond Serena. Heavy footsteps paced across the floorboards, pausing as if indecisive what trek to take—then resumed with determination towards the front door.

"What the hell?"

Jumping up to intersect the path of the intruder, Brett heard the steady tread before him. Then as if the figure passed directly through his body, the steps continued past Brett, out the open doorway.

"Stay right there!" he yelled over his shoulder while plunging through the door.

The wind slammed it shut behind him.

Serena clutched her arms about her. She stared at the door, willing it to open again. She willed Brett to return and not leave her alone for the next ghost. Its chilling cries were more haunting than the doleful steps of a man she could not mourn.

CHAPTER V

There had to be a logical explanation.

The stranger had to be lurking out there somewhere. This man, this psycho, who stole into Serena's apartment to assault her while she was alone and defenseless. The thought burned inside Brett.

He reached the bottom step and scanned the vacant deck. Floodlights cast an eerie glow against the low-lying fog, providing enough light for him to explore the base of the sloping hills. No sign of an intruder. No tread marks in the thin coat of snow that had just begun to form.

Brett's fist curled around the balustrade as his gaze penetrated the slats between the steps, hoping for a glimpse of the prowler. He was tempted to give chase, search the grounds of O'Flanagans, but the thought of leaving Serena alone upstairs troubled him.

Serena.

Brett's neck craned up the stairs. If he hadn't been here— she could have been hurt. Or worse.

His frown intensified with each step of ascent. Through the window he could see he. He entered and crossed to her side, staggered by the fresh stream of tears that gleamed down her cheeks. He lowered to the edge of the cushion, clasping her hand in his, rubbing the fingers to provide warmth. With a pained expression, he whispered, "I couldn't find him."

To his astonishment, Serena began to laugh. A hushed chuckle.

Brett felt her fingers clench in his and worried that she had gone into shock from the exposure.

"What's so funny?"

Serena's laughter stopped, but the bright countenance remained. "You heard him?"

"Who?" Fear for her made Brett's voice harsher than intended. "The man that was just in here?"

"You know it's not safe up here," he censured. "Everyone knows your patterns, and anybody could sneak up those stairs and break in while you're working down below. If I wasn't here, I'd hate to imagine what could have happened to you."

"You heard him," she repeated in awe.

"Yes I heard him," Brett said roughly. "And it's nothing to laugh about. You should be a little more concerned. A man was just staked out in your house." Brett almost touched her. "Dammit, Serena."

Serena couldn't help it. Another chuckle bubbled from her lips. If Brett heard the footsteps too, that proved that she was not going insane. Someone else heard them. Her ghost was real—not the sinister byproduct of madness.

She sobered, recalling that Brett had not heard the other specter that haunted her.

But then again, wasn't that her own private ghost?

"He's here every night."

"What?" Brett sat back, frowning.

"Alan. He's here every night. That's why I want the lights on. Wouldn't you? Wouldn't you be afraid of the dark if a ghost visited you every night?"

Brett released his grip on Serena to shove his hands up into his hair. "You're telling me Alan's ghost drops by for a visit every night?"

Serena slumped back against the cushions of the loveseat, but felt remarkably lucid.

"I know you think I'm insane. I did too. But you heard him—he's not just in my imagination." She drew her knees up and rested her arms atop them. "At this point I really don't care if you believe me or not, Brett. You haven't believed anything I've said, so why should things change now?"

Flinching at the accusation, Brett stood up.

"Look, if you think this crazy tale is going to sidetrack me from finding the truth—"

Brett's bravado seemed to vanish the longer he looked at her. He stifled a curse and sat back down beside her.

"Well, it looks like you're taking on a boarder." His voice was gruff. "I hate that motel by the interstate, and I want to be here tomorrow to hear your *ghost* when it arrives."

Serena thought of protesting. This had been her private battle. She snuck a quick look at Brett's brooding face, the dark shadows and absorbing eyes—eyes that made her heart hammer when he looked at her. She wasn't comfortable with the notion of sleeping under the same roof as him, but then again, when did she ever sleep? Perhaps with someone else around she might feel safer. After all, didn't she feel it already? Right here with Brett so close, his arm brushing against her leg, the contact grounding her, making her feel that she was no longer surrounded by death.

"Really Brett," she managed. "I'm sure that's the last thing you want to do."

"It's not up for debate."

"Fine," Serena looked away. "But I keep lots of lights on at night, and I don't want to hear any complaints."

"Maybe if I'm here," his voice lowered, "you won't need all those lights."

In the background, the Grandfather clock ticked in time with Serena's pulse.

"Why don't you try to get some rest?" Brett suggested.

Serena swung her legs onto the floor, and for a moment felt as though all power had fled her. One deep breath and she tried for the energy to cross the loft and reach her bedroom.

"Do you want a hand?" he offered.

She shook her head and used her arms to propel herself upright, but then began to sway, seeking support in the closest thing she could find. Brett was there, one hand slipping around her waist, the other circling her wrist to steady her.

"You could have frozen to death out there." His voice was hoarse. "You obviously haven't been getting much sleep, you could have succumbed to hypothermia—" His grip on her tightened.

"Why did you do it, Serena? Why did you run from me? You should have just said it was none of my damn business."

If she was in possession of all her faculties, she would have wrenched from Brett's grip and lashed out. But she was too tired to fight him, and with the urge for battle doused, she could only whisper in agony, "It was an accident."

Would the pain ever go away? "A terrible accident," she repeated.

"Shh," Brett said. "Don't talk about it." His hand moved from her waist to splay across the small of her back.

As if Brett's palm had the power to heal, warmth streamed from it and trekked up her spine. She let him help her to her bedroom, knowing full well she could make it on her own. The opportunity to lean on someone else for a change was something too tempting to pass up, let alone the solid shoulder of Brett Murphy.

Only a few moments ago Serena had divulged that the ghost of her dead husband visited her every night. It was no wonder Brett supported her. He must have thought she'd gone completely mad.

But he'd heard it too. Brett heard her ghost.
How mad could she be?

"Serena!"
Brett bolted upright. He squinted against the sun. The front door vibrated under the insistent knock, which repeated

over and over. Launching off the loveseat, he hauled it open. "What!"

Rebecca's mouth gaped. Her eyes slid down Brett's chest as he glanced down to see his shirt was halfway out of his pants.

"I—um—" Rebecca faltered. "I'm looking for Serena."

"I gathered that," he scowled. "She's sleeping."

The redhead's lips opened and closed like a guppy as she tried to glimpse beyond him.

"It's okay, Brett." A soft whisper prompted him to relent and step aside. "I'm up."

Brett searched Serena's face for effects from last night. Her eyes were puffy, but there was more color in her cheeks. That flush gave him concern. He brushed the back of his hand against her skin in search of fever, and caught the slight flare in her sun-spiked eyes.

Satisfied that she had not suffered any serious health repercussions, Brett took his hand away from the promise of her flesh and retreated into the kitchen, mumbling about coffee along the way.

"Hi." Serena motioned Rebecca towards one of the loveseats.

"Don't you dare *hi* me, Serena O'Flanagan Murphy."

Cabinet doors slammed in the kitchen. Serena cocked her head towards the sound, and smiled.

"Get your deprived, small-town, romance-novel reading mind out of the gutter, Becky," Serena said. "Brett— I fell last night, and if he hadn't found me—"

"Fell?" Rebecca leaned forward to grasp Serena's hand. "What happened?"

"It's a long story."

Brett set down three mugs on the dining room table with no intention of serving them. Serena smiled at the gesture.

"And he felt it necessary to spend the night and keep an eye on you?" Rebecca challenged.

"Yes."

Rebecca stammered. "I see."

"I'm leaving." Brett hoisted his suede jacket off the chair. "I'll see you later," he added.

Serena rushed to reach the front door before him, but once she got there, she brushed the curtain aside and pretended to study the weather.

What could she say? In the harsh light of morning, her phantoms seamed surreal.

Yet Brett had heard them too.

"You don't have to come back tonight." Her throat caught.

The scowl disappeared from Brett's face.

"I know I don't," his voice was husky. "But I'm going to."

Locked by Brett's gaze, she wanted to thank him, but something in that grave expression said it was unnecessary.

"*I'm going to*," he repeated for only her to hear.

When Brett looked at her that way, she felt vulnerable to the core.

God help her, it felt good.

Serena watched Brett start down the staircase and then sagged against the door jamb with relief, knowing that he would return tonight.

"Okay woman, spill it."

Serena turned towards the petite ball of energy that bounced up and down on the couch with scarcely contained curiosity.

"Calm down, Becky," she said. "He's Alan's brother. He's concerned about finding the truth. So am I."

"How friggin noble." Rebecca snorted. "He's very hot."

Serena cleared her throat and on reflex, reached for the blanket on the floor, folding it in quarters and draping it over the chair. "He doesn't much look like Alan, does he?"

"Is that your way of saying Alan wasn't hot?"

"You're talking about a husband that I just recently lost." Serena reprimanded. "And I never said Brett was *hot*."

"Well," Rebecca drawled, "this is the most animated I've seen you in a month. Whatever Brett Murphy is doing here, it's good to see some color in your cheeks again. For that, it's worth it." Setting her coffee down, she declared, "of course, *I will* get all the juicy details out of you."

Alone, Serena stood in the center of the living room. Last night she had fallen into an exhausted sleep and this was the first opportunity she had to digest what transpired. When Brett charged her with Alan's accusations—Alan must have told Brett that she had gotten rid of the baby— not miscarried. Even now Serena clenched her coffee cup so tightly, that if she were any stronger it would shatter. Why did her husband hate her so much? And extending that hatred to his brother only compounded the matter.

If only she hadn't stumbled last night—if only Brett hadn't found her—this would all be over and she would be asleep right now.

Frowning, Serena set the coffee cup down so that circulation would return to her fingers.

Alan would just love that, wouldn't he? He'd just love it if she curled up and died from despair.

Across the room, behind her parents' picture, Alan's smiling face taunted her.

"You can't hurt me anymore," she vowed.

But he did. Every night when he returned to torment her, it hurt. Perhaps tonight she would be stronger.

She would not be alone.

It was early. The sign on the door said CLOSED in handwritten letters. Pounding on the front door of the shop, Brett considered that Harriet might not be within earshot. Several seconds passed unanswered before he repeated the noise. He was startled when the door yanked open so swiftly a vacuum was created, sucking him in along with a swirl of dirt.

"You again." The disheveled woman raked her glance up and down his body, feigning contempt. Harriet shook her head and then stepped back to allow him full entry.

"Got a yearn to head out fishing this morning?" she barked.

"Not exactly."

"You better damn well buy something before you leave this store."

Harriet's face was puffed up with scorn, her chapped hands resting on wide hips. But Brett was on to her. Beneath this façade he witnessed the first hints of a derisive grin.

Automatically, he reached for the closest item at hand, which ended up being the replica of a wriggling black eel intended to lure some innocent creature into captivity. Holding the item in the air for Harriet's inspection, he heard her snort.

"Five bucks." Harriet turned her back to him and shuffled behind the cash register.

Brett studied the twisted bait incredulously. "Five bucks for this?"

Harriet arched a gray eyebrow and crossed her bulky arms. "Five bucks," she repeated.

"Do you even know what to do with that thing?" Harriett challenged, ringing up the sale.

I have some ideas, he thought, but refused to take the bait, so to speak.

Not offered a bag, Brett stuffed his purchase into his jacket pocket and then splayed his hands atop the formica counter. He gave Harriet his most absorbed stare, to which she just uttered a *hmmmph* and crossed her arms.

"I didn't think it was going to be that easy to get rid of you."

He relented with a grin. "Come on, Harriet—"

"*Ms. Morgan.*"

"Of course," he continued. "I'm just trying to find out what happened here. What happened to the marriage between my brother and Serena? I know I was neglectful in staying away so long, but till the very end, the conversations with Alan had seemed positive ones. How did it crumble so fast?"

Settling down atop her swivel bench, Harriet glanced at the clock. She stared across the counter at Brett, and finally lost an apparent inner conflict to remain silent.

"You know Alan didn't want to come up here, of course," Harriet started. "He wanted to stay in the city. But Serena finally convinced him that there was land for the taking in this area, and that he could make a good start in Victory Cove. I think from that moment on, Alan began to resent her. He resented that she led a happy life up here and that he was an outsidah."

Maine's brittle wind jarred the glass panes of the front door, enough to cause a soft jingle of the strung bells.

"The O'Flanagans now," Harriet continued, "they couldn't alienate a soul. They welcomed Alan as family, but he didn't seem to notice. As the years passed, he grew restless and found more and more excuses to leave the Cove. Serena knew that she asked a lot of him to come to this remote village, so she nevah tried to stop him from taking his business trips. At first Alan might be gone a week or two, then it became two or three months at a time."

Harriet shook her head. "We all saw the pain on Rena's face, but pride kept her going, pride and people that loved her."

"Why didn't she leave him?"

"Bull-headed damn woman." Harriet cursed. "She didn't want to admit failure. She was consumed with making their marriage work. She kept thinking he would grow out of the phase he was in."

"And I bet she thought the baby was going to solve everything."

Stricken by Brett's words, Harriet's eyes seemed evasive. "How did you know about the baby?"

"Serena told me."

"I find that hard to believe." Harriet frowned. "It's not something she evah talks about." She eyed him again. "No one even knew that she was pregnant. I knew though. She couldn't hide the signs from me. I brought it up, and she finally confided in me. It was a surprise to her." The shop owner blushed. "With Alan gone so often, the occasions for such a thing to happen were rare—"

Harriet cleared her throat with a gruff cough. "But given this gift, yes, she did see it as a chance to rebuild their relationship. She couldn't wait for Alan to get home so she could tell him."

Harriet's head tucked down, enhancing one of her chins.

Brett leaned on the counter, the tale playing out for him like a movie.

God help him—he dreaded its conclusion.

"What happened?"

Head up and arms crossed, wrinkles of pain surrounded Harriet's eyes. "No one knows about any of this, Mr. Murphy. Even Serena's parents never knew she was pregnant. I am trusting that you will keep this between us."

His nod was sincere.

"All I can tell you is that Alan and Serena left on *O'Flanagans Stew* that morning with a baby in her belly. When she returned, she started having bad pains and next thing I knew she was in the hospital." Mist filled Harriet's eyes. "She hasn't been the same since. I have tried to pry it out of her, to ask what happened out there, but she won't talk about it. She just walks away. If the baby was only a month or two along—well these things happen. But Serena was well into her fourth month, something drastic had to occur."

Harriet unclenched her arms and dropped her hands to the faded polyester at her knees. She looked up. "I know he's your brothah, so I don't mean to offend you, but I can't help thinking that when Serena told Alan about the baby—he was less than happy about the news."

The implication hung heavy in the hush of the tackle shop. And in that protracted silence, Brett found the answer he was looking for. The knowledge saddened him. It angered him. He wanted to escape this coastal village. He wanted to head out on the Interstate and never look back.

"I appreciate your time, Ms. Morgan."

Brett turned towards the front door, but Harriet's voice halted him.

"Don't hurt her."

Brett stopped, pained that no one cared that his brother was dead. No one sought to even pursue the matter.

Yet the grief that plagued Brett the most was his own betrayal, conceding that his brother was capable of these accusations. And yes, the guilt. If he had just had the courage to steal Serena away that day, she would have been spared.

Embittered, Brett answered, "I'll try not to."

Elbows resting on the bar, Rebecca cupped her face in her hands, and gave Serena a tentative smile. "So it's just us now. Are you going to fill me in on what Brett Murphy was doing in your apartment this morning—looking shall we say, pleasantly rumpled?"

The heat in Serena's cheeks must have stemmed from lifting the heavy tray. Her chuckle was forced. "I told you why he was there. Quit looking for gossip, Miss Sorrenson."

"Well, I just think that—" Rebecca's voice halted as a telltale breeze fluttered the stack of napkins near her hand. She turned towards the door to find the daunting figure of Brett Murphy. With a gurgle low in her throat, Rebecca slipped from her bar stool.

"Rena honey, I'd love to stay and chat, but I've just had it. Are you sure you're okay cleaning up that mess?"

Baffled by Rebecca's hasty flight, Serena acknowledged Brett with a tip of her head and answered, "I'll be fine. Go get some rest. It's going to be like this through the weekend."

Rebecca grabbed her scarf and wound it about her neck. She nodded at Serena and plowed past Brett.

"Was it something I said?" Brett's eyebrow arched.

He cleared his throat. "I wanted to get here earlier. I was afraid you'd be upstairs already."

"Didn't want to miss any of the action up there?" Serena's voice was spiteful, but not to him, rather the insanity that plagued her. "Don't worry, no matter what time I come home at night, the ghost accommodates my schedule."

"I wanted to be here," he stepped up to the bar, "because I didn't want you going upstairs alone."

Serena's emotions betrayed her with the slight tremor of her lip. She broke from Brett's gaze and slipped through the service panel to attack the mess in the dining room.

"I won't be long." She brushed her hands against her thighs.

"Let me help." Brett offered.

Before she could object, Brett reached for the loaded tray and conveyed the clanging mass of dishware to the counter. Hesitant, she followed, passing by him to slide behind the bar and dump her pile into a sink full of suds.

Amidst a shower of bubbles Serena glanced up and asked, "Can I get you anything while you're waiting?"

Brett's grin was quick. "You've got your hands full. How 'bout I come back there and pour it myself?"

Before she could react, Brett ducked beneath the panel. Now he was standing next to her, so close she could smell a hint of musk and ocean.

Brett reached for a mug and tugged the tap nozzle. He set the glass down and hoisted up the sleeves of his black pullover sweater, revealing strong forearms that she tried not to stare at. To her surprise, he dipped those arms into the mass of foam.

"You—you don't have to do that," Serena stammered.

The turbulent clouds in Brett's eyes abated. "It's actually kind of relaxing," he said. "I don't mind."

Feeling the tension in her shoulders ease, she yielded to a grin. "Ten-fifty an hour and you can have all the relaxation you want."

"Where does this go?" Brett held up a long-stemmed wineglass for Serena's inspection. Following her tilted head, he reached up towards the other flutes hanging in rows above the cash register.

Serena was in his way so he stretched over her to slide the stem of the glass into its wooden channel. In doing so, he became conscious that he was draped over her, involuntarily pressing Serena back against the counter.

In slow motion, his arm dropped. He met wide eyes brimming with incredulity. Without considering the move, his hand settled on Serena's arm, his fingers dusting around it. He felt a tremor course through her.

Managing restraint, Brett cleared his throat and stepped back. Temptation still licked at his fingertips so he reached for a dirty dinner plate to occupy them.

Serena dragged in a breath and touched her hand to her face. For one crazy moment she thought Brett was going to kiss her.

But that thought was ludicrous, wasn't it? He was only here to keep an eye on her, to see if she revealed anything about Alan.

"I guess that's it." Brett interrupted her musing.

Serena jerked her eyes up towards the clock. Half past eleven.

Would her ghosts still be up?

"Are you sure about this?" she hesitated, "It's probably inconvenient to you."

Brett reached into one of the booths to hoist an overnight bag over his shoulder. He reassured her with a wink.

"No, Serena, I don't think I'll be inconvenienced."

CHAPTER VI

"I'll get the fire going."

Brett stoked the flames to life. It was a source that drew
Serena to his side as she stood with her hands fanned out
above the heat.

In his periphery, he studied her, noticing the tense set of
her shoulders and the worried frown. He crossed his arms and
kept his eyes averted. "I know this is awkward for you."

On an absurd laugh, Serena brushed past him to reach for
his overnight bag. Brett pursued, following her into one of the
small bedrooms. The ceiling was angled, with a dormer
window overlooking the latent town of Victory Cove. Brass
oil lamps atop lace doilies cast dual arcs of gold across the
wooden floor. Above the bed spanned a vivid painting of a
clipper ship—so vivid that he could nearly feel the sway of its
deck beneath his feet.

A final glance around the bedroom and Brett felt as if he
had been transported to an era long ago, when a weary sailor
just back from months at sea bedded down in this very room.

"Will this do? I've kept it clean, but other than that, it
hasn't been inhabited in a long time."

He smiled at her awkwardness, aware that the room was
so confining they were forced to be close. "It's perfect." Then
he added, "Serena, you know why I'm doing this don't you?"

Serena's chin tilted up. "Yes."

"Oh really?"

"To keep an eye on me," she said. "Maybe I might say
something, reveal something incriminating."

"Maybe," he said quietly. "Or maybe it's because I realize
that I've been too judgmental. Maybe, just maybe, I was
wrong about some of my accusations." His gaze dipped to the

shadows beneath Serena's eyes. "Maybe I want to see you get a decent night's sleep."

Serena felt edgy. Her glance fled to the black night beyond the window. But in that glass pane, she did not see the night. She saw their reflection.

Her figure was daunted by the giant man behind her. Brett filled the alcove, making it seem even smaller, and he was so close that she could feel his jacket pressing against her back.

"I don't think that's in the cards for me, but—"

Serena froze, her eyes darting to the doorway. The sound sent a jolt through her as she clutched the dresser for support.

Brett came alert. He reached for her arms and gripped them with force.

In the mirror their eyes locked.

"*Stay here,*" he ordered.

Brett heard it too. The unmistakable footfall that echoed from the hall. A solemn invasion. Rooted, his gaze shifted, awaiting something to materialize. He listened as the pace crossed the floor, and in disbelief heard the ghostly gait vanish through the door and into the night.

For a moment he expected Serena's frilly yellow curtains to billow in the breeze, but they remained still. With a jerk, he broke from his stupor and vaulted towards the door. At the bottom of the stairs his gaze shifted, scanning the arc of light. He peered through the stairwell and raged to discover moist footprints trailing down the center of each step.

Brett slipped into the shadows, circling the foundation of O'Flanagans. A cloudbank obscured the moon as a black void blanketed the frigid ground. Only his breath broke the raw silence.

Starting off at a jog, he rounded the far corner of the inn and lingered beneath the awning. Above him, the

O'Flanagans sign rocked in the wind. Dangling from rusted chains, its plaintive screech nearly muted the dull tread resonating from the shadows. An overhead streetlight disclosed a figure in the distance, the body and head obscured by a slicker and hood. Hunched against the bitter cold, the nebulous profile revealed little, and into the darkness the silhouette vanished like a vapor of mist.

Like a ghost.

Brett started to give chase, but thoughts of Serena slowed his pace to a halt. She was alone, vulnerable, and with a prophetic sense, Brett felt that he would encounter this specter again. And when he did, he would make him pay for the damage and suffering he had witnessed in Serena's eyes.

Brett marked the trail as he ascended the staircase. He calculated the source as a pair of men's boots, the pattern of the heel now evaporating into illegibility. Standing outside the door, staring at the yellow-frilled curtains, he was plagued with thoughts of what could have happened had he not been here.

Lost in deliberation, a motion caught his attention through the filmy material. Alarmed, he yanked the door open and rushed across the room to the figure huddled on the floor.

Brett's heart pounded as he crouched down beside Serena, taking in the protective state of arms locked around shins. Her cheek rested atop her knees as tears streamed down her face and her body rocked back and forth.

"Serena!" He touched her, running his thumb across the moist skin.

"It's okay." He was crazy with concern. "It's going to be okay. I found your ghost."

Bleary eyes opened as Serena whispered, "My baby?"

Jolted, Brett pitched back on his heels and reached a hand to the wall for support.

Serena's eyelashes fluttered down, locking him out. Pain and anger assailed Brett as he cursed whoever was attacking this woman's emotions. He regained enough control to hook an arm beneath her knees, and loop one behind her back, lifting her with ease.

Making his way to the love seat, Brett draped Serena across his lap where he held her until the tears subsided.

Lucidity returned with the heat of embarrassment. Serena shifted to stand, but strong arms locked around her, securing her in a masculine embrace.

"No, not yet." Brett whispered.

Shivering, yet unnaturally warm in this new haven, Serena cleared her throat.

"Sorry 'bout that," she choked. "Sometimes I just lose it. My grip on reality is tenuous at best."

When Brett didn't respond, Serena continued. "You should go back to Boston, Brett. Forget about your crazy sister in-law. Go home and grieve for your brother, have a service, do something special for him, and please try and forget how you saw me tonight."

"Are you done?" Brett spoke gently, his palm still splayed across her thigh as if he thought she might flee.

"Well," Stunned—at a loss for words—humiliated that he had found her in such a state—Serena struggled for something objective to say. "Well, er—yes."

Brett squelched his grin, but Serena caught it. She almost smiled.

With his arms around her, Serena began to feel warmth permeate her body. It was addictive, compounded by the masculine scent of him. When she felt Brett's fingers comb through her hair, she closed her eyes and caved completely against his shoulder.

"Why were you crying, Serena?"

Serena listened to Brett and thought his voice was soft, and his touch so gentle. Beneath her ear she could hear the rhythmic beat of his heart.

"Your ghost will not haunt you anymore." His whisper rumbled deep in his chest. "I'll find him and put a stop to it."

Weary from expelled tears–not fully comprehending him, Serena whispered sleepily, "He doesn't scare me anymore— it—it's the other one."

Brett tipped his finger under Serena's chin, lifting her face, considering her with intense gray eyes.

"What other one?" His voice was low, lethal if used in any other vein than the concern it expressed.

Serena's glance slid towards the fire, and her body tensed again.

"No," Brett commanded. "Talk to me, Serena. I want to help you."

"Why?" she pleaded and struggled to be set free.

Brett's arms locked, but his voice was assuring, luring her back towards the security he offered. Serena fought the temptation. She struggled upright as much as his hold would allow.

"How do you know my ghost won't hurt me anymore? What did you find out there?"

"I found," he frowned, "that your *ghost* wears a size eleven boot."

Reeling, Serena clutched Brett's forearm for support. She felt the muscle jolt.

"I followed the sound outside, and on the steps there was a trail, as if someone had just tramped through the wet grass in boots and came up that staircase." His voice turned cold. "Someone hell bent on scaring you."

Brett's grip tightened. "I almost missed him, but out front there was a figure in a raincoat, heading the other way. I would have gone after him, but I didn't want to leave you alone up here."

"You—you're saying it was a man—a real man? But, but you've been here, how do you explain it?" Wildly, Serena explored the shadows that concealed a ghost's tread. "How'd he do it?"

Brett looked past Serena, seeking the murky corners of the ceiling, the ornate latticework that could harbor any mechanical device. At first light he would scour this apartment and locate the source of Serena's madness. Till then there were questions to be addressed.

"With a little ingenuity anything can be achieved," he reasoned. "Why would someone want to scare you like this? Do you have any enemies?"

"Enemies?" Serena stared into the fire. "I wouldn't say I have enemies. The only people who've ever had it out for me are Alan—and you."

This time when Serena hastened to rise, Brett let her go.

"I'm not your enemy, Serena."

Brett rose. The motion forced Serena to tilt her head back to look up at him. He dominated her, but she stood her ground.

"Look at me, Serena." The tip of his knuckle softly grazed her chin. "Do you really think I'm an enemy?"

She stared up at him.

"Brett—I—"

Brett's hands dropped to Serena's arms. "Do you think I'm your enemy?"

"You—you insinuated that I killed him," she choked, "you, oh God, what you said on the deck about the baby—"

Brett's grip was now used to haul Serena against his chest, to keep her from saying the words.

"Oh, Christ, I'm so sorry. I didn't know." He held her tight against him and whispered into her hair, "I made the mistake of listening to Alan. *I was wrong.*"

Serena closed her eyes and felt his strength envelope her. This refuge was so warm. It staved off the chill that permanently racked her body. She allowed herself to stay in the embrace for a few seconds too long, and then drew back to ask, "And how do you know that you're wrong?"

Brett stared at her for a moment. "Your eyes," he said quietly, "and when I found you just a few moments ago—it was your voice."

"Maybe I'm just a real good actress." She tossed out bitterly, scared by how close Brett had gotten, scared at how good it felt.

Intent now on alienating him, if only to preserve their tenuous status, Serena retreated several steps.

"Maybe I paid someone to haunt me," the words lost their impact when her voice failed her, "all as an elaborate hoax to convince you of my innocence."

Serena's withdrawal drew her back against a three-tiered plant stand beside the bay window. Touching the piece for support, she swiveled towards the glass, gazing out at the near full moon that finally broke free from the clouds. It cast a brilliant sliver of light across the black sea.

In the darkness she saw Brett's silhouette advance behind her, but there was nowhere to go, and she was too tired to flee.

Brett placed his hands on her shoulders. When his fingers began to knead at the tension there she thought she might collapse. He spoke softly against her ear.

"I was suspicious, yes, but I wanted someone to lash out at—someone to explain to me what has been a mystery so far. I was hurt that Alan commanded no respect or remorse over his loss, and yes I wanted to blame you for that. I am guilty of these things. But Serena," Brett touched her hair. "I have never been, nor will I ever be your enemy."

Serena's eyelashes pressed firmly down against her cheeks, hoping to lock out the sight of the couple in the window. She leaned back and felt Brett's hands slip down her arms, drawing her closer. For the briefest second she welcomed that embrace. For just a whisper of time, she felt every hard inch of him pressed against her back.

It was good.

It was wrong.

Serena shook her head and wrenched away.

"I—I'm very tired. I—I have to try and get some rest."

"Yes, you do," he whispered, setting her at ease by widening the gap between them.

Serena fled to her room. With her door closed, she leaned against it to draw in a deep breath. According to Brett, one of her ghosts was real. A man intent on terrifying her, and for what reason? For what possible reason could someone hate her that much?

Only one person capable of such loathing came to mind.

But he was dead.

"Serena." Boom, boom, boom. "*Serena!*"

Dammit to hell, Brett muttered as he erupted from his light sleep to put a stop to the annoying thud at the front door.

Don't people let this woman alone?

Brett pondered the tall silhouette concealed behind the veil of gold curtains as Serena opened her bedroom door.

"It's okay, Brett, I've got it."

One ankle hooked over the other, Brett leaned against the wall, his stance seemingly casual as he watched Serena pass. His eyes, however, were alert and all his muscles were honed to attack should that shadow prove to be Serena's tormenter.

"Serena, oh my God, I just had to talk to you. I've been up all night thinking about a theme for next Thursday. I've got such brilliant plans."

Reaching her hands up into her tangled hair, Serena stifled a yawn and managed a plaintive smile for her wayward maitre de.

"Theme? I was more or less thinking we'd go with—oh, I don't know—something like, *Thanksgiving*."

Simon's hand dismissed that notion. "That's so boring." Then his eyes alighted on Brett and flared.

Simon's fingers rose to his mouth. "Oh my." He glanced at Serena. "I guess I've come at a bad time."

Serena tried to draw her gaze from Brett as well, hypnotized by the smoky eyes that languorously followed her. Heat tinged her cheeks when she connected with them. She saw what must have rattled Simon. Brett's shirt was unbuttoned most of the way, revealing a sparse trail of dark hair that dipped down a ladder of muscles. God, he looked good.

"No—no," she stammered. "Not at all. Umm, Simon you've met Brett Murphy haven't you?"

"Alan's brother?" Simon stepped closer, cocking his head, staring until Brett shifted uneasily. "No, I don't believe I've had the pleasure." He extended his hand and Brett obligingly returned the shake. "You don't look much like Alan."

"I've been told that before." Brett muttered.

"Yes—well, Brett's here to help me out this morning. I'll be downstairs in a little bit." Serena reached the front door and grabbed the knob, the gesture blatant enough to cause anyone to retreat.

Simon caught the hint and hefted a pale eyebrow. Grinning at his boss, he darted a hasty glance over his shoulder. Then, reluctantly, Simon followed Serena's lead and stepped outside.

"No rush." Simon leered. With a twist, he jogged down the steps, leaving Serena blushing to her toes.

"Damn." She slammed the door shut and marched into the kitchen.

Brett propelled himself off the wall with a shrug of his shoulder. He ambled in behind Serena, and reached over her head for the mugs.

"Something wrong?" Brett tried to keep the smirk off, but Serena looked so riled he couldn't help himself.

"No, nothing's wrong." She grabbed his offered mug with force, having noticed his amused grin.

"I wouldn't look so damn smug if I were you." Her gaze dropped down his chest, and Brett found he enjoyed that womanly perusal. "I do believe Simon likes you."

Brett struggled not to laugh.

"I'm flattered," he replied.

Serena chuckled. She poured coffee into his mug and he saw her mirth quickly segue into doubt.

"Are you sure, Brett? Are you sure it was someone real?"

"You mean, am I sure you're not going crazy?"

Plaintive green eyes spiked by the sun's golden rays awaited his reply with such intensity Brett didn't dare hesitate.

"He was real, Serena. Someone is deliberately messing with you."

Brett sipped his coffee and set the mug down. "And this morning," he declared, "I'm going to search this place for a recording device to prove it."

Serena released her withheld breath as her shoulders slumped. Her head dropped too, until Brett's touch on her arm jarred her. She looked up at him.

"Don't look so glum sweetie," Brett whispered. "At least you aren't the object of a gay man's lust."

The laugh from Serena's lips warmed the loft.

Brett craned his neck to search inside the window frame, squinting against the glare of the sun as his breath clouded the glass panel. "We're in agreement that the noise seems to stem from this room, right?"

Arms crossed, Serena's eyes restlessly scanned the corners of the room. Sensing her unease, he allowed the short navy drape to fall back into pleats as he searched her face. It glowed from her recent shower, yet still harbored traces of fatigue.

"I'm sorry," he added softly.

Serena shrugged, but the gesture did not conceal her apprehension. "I still don't believe someone would do this. I mean, how did they get in here and set this up?"

"Don't be naïve, Serena. You're downstairs nearly all day and night," he said. "It's simple enough to do. But I'll tell you…whoever did this is a pro, because I can't find anything in here."

Folding to her knees, Serena stooped over to peer at the cobwebs beneath the loveseat. Her breath disturbed the fine dust as she spoke. "What should I be looking for?"

Serena's shiny crown of hair fell forward as she skimmed the wooden legs. Brett noticed the revealing tremor in her fingers. He crouched down beside her and placed a hand on each shoulder to pull her up to his level, and ducked his head to produce a wan smile. "Why don't you go downstairs—I'll take care of this."

Serena sat back against her heels and searched his eyes.

"This is my house," she challenged, "and my problem."

"You're my sister in-law," Brett countered. "He was my brother, and I want to know what's going on here. Serena goddammit, trust me."

"Why should I?" She tipped her head in aggression but her eyes were plaintive.

Brett roved that tilted chin, and the soft trembling lips— so close that all he had to do was slant his head and seize her mouth, showing her exactly why she should trust him. The impulse was so strong, he nearly yielded to it.

"You're absolutely right," he agreed. "You haven't seen me in ten years. Why should you trust me?"

Brett's frustration was fueled by a brief glimpse of Serena's wedding photo. He hoisted himself up and shoved a hand out to assist her.

Serena ignored the offer and rose. For several heartbeats they stared each other down until she drew in a long breath and uttered. "I have work to do. If you need me, I'll be downstairs. Kindly lock up when you're done."

"Okay."

Serena turned her back on him.

"Wait," Brett drew in a deep breath, relieved to see her stop. "I'm going to ask you something, and I don't want you to get angry."

She crossed her arms. "What?"

"I want to look through Alan's papers. I want to know what he was working on just before the accident. He could have been in over his head. This—this—*man* pretending to be your ghost might be after something he left behind."

To Brett's astonishment Serena began to laugh. Her fingers clamped over her lips to stifle the stark noise.

"What's so funny?"

"Go ahead, search all you want. I think about all you'll find are a couple of his shirts." The humor fled her eyes.

"When my parents moved to Florida, Alan and I moved into this loft. Ten years of marriage and he had very few personal affects to bring with him. I found it odd, but I was too busy trying to run a business." She sighed. "Tax time was hell around here. I couldn't even get him to produce any documented source of income. There was never any paperwork here," she emphasized. "I'm sure it exists somewhere, wherever he disappeared to for all those months, but go ahead, Brett." She flung her arm in disdain and marched to the front door. "Have at it."

"Serena."

She didn't make it fast enough. With her hand on the doorknob, her head dropped. A willowy figure in blue jeans, looking frail despite shoulders pinned back stiffly.

"I'll be down around the same time tonight." He hesitated when there was no response. "I'll help with the dishes again."

Only a brief nod indicated Serena even listened. The door opened, and the Atlantic gust assaulted Brett with a chill that stole his breath.

And into that cold fist, Serena disappeared.

CHAPTER VII

Brett focused on the slick stretch of blacktop, the drone of the windshield wipers hypnotizing him as he maneuvered the Jeep around a sharp turn. His constant badgering of the police had finally paid off by providing a list of names involved in Alan's muddled business ventures—the endeavors that had landed him in jail. Both victims and benefactors were obtainable only because Brett argued that since Alan was dead he certainly bore no threat to these people. When asked what possible reason he would want such contacts, Brett simply indicated it was to express regret over his brother's business strategy, and to apologize. What he had though, was something tangible to research—a potential source for Serena's ghost.

A steady rainfall pooled with dusk, making visibility virtually nil. Brett flipped on the fog lights. All he could discern in the murky glow was the sinister profile of the lighthouse. As he passed by it, he contemplated the history of the statuesque structure. It conjured up images of tall ships evading the craggy obstacles of the cove. He imagined what it would have been like to live in that time, to have a woman with long fawn-colored hair, waiting for his ship to return.

It was near dark as Brett pulled into the parking lot behind O'Flanagans. Head hunched against the onslaught of rain, he approached the back door of the tavern.

For a moment he stood outside and listened to the muffled sounds of music and laughter. He was anxious to get in there and be a part of it.

He was eager to see its owner.

Brett was behind the bar, stacking dishes and loading the sink, conscious of Serena inserting a plate between his crooked arm. Over his shoulder he talked against the flow of water.

"Why don't you hire anyone to do this?"

Pausing in her torrent of activity, Serena shrugged and smiled. "Don't think of me as a martyr. I've got plenty of staff, but they're all young, and I like to see them on their way home by ten. I can handle what's left after that—and now I have you."

"That you do. But—"

"I know." She looked away, emptying the cash register into a cloth bag with a padlock secured to the zipper. "It's a temporary thing."

"I don't like the idea that you're in here alone, dealing with money like that—late at night."

"I've been doing this for years, Brett. The only person to ever come in here and take money out of the register was my husband, and I certainly shouldn't have been afraid of him, should I?"

Serena seemed to want to pick a fight. Perhaps she too felt the shift of balance between them.

Brett frowned, angry with her for being so stubborn and not seeing the danger she placed herself in every night. Who was going to look after her when he was gone?

And when had it become his job?

"I'm sorry. I've just been a little tense." Serena's soft voice beckoned.

Brett glanced over and caught her defeated look.

Who was he kidding? He had readily taken on the job.

"I've just been so edgy." She busied her hands by stacking pitchers beneath the bar. "My imagination is out of hand lately. Why, if it weren't for you hearing my ghost, I'd probably be locked away by now."

"Your ghost is pretty clever," Brett mused. "I couldn't find anything in your loft this morning. I've got a few leads on some of Alan's deals which went sour—people who could potentially hold a grudge."

"And that grudge would extend to me?" Serena's eyes narrowed. "Guilt by association, is that it?"

"Who's on this list?" She pushed. "Parker Banfield? He's the one who sold his land for ten grand only to watch Alan make a hundred and fifty percent profit on it. Or is it John Morse?" A shiver coursed through her. "I'm not even going to go into what Alan got involved with there. Or is it—"

"What did Alan do with this John Morse?"

Serena visibly fretted.

Brett leaned his hip against the sink, crossing his arms in anticipation until she submitted. "John is from the Pasamaquoddy Tribe.

Brett's nod prompted her to elaborate.

"The Pasamaquoddy receive federal dollars in order to acquire their own land back. Alan hooked up with John, hoping to pull a scam on the government. Because the tribe has sovereignty over tribal land, they are exempt to certain laws. Alan just saw this as a great opportunity—for what, I was never privy to the details. But when he was gone for those month-long spells, more often than not he was with John Morse."

"I need to start on these dishes." Brett's voice was brusque.

Hands ensconced in foamy liquid, Brett tried to focus on the information Serena just detailed. He accepted that he had turned a blind eye to Alan's private endeavors. Now he must face the repercussions of that ignorance.

"What are you thinking about?"

Brett glanced up from the pan he was taking all his frustration out on. If anything, the copper bottom sure shined.

"I was thinking about that name—John Morse. I heard Alan mention him."

"I'm sure you did," Serena said. "He's Alan's best friend."

"If they're so chummy, why hasn't he been around here? Did he show up for the service? If they're such good friends, has he stopped by to offer you any assistance, any insight on what might have happened?"

"No. I wouldn't want him around here though. He always made me uncomfortable. I mean, the man has a permanent sneer stitched on his face."

Serena reached for a towel near Brett. Perhaps it was her close proximity that set him on edge. Suddenly, the pile of dishes slipped from Brett's slick fingers and crashed into the water. A wave erupted and surged in an arc that splashed Serena from neck to waist. Her scream of surprise quickly turned to a peal of laughter as she stared down at her drenched shirt.

Brett couldn't resist a laugh, but his gaze turned heated as he fixed on the results of the mishap. Serena had removed her sweater earlier, the kitchen still hot from the ovens. She now wore only a simple cotton top with the sleeves rolled up to her elbows. Completely sodden, the material was sheer. Curse him to hell for staring, but he could see her nipples and the sight made him growl. He tried to conceal it with a cough.

The affect Serena had on him was staggering. The cravings she triggered were insatiable. He was a condemned man for wanting something that had belonged to his brother.

"Well," Serena announced with a chuckle as she reached for one of the napkins to dab uselessly at her soaked shirt. "On that note, I guess we're done here for tonight."

Serena glanced up, amused, but her humor faded as she caught the naked desire in Brett's eyes. Held immobile by his stare, she gulped and clutched the damp napkin tight to her chest.

Brett looked lethal, with long black lashes lowered across stormy eyes. Those eyes roved over her with yearning. It was as bold a caress as his large hands could have produced, and she felt it as surely as if his fingers branded her.

Brett cleared his throat.

"Sorry about that," his voice came out husky. "You're right, that should do it. I know it's a quick jaunt upstairs, but you better put a jacket on."

Brett was trying to sound gruff, authoritative, but the note of concern was evident to her. She secreted a smile and turned her back to him while hoisting her thick sweater over her head. "All set."

Any awkward discomfort was dispelled as soon as Serena switched off the lights of O'Flanagans and faced the prospect of going upstairs where her ghosts—be they real or products of failing sanity, awaited. Brett held her up in the doorway with a splayed hand as he inspected the shadows beneath the stairwell. Satisfied, he prompted her ahead.

Serena replaced the soaked shirt with a blue knit top, and stood on the warped corner of the throw rug, wringing her hands. She stared at the long arch of Brett's back, watching the fire glow over wide shoulders and muscular outstretched arms. Eclipsed by that golden glow, he looked like a deity sent down to protect her.

"Do you want some coffee?" she asked.

Brett rose, turning towards her with the fire radiating off his frame. She drew in a breath and battled the urge to retreat.

Measuring her reaction, Brett shook his head. "I'm not going to bite."

"Of—of course not. I'm just jittery, it happens this time of night."

Some of the heat in his eyes abated. He approached her and placed his hands on her shoulders. "Why don't you curl up on the couch, and I'll make us that coffee?"

For the briefest moment Serena wallowed in that tone of tenderness, wanting to believe it was real.

Insecurity settled in.

"Don't treat me like an invalid. I've been dealing with this by myself for a month now, and I've been just fine."

"Have you?" Brett challenged quietly. "You weigh next to nothing. You have circles under your eyes. Every morning your eyelids are swollen from crying. Are you fine?"

Serena broke his gaze and sought the flames as a diversion. "Well, doesn't that just paint a flattering picture of me? Poor ole Serena, looks like death herself."

Surly with exasperation, Brett sighed. "Dammit woman, sit down and relax."

Realizing how ridiculous they both sounded, Brett relented with a grin and released his grip. Serena dropped onto the couch.

"Are you sure I can't help?" she offered wearily, her head already sagging against the arm of the love seat.

"Just stay there."

Familiar now with the kitchen, Brett moved efficiently, all the time berating his behavior. Serena needed protection. She needed answers. She didn't need a lecherous brother in-law. He had to stay resolved to the fact that there would never be anything between them.

Brett rested his hands on the counter, regrouped, and returned to the living room with two steaming cups in hand.

Serena was asleep.

In some way he felt victorious that she succumbed to this one weakness in his presence.

Sinking onto the adjacent love seat, Brett sipped his coffee and stared at the smoldering logs. He considered feeding the charred pit with more kindling.

Lost in thought, replaying in his mind the facts he had learned today and the list of people he intended to visit tomorrow, Brett jolted as Serena sprang erect.

Her eyes shot wide open.

"What is it?" Such was the panic in her gaping stare, he felt dread clench his stomach.

"*He's here,*" she whispered in a detached voice.

Instinctively, Brett came to his feet, listening for any trace of the invader. The loft was silent apart from the crackling of the fire and the distant rumble of the ocean.

Serena's gaze was unfocused and he considered touching her to see if she was truly awake, but then he heard it—the methodic footfalls emanating from behind her. Their path was deliberate. Brett was already certain of their destination as he hastened towards the front door.

There seemed no mechanical source for this unsolicited visitor. It stemmed from the very floor beneath him, crossing wooden planks out into the night. With a growl, he hurled open the door and raced down the steps, determined this time to catch the culprit.

At the base of the stairwell, Brett wavered. The haunting memory of Serena's oblique gaze troubled him. And the sound that ensued from above made him sick.

"No!" He tried to deny the sound.

With dread he vaulted up the stairs.

CHAPTER VII

Alan was gone.

Serena was relieved to hear him leave. In fact, that that had always been the case.

Yet it was at this moment, this dreadful silence before the arrival of her next phantom that Serena recognized the icy tendrils of fear. When her ghost arrived today, it assaulted her not with the anticipated wails of anguish, but something much more dramatic.

Laughter.

Serena's hands lashed out before her to hold the sound at bay, but the child's echoes of mirth dipped into her soul, permitting a glimpse of a life taken. She moaned, but the childish giggles prevailed, a singsong laughter that had her teetering on the edge. Incoherent pleas fell from her lips as she hugged her arms about her and rocked back and forth, ignorant of the tears coursing down her cheeks.

That was how Brett found Serena as he paused at the doorway, shocked by an infant's sound of merriment interlaced with Serena's weeping. Brett launched at her, landing hard on his knee, cupping her face in his hands.

"Serena!"

She was lost to him.

"Goddamn you," Brett cursed the source of this hoax.

His fingers bit into Serena's shoulders, a vain attempt to break through to her.

"Serena, look at me!"

Moist eyes stared through him. It was a vacant gaze he would never forget.

Serena was crooning to the infant.

"Honey, look at me." Helpless, his thumbs brushed at the tears coursing down her cheeks.

Powerless to stop this torture, Brett searched in vain for a way to invade her daze—a way to penetrate her torment. The invasive ring of laughter thwarted all his efforts. Distraught, his fingers wound into Serena's hair.

Any indecision was lost to this sense of urgency. In a move fueled by despair, he yanked Serena's mouth to his.

Brett thought the shock of the act might penetrate Serena's anguish. Initially, she was cold and unresponsive. He swiped his lips against hers and tasted her tears, licking them away, using his roaming hands and unleashed passion to distract her.

If God struck him dead for this, so be it. If Serena herself wanted to kill him as a result of this, that was understandable. If she was coherent enough to hate him—that would be satisfaction enough.

But right now he still tasted her sobs.

Rough and insistent, Brett's kisses became a constant. His hands tangled in Serena's hair, capturing her into compliance until gradually he felt her respond. When the soft tip of her tongue emerged to graze his bottom lip, Brett jolted, but he held her steady. Serena's mouth opened under his as he heard a soft rumble of desire purr deep in her throat. The warm invitation was just too much to pass up. He greedily partook.

Cool white fingers caught his collar as Serena kissed him back. Tiny whimpers of despair or yearning were the only discernable sound, while he distantly acknowledged the child's laughter had ceased. He was not gallant enough to withdraw yet, and couldn't have done so if he wanted to; such was Serena's hold on him. Taut fingers gripped his shirt, her soft lips responding to his every touch.

Brett's knees spread apart as he hauled her between his thighs, pulling her closer, nearly onto his lap. The wanton embrace made his kiss intensify and it also altered Serena's whimper into a husky groan.

He had to stop.

If he didn't stop, he would lie her down on the floor and kiss her until there were no more ghosts, no more pain—*just him.*

Instead, Brett brushed a last stroke across Serena's mouth, a gentle caress that made his stomach clench with desire. His forehead rested against hers, the sounds of their uneven breath united. Once Brett felt his heart slow down to a safe enough pace, he scooped Serena into his arms and carried her to the loveseat, nestling her onto his lap.

A sob wrenched from Serena's lips. She ducked her head against Brett's throat, her fingers still clutching the fabric around his collar. Weeping anew, she clung to him, expelling all the tears that had been trapped inside since that dreadful day aboard *O'Flanagans Stew*. Her cries extended to the grief she had not permitted herself after Alan's death—these tears healthy and cleansing.

Dreamily, she was conscious that she was not alone. She was warm, secure, comforted—and seized a hold of those sensations, using them as steps to climb back to the present.

"Brett?" Drops clung to her eyelashes as Serena pushed against Brett's shoulders in order to search his face.

"I'm here," His voice was hoarse.

Disoriented, briefly catching familiar scents—the fireplace, the sea, and the rugged combination of musk and soap that was uniquely Brett's, her eyes opened fully.

Serena acknowledged her position collapsed against Brett's body, feeling his arms encircle her protectively.

She should run from this embrace. It felt too good.

Instead, Serena relaxed against Brett's chest. For just a moment—just a moment to subdue the racing of her heart, and the lingering traces of panic. She knew only that in this haven she felt a remarkable sense of relief, and a tingling in the pit of her stomach—akin to anticipation. These new sensations muddled her thoughts.

"Wh-what happened? Did you catch him?"

Serena remembered that much. *Brett storming out the door—the distant echo of his steps fading down the stairs.*

Brett reached up to brush a tear off her cheek.

"No," he said. "But I did hear your other ghost."

When Serena would have retreated, Brett's arm prevented her, locking her against him. He continued softly. "Why didn't you tell me sooner? Why did you live through that hell by yourself?"

"I—it—I thought it was all in my head." Fumbling for the words to describe the pain, Serena managed to add, "Guilt."

"Guilt?" His voice was hoarse. "You are guilty of nothing. You are a victim. I see that, and I'm sorry I didn't recognize it sooner. You're second ghost isn't real either, Serena. And now you aren't dealing with it alone anymore."

Serena's withheld breath released against Brett's neck, reassured by his confident tone. She should struggle. This wasn't right—them being so close, but she was too weak to fight, and had little inclination to do so.

So safe. She felt so safe.

Serena closed her eyes and fell asleep.

Groggy, Brett squinted against the sun filtering through the windows. On the other side of the wall he heard Serena start the shower. At least she had made it through the night with only a minimal amount of agitation discernable from across the hall.

Brett dropped his feet to the floor and rubbed his hands over his face, fingers digging into gritty eyes. He stood up and caught a glimpse of his haggard expression in the mirror and flinched at the image. Hell, if he greeted Serena this way, she would surely flee in terror. Grabbing the black sweater he had tossed at the foot of the bed last night, he hoisted it over his head.

The front door was empty. No boisterous morning visitors.

"You look like you had a rough night."

The voice itself sounded rough, hoarse from spent tears and emotion, yet there was a hint of affection mingled in Serena's words.

Brett turned to look at the fresh vision whose hair was a shade darker from dampness. Void of makeup, Serena's skin bore a healthy glow that enhanced the jade flecks in her eyes. She was barefoot in thick wool socks, her jeans faded from years of washing. The New England Patriots jersey, judging by its old logo, had definitely seen its prime. *She was beautiful.* And he felt as awkward and awestruck as when he stood before her on her wedding day.

Muttering an ambiguous reply, Brett turned his back and addressed the switch on the coffee maker.

"Brett." Her voice brought him around again. "Thank you."

Brett nodded gruffly. "I didn't do anything."

That was the truth. He felt discouraged because he hadn't found a trace of Serena's enemy.

Serena slid onto one of the long picnic benches and rested her elbows on the table, cupping the side of her head in her hand.

"Well—" She seemed uncomfortable at first, and then looked at him so frankly that Brett felt his heart stammer.

"I hadn't cried for Alan yet," Serena admitted. "I still have a hard time believing he's gone—I keep looking for him—"

"Your sea vigils at night?"

"Yes," she chuckled awkwardly. "I guess you thought I was crazy?"

"Initially." Brett smiled and slid onto the bench across from her.

"But me being here, isn't that my own vigil?" He didn't wait for her to answer. "Serena," he breathed in. "The baby. I'm so sorry about the baby. If I could take back the things I've said—"

Her upheld hand cut him off as Brett sullenly acknowledged the simple gold band on her ring finger.

"You helped me more than you can imagine," she said. "If you weren't here last night—if I were to continue believing that the ghost of my child haunted me," Serena shrugged, but the gesture was not casual. "I don't know if I'd even be coherent right now. And—" her hand thumped against the floral tablecloth. "I'm not working the lunch crowd today."

"Good for you, it's about time you took some time off."

"Don't be so hasty in your approval. I took the day off because I'm coming with you to review that list you got from the sheriff."

The cup Brett held came back down.

"Now wait a minute, Serena. I mean it. You should be resting, not antagonizing yourself by talking with Alan's—"

"*Business* partners, accomplices, enemies," she sighed. "I don't romanticize my husband. I accept what he was and hope to someday not blame myself for his downfall."

Brett's scowl increased. "Alan was destined for trouble. I tried to keep him out of it during our school years, but when he became an adult it was almost impossible. The day of your wedding," he met her gaze. "I tried to," he hesitated. "I wanted to warn you—warn you about what you were getting yourself into." The words wrenched from him. "If only I did."

Serena stared.

Brett would have given anything to know what she was thinking.

"It's in the past Brett," she declared. "And if I'm going to truly put Alan to rest, I need to know what happened to him."

Brett rubbed a hand over his eyes, swiping at the lingering traces of fatigue. "You said you cried for Alan last night. If he hurt you so much—then why?"

A ray of sunshine darted through the front window and trailed off down the hallway. Serena tilted her head to catch a trace of its warmth and then sighed.

"He was young, he was troubled, and he was my husband. As infrequently as he played the role, Alan was still my husband."

"Okay," Brett yielded. "We'll go together. But give me a couple minutes," he muttered. "I sure as hell need a shower."

Brett rose and felt Serena's eyes on his back. Just before he shut the bathroom door, she called out his name.

"Hmmm?" His hand was on the doorframe, his head crooked around the corner.

"Brett," Serena began in such a soft voice that he had to strain to make out the words.

"Everything is such a blur from last night. I don't think I've ever been so—so distraught. But I fell asleep afterward, and I only fell asleep because I felt safe." She took a deep breath. "Brett, I have to ask—did you kiss me last night?"

Oh God.

He was a thirty-six year old man. An intimidating figure on the New York Stock Exchange. A cunning broker that firms sought out for his expertise. Yet now he was just a man fumbling for a reply.

"Well—I—" he cleared his throat, "you were bordering on hysteria. I didn't know what to do to bring you back—I—"

Amusement tickled the corners of Serena's lips. She put an end to his misery. "It worked."

Brett cleared his throat and nodded. As he turned around, he caught a glimpse of his grin in the bathroom mirror.

Murphy, you better watch yourself.

Within a half hour they were out on the coastal highway, winding downhill towards the seaboard settlement of Victory Cove. The high cliffs that were a staple near O'Flanagans tapered down to a horseshoe inlet. An elevated road, fortified by rocks separated the Atlantic from quaint wooden shops and seafood restaurants.

"John Morse lives just past town." Serena pointed through the windshield. "It's a nasty little shack near the water. I've never been in it, but I've seen Alan's car parked there."

Even the bright autumn sun did little to enhance the weary establishment settled on a crag of rock. Brett pulled down a rutted driveway and eyed the old pickup truck with one tire lodged in a slick of mud. He shot a doubtful glance at Serena.

"Will it do me any good to ask you to stay here?"

Her hand was already on the door, one leg slipped out, searching for a dry place to set down. "Of course not."

They heard the television before they reached the steps. Several planks were missing on the porch, and so was any indication of hospitality. A familiar commercial, loud and invasive camouflaged the shriek of decaying timber as they reached the door.

Brett wished Serena had stayed in the car. His apprehension was escalating. He cast one last skeptical glance in her direction, and pounded his fist against the screen frame. By the third rap, the door swung inward.

John Morse was a burly character, with straight black hair pulled back into a ponytail that leaked dark strands around high, pitted cheekbones. Ebony eyes narrowed until a glint of recognition sparked at the sight of Serena. The man sneered.

On instinct, Brett positioned himself in front of Serena.

"What do you want?" Morse snarled.

"A few minutes of your time." Brett began, sensing a battle. "We have some questions."

"And why the hell would I answer any of your questions?" His glare swerved to Serena. "Your husband isn't even gone a month and already you're whoring yourself out to the first man you see."

Brett moved so fast that everyone was startled, most particularly John Morse when he found himself pinned against the wall.

"Let me clarify," Brett continued in a steely voice that matched his grip. "You *are* going to answer a few questions for us. You *are* going to tell us what happened to my brother the day he disappeared, and you *are* going to tell me exactly what Alan was involved in."

Morse managed a brief nod before Brett released him.

Rubbing at the pain in his throat, Morse reassessed Brett.

"Well isn't this just special," Morse's voice was slightly off. "The brother who never gave a damn, along with the wife who never gave a damn—and now you're all acting downright concerned. It does the heart good to see the love of family."

Brett held back from throwing the man against the wall again. It didn't help that he was sensitive to the accusations, a sensitivity that only broadened his anger.

"Your opinion of me means squat." Brett said in a tight voice. "I know you and Alan were in trouble with the government. Why don't you elaborate?"

"Why don't you—" John's words were arrested by Brett's threatening step forward.

Morse cleared his throat and shrugged his shoulders. "It was Al's idea. He thought we could beat the system—con the government out of some federal aid," he snorted. "He had grand ideas of building a casino on tribal land."

"That's ridiculous," Brett argued. "Do you know what it takes to obtain sanction for a casino? And besides, Alan's white. That's a tribal issue."

"You seem pretty informed."

"I'm in a business to be informed." Brett said.

"Alright, so you're right. But Alan had the backing of many Pasamaquoddy. I believe he could have done it—if someone hadn't of killed him." Black eyes swerved suspiciously towards Serena as she crossed her arms and glared back.

"What makes you think he was killed?" Serena challenged.

"Come on lady, don't be naïve." Morse barked. "If he wasn't already an enemy of the government, he was surely an enemy of several other tribes. The Penobscot didn't like the trouble Alan stirred up. They were vying for the same grant. Surely you can imagine he wasn't too popular."

"Well you seem to look unscathed," Brett mused. "Aren't you worried?"

"I wasn't, until somebody just assaulted me on my doorstep. Kinda odd that Alan disappears and you suddenly surface, don't you think?"

"Kind of." Brett clenched his fist. "What do you know about that day? When did you see Alan last?"

"I already talked to the police. Ask them."

"I'm asking you, because I know damn well you didn't tell them anything."

Morse heaved a sigh. "I don't know. Alan came over here in a huff. Something happened, but he was too mad to even get into it." Tossing his head towards a three-legged kitchen table propped against the windowsill, Morse muttered. "Broke my damn table—kicked the leg right off of it. Said somebody was gonna pay, but didn't go into what was bugging him. I was well into a bottle of whisky, so I just ignored him," he rolled his eyes. "I mean if you know Alan, his tantrums are pretty common."

"Did Alan say where he was going?"

Morse shook his head. "Didn't say, but I guess it's not too hard to figure out he went to his boat, now is it?"

Brett cupped Serena's elbow and said, "Come on, we're not getting anything here."

Before stepping off the porch, Brett turned to Morse. "If I were you, I'd lay low for awhile."

Tipping up his chin, Morse smirked. "If I were *you*, I'd watch out for the little missus. Whoever did this to Alan might believe that he confided too much information to his wife, and—"

There was no need to continue. The point was made.

"You're awfully quiet," Brett said. "Are you okay?"

Serena seemed absorbed by the pattern of the windshield wipers. "Umm hmm."

It had been a long day, and the Alan battering had apparently taken its toll on her. Brett glanced over again and studied Serena's silhouette in the glow of the dashboard. Her chin was set, but a slight quiver at the corner of her mouth indicated that she toyed with speaking.

"There was nothing you could do," he tried to reassure. "Don't take everything he said seriously."

Serena tipped her head back against the headrest. "Do you think it's true? Do you think Alan could have been in so much trouble he was killed because of it? My God—"

Silent in his own deliberation, Brett considered Serena's question and squeezed the steering wheel.

It was pointless for them to sit and swap self-condemnation tales. They were both guilty of ignorance when it came to Alan, but both were by design and self-preservation. Now, Brett's primary concern was John Morse's haunting advice that someone may be after Serena. The ghosts that plagued the loft at night validated that.

"What do I have to do to get you out of working in the tavern tonight?"

Brett wanted Serena close to him, and not with a group of strangers, amongst which a murderer could easily blend. "How about if I offer to cook dinner?"

Serena's laugh was pleasant, but it did not make it to her eyes. "What can you cook?"

"If it comes in a box, I can make it."

Serena glanced at her watch. "I'll tell you what, I have to check in downstairs, but my curiosity is piqued enough to consider your offer—that is if you can wait till later to eat?"

Brooding over the decision to remain in the restaurant with Serena and monitor its patrons, or to scour the apartment in search of audio mechanisms—it finally registered that she had accepted his invitation.

Suddenly, Brett felt awkward. He knew Serena wasn't looking for a romantic candlelit dinner—more likely a summit to discuss today's events, and devise a game plan. When she looked at him, she saw only Alan's older brother.

The Jeep rolled to a halt beside the stairwell, and Brett yanked the emergency brake, inhaling the scent of honeysuckle and warmth, knowing both emanated from the woman by his side.

Slanting a glance at her, he managed a husky, "Late is fine. It'll take me that long to figure out what the hell I'm going to cook that can come anything close to the food downstairs."

Serena climbed out the door and then smiled at him over the hood of the vehicle. "Well, you're in luck. Everything I have upstairs comes from a box. Cookies, some macaroni and cheese, and cereal. Lots of cereal."

"What type?"

"Wheaties."

Serena walked alongside Brett and darted a glimpse at his profile, misted by the rain. Beside him she felt small. It was a pleasant sensation and it reminded her of how she had felt in his embrace.

"Is the milk fresh?" Brett asked with a wry grin.

Serena focused on his lips.

"No," she whispered.

Brett reached the door and paused a moment to make room for her to step alongside him under the awning. The vinyl flap sheltered them from the rain.

"If you let me borrow some from downstairs, I think Wheaties sound perfect for a late night meal."

In the tight alcove, Serena had no room to maneuver, and to keep from getting wet, she moved up close to Brett, close enough to brush against the front of his jacket. He still did not turn and open the door.

"That would be letting you off too easy." She teased and tipped her head back to look into his eyes.

The rain was an afterthought as she felt the heat of Brett's body and the heaviness of his stare. She was aware of his hand slipping around her back, and in response hers landed on his chest. His head lowered close enough that his breath tickled her lips and warded off the raw chill around them.

At that moment, someone thrust open the door behind them and Brett crashed into her.

"Excuse me." A middle aged woman apologized as she yanked the hood of her jacket over her head and hastened out into the rain.

Holding onto one of the metal poles that supported the awning, Brett sought balance and loomed over Serena.

"Get inside," he whispered.

Trapped in the open folds of his raincoat, Serena raised another hand to his chest, telling herself that it was only to steady him. Her fingers settled on solid muscle beneath his sweater, where she could feel his heart beat a quickened pace to match her own. It stimulated and unnerved her—so much so that she yanked her hand back.

Left uneasy by the brief spell, Serena slipped past Brett into the glowing haven of O'Flanagans. Inside, she felt the heat of the dining room fireplace assault her flushed cheeks. She dipped beneath the service panel, and emerged behind the bar where confidence returned.

CHAPTER VIX

"You had to stay down there till closing, didn't you?" Brett scolded. "I made you dinner. Wheaties."

Serena pulled off her sweater and hung it from a wooden coat rack near the front door. She stood before him in a black turtleneck and jeans, with her cheeks red from the cold, and her hair mussed from the wind. She eyed the two cereal bowls and rubbed her hands together, either for warmth or the prospect of food. Then she wrinkled her nose at him in response to the reprimand.

Brett laughed. "It's a good thing I didn't pour the milk two hours ago when I thought you were coming upstairs."

"Soggy wheaties turn me on," she teased.

"Well hell, if I had known that, I could have filled up the bathtub—"

Serena's hand curtailed him. "Alright, alright, just give me a spoon will you, I'm starved."

Brett grabbed two spoons out of the drawer, and rounded the counter to settle on the picnic bench across from her.

Serena delved into the cereal, until three spoonfuls later she realized that she was the only one eating.

"Arrren yuu wungry?" With a forceful gulp she swallowed the rest and repeated, "Aren't you hungry?" Then she considered the stark look in Brett's eyes. "Did you find something?" she asked. "A recorder?"

Brett cleared his throat and forced an affable expression back on his face. If he didn't stop lusting after his sister in-law, he was going to get into a lot of trouble.

Truth be told, his search wasn't lucrative. Instinctively, he glanced at the clock to see how much longer till their ghost returned. As much as he enjoyed Serena's newfound comfort around him, it was time to put frivolous repartee behind and prepare for their nightly caller.

"Serena, if and when those footsteps start tonight, I want you to listen to them. I mean really *listen*. You have the advantage. You know this loft inside and out. Tell me what you hear. Tell me what's wrong with them. Are they accurate?" His eyes left hers to span the living room. "You know where the planks creek on the floor, the weak spots, try and gauge where they're coming from, or if they were even produced in this house."

Serena set her spoon down and shoved the bowl away.

"Oh no you don't."

Startled by his rebuke, she glanced up. Brett came around the table to sit beside her.

"What?" She flinched.

He drew up a foot away from her and stifled a curse. "First, don't shy away from me like that." His voice grew soft. "I'm not going to hurt you."

Visibly relaxing, Serena offered him a shamefaced smile. "And second?"

Brett left a decent gap between them. He tipped his head towards the porcelain bowl. "You are going to finish that."

Serena followed his gaze to the sodden mass.

"Soggy wheaties," Brett reminded her.

She continued to scrutinize the clump of bran and milk, and wrinkled her nose. "I lied."

"Then what *does* turn you on, Serena?"

Serena's head snapped at the soft lure of Brett's voice. She was pinned by stormy eyes that washed over her with a gale force. Brett had not moved, but she felt his close proximity, aware of his warmth, sensing something so raw and elemental that she wanted to connect with. Of its own volition, her hand rose until the tips of her fingers skimmed the dark stubble framing his jaw. Gray eyes continued to watch her. Steady. Solemn. Hot.

Brett reached up to enfold Serena's hand in his and turned it to brush a soft kiss against her palm. Then he guided her trembling fingers back to the table and around the handle of the spoon.

"Eat," he ordered in a husky voice.

With her eyes fixed on him, she hesitantly raised the spoon, managing a brief mouthful as he nodded his encouragement.

Her spine stiffened. The spoon crashed down into the bowl of milk.

Brett's head jerked at the sound of footsteps.

"Serena!" His voice was raw. "Listen to it."

Her first instinct was to cover her ears, but Brett grabbed her arms. "Listen. Tell me what you hear."

Eyebrows furrowed, Serena searched past Brett into the living room, then wrenched from his grip to approach the phantom steps.

What did she hear?

She heard Alan crossing the living room in slow, deliberate steps. It was another of his endeavors to sneak out the front door, hoping not to be overheard from the bathroom where she stared at her distraught reflection in the mirror.

Serena's eyes closed now, listening to the past, listening to the present—what was wrong between the two?

There was a hollow sound to the heavy stride that she had not detected before.

Serena crouched down in time to heed the steps as they passed before her. Splaying her fingers on the wooden floorboards, she leaned forward and listened to them fade.

"What is it?" Brett ducked down beside her.

Focused, she replayed the eerie tread in her mind.

"It—it didn't sound natural. I mean, if I wasn't really paying attention, I could swear it was Alan walking out the front door," she shook off a chill, "it *did* sound like his footsteps. But it sounded hollow, like an echo." She glanced at her fingers on the polished floorboards. "It seemed like it came from downstairs."

"Downstairs." Brett repeated. "What's down there? I noticed that the stairs outside don't stop on the second floor, how do you get downstairs?"

Brett followed Serena's glance to an unmarked door in the hall.

"That's the inner stairwell. We used to live down there, Alan and I." Serena explained. "My parents stayed up here in the loft, but once they left for Florida, I pretty much closed off the second floor."

She rose and clutched her arms about her to ward off a chill. "I had aspirations of turning the second floor into a real Inn, renting out the rooms to weary tourists and all."

"That doesn't sound so ludicrous." Brett reached the stairwell door, twisting the brass knob, but found it was locked.

With a steadying breath, Serena sought to moderate her thunderous heartbeat. She probed through a ceramic curio box on the coffee table and grabbed the key, but immediately dropped it at the sound of an infant's laughter pervading the still loft.

Brett crossed the floor in three strides, reaching for her shoulders, forcing her to look at him.

"It's a cruel trick. Don't cave into it, Serena. That's what he wants."

"It *is* a cruel trick," she cried.

Brett's arms enfolded her as if he sought to shelter her from the haunting mirth. His broad chest, so warm and powerful beneath her cheek proved to distract her from the invasive sound.

At length, Brett set her back and stooped to retrieve the key. His hand reached for hers and their fingers meshed. They stared at that simple connection.

With a gentle squeeze, he whispered. "I'm going to put a stop to this, but I need you. Can you hang in there with me?"

The baby emitted a string of cooing giggles. It was a hoax Serena reminded herself—a malicious joke, and the only way to end this daily torture was to trace its source.

She clutched his fingers. "Come on."

A single bulb mounted high on the angled ceiling cast a yellow hue on the wallpaper. Along the border of the wooden steps the aged paper curled away from the wall. Serena made *tsking* noises at the state of disrepair as she flattened her hand against the course material.

"We haven't used these stairs much," she whispered. Anything louder than a whisper would have reverberated enough to peel the cracked wallpaper.

"The middle floor has been closed off," she said. "I guess I've neglected it."

Honestly, she did not want to come downstairs and address the memories. She had ventured down here once a month ago to locate some personal effects for Alan's service, but there was nothing sentimental she could find to bury in his empty coffin.

Using the same key, Serena unlocked a door at the first landing as Brett surveyed the shadowed route down to the restaurant. When the door swung inward on squealing hinges, he stopped her with a light touch on the shoulder and then moved past to survey the dark chamber.

"I can't see a damn thing," he cursed, using one hand for leverage, the other secured around her forearm.

"The electricity is off on this level. We were being cheap." She brushed by him. "Hold on."

Distressed by her disappearance, Brett called out Serena's name. Her face appeared before him, glowing in the wake of candlelight. She clutched a thick vanilla candle melted at an uneven angle so that half the room shone brighter than the other.

In that flickering ring of light, Brett was able to discern a family room with its few pieces of furniture sheltered in dusty sheets.

Ghosts.

Acclimating to the darkness, only large objects were recognizable, and these Brett warily steered around. Taking the candle from Serena's hand, he held it up towards the ceiling to inspect the chain of cobwebs linked in such a fashion that no mortal could have tampered with them.

"Is this room directly beneath the living room?" Brett cringed at the echo of his words.

"Not exactly. There's a small kitchen through that archway. The floor plans aren't similar at all, and the third floor was an attic till about thirty years ago."

Serena guided him towards the entry of a galley-styled kitchen. Here, the dark was impenetrable, with no window to cast even the subtlest glow. Brett set the candle down on the counter, snapping his hand back from the hot wax that trickled down to scorch his flesh.

"Are you okay?" Serena whispered.

"Yeah," He reached for the first cabinet. "Is there a dish or something I can set that on?"

Brett sensed Serena's touch beside him. "Here."

Accepting the small saucer, he held the flare aloft and craned to examine the ceiling for the telltale track of wiring.

Nothing seemed amiss. Frustrated, he handed the candle back off to Serena.

"Hold this a second."

He hoisted onto the counter and reclaimed the candle, peering into the dusty alcove above the refrigerator. As much as he dreaded what might be lurking there, he thrust his hand into the tight space. The grill behind the icebox was cold to the touch, but not rigged with anything malicious. Still, he was convinced that the source of Serena's ghost lie in this room.

Impatient, Brett began tossing open cabinet doors, his fingers probing the remote corners, coming up empty except for a mousetrap that snapped near his pointer finger.

"Dammit!"

"Brett?"

"I'm okay. Wait, there's something here." It was a cable coiled in the recesses of the cabinet. He yanked the cord and heard a muffled crash upstairs.

"*Brett*?"

The urgency in Serena's voice pervaded as Brett reached for the candle to catch the taut shadows of apprehension around her lips.

"What is it? Did you hear something?"

Brett climbed down and positioned Serena behind him. He jabbed the light out into the family room, but saw only the harmless mounds of furniture.

"No." Her voice was tremulous. "Over there. On the counter."

Sweeping the candle back into the kitchen, it penetrated into the far corner to reveal two dim shadows atop the nicked formica. Advancing towards them, Brett was conscious of Serena's nails biting into his arm. Her other hand was on his hip as she molded herself against his back.

"It's a bag of corn chips?" Brett tried to justify the fear he felt in Serena's grasp, but wasn't going to dissuade the friction of her body.

"And a bottle of *Allagash*." she added, hoarsely.

"Yeah?"

"Alan drinks Allagash," she whispered. "And corn chips were his favorite snack."

"But this was his home, naturally there are going to be traces of him left behind. I know it must hurt, Serena—it must be hard on you to come down here and see signs of your husband, but—"

"No," Serena grabbed the beer bottle and held it up to the flame. Tilting the glass left and right, she watched a frothy ring of liquid slosh around the bottom.

"I was down here a month ago, just before Alan's service. These were not here. There's still condensation in this bottle. It would have evaporated if it was here that long."

Serena seized the bag of corn chips, where several chunks were still intact. "And the damn mice from the cabinets would have feasted on these."

In the diffused light, Brett saw rage darken Serena's face. He took the bottle from her hand and watched the liquid swirl around in the same pattern his thoughts whirled about in his head. Disbelief, incredulity, cynicism—and above all else, a growing resentment.

"Are you sure?" he asked. "Allagash is a local beer. It could belong to anyone. Maybe it belongs to this John Morse—if they're so buddy buddy, naturally they'd have the same tastes."

"I guess I don't know him well enough, but I think about anybody in Victory Cove will testify to the fact that Morse won't drink anything tamer than whisky."

Brett's curse was enunciated clearly as he slammed the bottle back down, wishing it would break. It didn't—which only nurtured his anger.

"Well, Serena," his voice was cold, "maybe your ghost is more real than you think."

Serena wrapped her arms about her. "What do you mean?"

"What if Alan is still alive?"

In the family room, the Atlantic's fierce wind rattled the windowpanes, making his already ominous voice even more compelling. "What if it really *is* Alan that's haunting you?"

Brett reached for both her arms.

"Tell me, Serena, do you think Alan is capable of this?"

The question might have been verbalized to her, but the query rooted inside his mind.

CHAPTER X

Alan—still alive?

The thought rolled in Serena's head, inciting an attack of nausea. Would he do this? Would he be malicious enough to drive her towards the brink of madness? Would he prey on her vulnerability at a time of such despair?

Alan, alive.

Was that such a startling revelation? Hadn't she felt him all along? Wasn't that why she sought the cliffs each night, hoping for closure?

"Yes," Serena choked. "Yes, he could do this."

Strong fingers touched her jaw, dragging her from anguish. In the candlelight Brett's features were eclipsed, but his touch stole through her.

"Look at me." His free hand reached up to cup her face, his thumb gently tracing it.

"Serena, you're not safe. I know what Alan's capable of, and I know when he's got it out for someone—he will carry it out to the end. We've got to go to the police."

Serena laughed. "And say what? A corpse is chasing me? They've pronounced him dead—as in the subject is closed. You've worked with them. Haven't the police been very closed-book on this?"

Brett released her and hoisted a hand through his hair. "Yes, but my brother is not right. He's—" the word took a second to form, "dangerous. I'm just going to have to make them understand that."

No amount of darkness could conceal the pain or disillusion in his voice. Serena reached for his hand. These were the same emotions racing through her veins, pulsing where Brett's fingers grazed her wrist.

"We're losing the candle," she whispered. "Come on, let's go back upstairs. I don't want to be here anymore."

Brett seemed preoccupied with remorse. Mechanically, he took the lead, candle aloft in one hand, his other gripping hers tenaciously. They mounted the stairs in silence until a thin band of light was distinguished at the base of the door.

Desperate now, Serena wanted nothing more than to return to her radiant loft and leave behind this pit of shadows and anguish.

"Well, I guess I really know how to wine and dine a woman, huh?" Brett inched his thigh into a half-seated position on the edge of the dining room table.

"You've virtually swept me off my feet."

What had been fun baiting suddenly lost its allure.

Trying to ease the beginning signs of a headache, Brett rubbed the apex of his nose and mumbled something.

"What?" Serena asked.

"I'm sorry."

"Sorry?"

"Yes, sorry. Sorry that I didn't stop you from marrying him. I wanted to, you know." He let loose a pent-up breath. "Isn't that selfish? I stood in that hall, staring at you, willing myself to say the words—*don't do it.*"

Serena touched the wall. "Why?" she whispered.

For a moment, Brett just looked at her.

"Because I knew he'd hurt you. I knew what type of person Alan was—that love was something I didn't think him capable of. I knew he would use you, and when he was tired—" Brett's eyes cut through the dark. "Because *I* wanted you."

Unnaturally loud, the tick tock of the Grandfather clock beat in time with Serena's heart. She opened her mouth, but Brett had already launched off the table.

"Never mind," he growled. "Forget I ever said that."

She didn't want to forget, but Brett was evading her gaze. He went so far as to stand up and inspect the loft. Fascinated by his broad shoulders and the long dip of his back, Serena watched him stoop down, his knee on the hardwood floor.

"Whoa," he said. "What have we here?"

Serena moved to stand over him.

"What is it?"

Brett righted the wooden figure adorned in a yellow slicker and hood. A craggy face looked up at them.

"Ya know," he smirked, "this guy looks like Coop Littlefield."

About to laugh because the statue really did look like Coop, Serena took notice of what Brett had seen. There was a barely visible hole inset between the narrow, painted lips. In addition, the statue had a tail, a cable that disappeared into the wall like a scurrying snake.

"Well, Miss Rena, I think we've found your ghost." Brett leaned back on his feet.

She stared in fascination at the statue. It was one of the pieces her parents had left behind. They figured flamingo sculptures would be more appropriate where they were heading.

"But how?" The thought that someone had been inside her apartment long enough to rig this apparatus staggered her.

"More important is *who*." Brett glared as he yanked the wire out of the fisherman.

"Look," he kicked the cable. "That puts an end to your nightly visitors."

Serena held a hand to her heart. Just like that, her ghosts were gone.

It wasn't that simple.

Brett must have read her thoughts. He reached for her arm. "Why don't you try to get some sleep? We'll deal with it all in the morning."

She nodded. She wanted that. She wanted to go hide in her room. She wanted to hide from the events on the second floor. She wanted to hide from this hollow fisherman with his illusory mouth. And she wanted to hide from Brett's compelling gray eyes and his gentle words.

With a whisper of acknowledgement to the man, Serena did just that.

Outside her window, Serena was aware that the wind had died down. She hoisted a long sleeved t-shirt over her head and then yanked off her jeans. She left on the thick wool socks to battle the bitter cold that lurked at the foot of the bed.

Lifting a hand towards the lantern on the nightstand, her fingers stopped short and retreated. Instead, she closed her eyes to shut out the dim light. Abruptly, her eyes flared, afraid of the darkness beneath her eyelids.

Alan was still alive.

She could feel it in the thunderous beating of her heart and the throbbing of her veins. Hands that clutched the quilt beneath her chin began to shake. Alan would torment her. He had already begun. Then he would come for her—and what he would do to her depended on how far over the edge he had finally gone.

Serena burrowed under the covers. In a whirl of anguish and fear, her last conscious thought before she fell asleep were the words Brett had uttered.

Because I wanted you.

Sleep was as elusive as answers.

Brett laced his hands behind his head and studied the grid pattern on the ceiling. The moon emerged to cast a luminous design—a chaotic checkerboard on which he had no clue which piece to move next.

Listening to the subtle groans of the old house and the distant sound of the breakers, he dissected each noise, however minute, for traces of an enemy. Restless and besieged with thoughts of Serena, he rose and approached her door.

The rustle of the quilt told him that even in slumber she tossed about in distress. His fingers brushed against the wood. He could go in there. Touch her. Offer solace.

That was a bad idea.

Brett continued down the hall, flinching as he induced a squeal from an aging floorboard. He stood poised, waiting to see if the noise disturbed Serena, but there was no sound from the other side of her door.

He reached the bay window and stared at the ocean beneath a three quarter moon. Waves crashed against the cliffs. The assault was methodical, reaching for the foundation of this house, attempting to draw it out to sea.

What happened to you, Alan?

This single thought bellowed over the raucous cadence of questions in his head.

Escaping a nightmare that left her breathing hard, Serena's eyes darted around the bedroom. A muffled sound, inconspicuous, but loud enough to make her flesh dimple had her swinging her legs off the bed. Controlling her quaking limbs, she found nothing amiss in her small room, but sensed trouble beyond the door. She approached it, listening to the squeak of ancient hinges as the panel swung inward.

She peered out into the hallway where shadows concealed all the demons of night. Damn Brett for not leaving a light on.

The lantern from her room cast a glow that ended uselessly outside her door. Still wary, she advanced into the hall.

Trembling fingers skimmed the wall for support until she reached the living room and saw the masculine silhouette profiled by the moon. Her intake of breath made the figure pivot, but his face remained cloaked in shadow.

"Alan," she gasped.

"No."

Shivering against panic, Serena lingered in her nightmares, but felt drawn towards the figure. On some lucid level, she realized that the shape was not Alan's—that the voice was not Alan's—but her nightmare still pervaded. Cautiously, she reached out to touch the shadow and gasped as a hand snatched her arm and drew her the rest of the way.

"I'm not Alan, Serena."

Serena was flat against his chest now, aware of his quickened heartbeat. She felt strong fingers wind under her hair and behind her neck.

Powerless, she was captured for lips that descended from the dark.

Brett slipped his arm behind Serena's back and felt the rigid tension in her spine. His fingertips traced down that taut column until she submitted and molded against him. All he wanted was to kiss Serena. He did so. A swift, hot assault of her mouth.

It tasted so sweet, but still like fear. He went slow. He would make this kiss last forever—just as long as she returned it.

In methodic sweeps, Brett brushed his lips across Serena's until she clung to him for support.

She whimpered. It was that tiny bleat of despair—or was it passion? It kept him in check. Still, Brett used his grip around Serena's back to haul her even closer, lifting her to her toes, the friction of the embrace nearly driving him to the brink.

This was what he had always wanted. *Serena.* Hot, in his arms. Kissing him. But he had wanted the whole package. The whole woman. Not just this sexy, half asleep vision. Because of this, his mouth continued to taste her with light swoops, intimate passes that made him grow harder by the second.

Lost in the rhythm, Brett was startled to discover that Serena's lips had opened, parting to offer her warmth. He groaned and used the grasp on her hair to tilt her head back so that he could brush a kiss on the pulse in her throat. His tongue lashed out to savor that tiny throb. Warm, silky flesh tasted like honeysuckle and lobster bisque, and he sipped it like it was a culinary masterpiece.

Serena gasped at the sensation, and Brett quickly returned to her mouth to swallow that soft breath. She whimpered again, but he could feel her body stir against him. Her arms laced behind his neck, pulling him down deeper into the kiss.

Obliged to deliver, Brett released her hair and reached to grip the hips that started to grind against him. Defying the initial resolve to simply taste her, he kissed Serena long and deep, his tongue inside her, stroking her into life.

Vaguely, Brett was aware that if his hand dropped only a few more inches he could caress the bare thighs rubbing against his jeans. But if he did that, he wouldn't stop. Instead, he tore away from her mouth and touched his forehead to hers.

"Who am I, Serena?" he murmured.

Deprived of his kiss, Serena moaned and tipped her head back, seeking Brett out. He evaded that temptation and whispered again, this time with his hands cupping either side of her face, so that when her eyes opened she would focus on him.

"*Who am I?*"

In the wake of the moon, Brett watched long lashes flutter and then open wide.

"Brett," she exhaled. "You're Brett."

God help him, but he had no defense against that ethereal voice. With a tortured groan, he crushed his mouth on hers. His hands slipped, his thumbs tracing the curve of her breasts—all the time acknowledging that what he was doing was insensitive, that he should have more control for both of them.

His taste. His touch.

The nightmare was long discarded and no confusion remained about the identity of the shadow that coveted her mouth.

Alan had never made her pulse beat so hard that she throbbed in the most private location. Alan had never taken the time to kiss her so thoroughly she found her limbs useless and relied on Brett's embrace for support. Alan's touch had never exacted the total abandon that consumed her. Serena's tongue sought warmth behind the barrier of Brett's teeth and was invited in with a sigh that might have been her name.

Tempted past the point of demure, she drove her fingers into his hair and stroked the length of her thigh between his. Bare flesh against denim, she felt the solid muscle that coursed down his leg. She could imagine that contact being flesh on flesh, and it made her frantic. Eager fingers searched the gap in his collar, seeking the warmth of his skin.

Serena reeled when Brett's kiss stopped.

"Are you sure, Serena?" His voice was husky.

"Brett." Fingers bunching into fists on his shoulders, Serena sought equilibrium both in mind and body.

"I know who you are—" she stammered. "I—it's wrong, I shouldn't be touching you—"

Brett's hands on her hips gently set her back, away from the evident reaction of his body. Once she was at a safe distance, he drove a merciless hand into his hair.

"Dammit." Air rushed between his lips. "Serena honey, you have nothing to feel guilty about. I just attacked you when you were at your weakest. Hell, look what you've been through tonight. I could see it in your eyes. The fear that you'd find Alan standing out here, and I just—" he hesitated, "I just wanted you to know it was *me*."

"Please don't cry." His voice was husky. "I would never purposely hurt you. You know that, don't you?"

How Serena hated the gap that separated them, yet if Brett touched her again she was unsure whether she would shatter or melt. In the dark, her head tipped forward in defeat.

Just this evening, she was presented with the possibility that her husband might still be alive, which meant that she was still married. If she had thought she was going mad during the past month, tonight she was certain of it.

"No," she began. "But I may hurt *you*."

When Brett would have stepped forward, she retreated. "If I asked you to stay away from me, it wouldn't be because I didn't want you." She shook her head. "I'm too old to play coy. I'm not going to stand here and deny that—that every time we look at each other there's—*heat.* I'm not going to deny that when you kiss me I feel something I've never felt before."

Serena took a deep breath. "Brett, I want to make love to you. What type of woman wants to sleep with her husband's brother?" Her voice challenged, but she didn't let him respond. "You, you deserve so much better than me."

It took great will, but Brett forced his hand back down to his side. He turned away from temptation and sought amnesty in the black ocean.

Given any other venue, Serena's admission of desire would have him confessing to the nights that she flooded his dreams. But Serena's words of self-condemnation were the very same words that echoed in his head.

"Look, I was wrong to kiss you," he said. "I know that. It was selfish, but God help me, if I had the chance to do it again—" he cleared his throat. "Right now, though, I'm more concerned about your safety than I am about all the things I want to do to you."

Testing his control, Brett turned around and reached out to touch Serena's arm. "We're going to the police tomorrow, okay?"

With a dispirited nod, Serena looked up. Her eyes were like the deepest shadows of the forest. A color he might expect to find on the shore of the Rhine, where the Brothers Grim wove many a dark tale.

"Go back to bed, Serena. Try and get some rest. Try not to think about this. Try—" Brett grappled for words, "Try to forget what just happened. We have a lot of work to do."

The tiniest nod served as acknowledgement. Brett watched Serena retreat down the hall, his hands hanging useless at his sides. Only when she disappeared behind her door did he turn back towards the living room.

Sinking down onto the loveseat, Brett crossed an ankle over his knee and kneaded the back of his neck. Preoccupied, he pondered the plant stand before him. Myriad sprigs of a fern, like dancing tribes, wiggled when a persistent breeze infiltrated the cracks around the window. He swiped a hand across his face and tried not to recall the actions which even now kept his body hard and hungry.

"Brett?"

Serena hovered in the shadows, just out of his reach.

"Hmm?" He came alert. "Are you okay?"

She didn't respond. She advanced a step. Her arm touched the frame of the sofa.

"I can't sleep in there—it's—" she waited. "I want to be out in the open, where I can react."

Precisely why he was sitting in the living room, Brett thought. Well, that and the fact that sleep was not in the cards for him.

But, wouldn't he feel safer knowing Serena was close by?

Brett extended his hand and touched Serena's outstretched fingers, coaxing her onto the couch.

"Come here," he whispered.

Serena alighted beside him, folding her bare legs beneath her and reaching for the knitted blanket. She draped it over her lap, but still remained rigid.

A grin tugged at Brett's lips. He dropped his foot off his knee and reclined, grabbing a pillow and throwing it across his thighs.

"Serena honey, you're tired. Just lay down," He patted the pillow and caught her incredulous look in the moonlight. "You sure as hell don't have to worry about me accosting you if that's what you're afraid of."

Ashamed by the stab of regret, Serena tried for a careless shrug as she stretched out and rested her head in Brett's lap. She struggled with the knowledge that only a thin padding separated her from his muscular thighs—thighs she had just shamelessly caressed. Thighs she wanted to stroke without the barrier of clothing.

"But you can't be comfortable," she protested, "and you need rest as much as I do."

Brett touched her hair. "I'm fine." His voice was husky. "More comfortable than I've been in years. Go to sleep, Serena."

Brett's gentle command lulled her eyes into closing as she breathed in his scent and realized that, indeed, it was the most comfortable she had felt in a long time.

"You put coffee on?"

Following the scent, Serena walked into the kitchen, slinking a towel over her t-shirt. She felt the cold sting of the tiles on her bare feet.

Hanging from a hook beneath the cabinet, her mug was blocked by a much disheveled and very sexy man. Serena scoured that image. Brett's blue cotton shirt was wrinkled, yanked out of faded jeans, and unbuttoned enough to glimpse a flat stomach. Her eyes lingered for too long until she jerked them up. His hair was matted on one side and faint lines creased the corners of his eyes—eyes that traced her every move with the focused intensity of a lion.

Speechless, Serena stood before Brett, waiting for him to shift aside and let her reach for the cup, but he did not budge. Heat rose to her cheeks as she caught him staring at her lips.

Brett cleared his throat, shuffled to his right, and reached to turn off the percolating coffee. Using the opportunity, he drew in a breath and tried to recover before looking at Serena again.

"What are you doing up this early?"

"If we're going to go to the police today," Serena reasoned. "I've got to get downstairs and get some work done first. I've still got food to order for Thanksgiving, it's only a few days away, and—"

Brett saw her throat pump as she swallowed. She must have interpreted his gaze. She must have sensed how much he wanted to kiss her.

God, how was he going to keep a level head and protect Serena when all he could think about was the taste of her lips?

He tried to break his trance by reaching for the coffee, but instead of grabbing the handle, his fingers wrapped around the pot itself. He bellowed and jerked his hand back.

"Brett!"

Serena reached for him, seizing his arm and tugging him towards the sink where she shoved his palm under a stream of cold water.

"Oww!" He howled. "Dammit woman, that hurts even more."

"Don't whine," Serena wrenched his wrist. "If the police ask you to fill out paperwork, what are you going to say, 'I can't, the damn blisters hurt too much?'"

Serena turned the faucet off and gently dabbed at his hand with the loose end of the towel dangling from her shoulder.

"I bloody well won't fill out any paperwork then."

Grunting his gratitude, Brett was mortified by the whole transaction. Serena's furtive smile fueled his humiliation.

"It wasn't that funny," he moped.

"Yes, actually it was."

He brooded some more until gradually they shared a smile. He reached up and brushed a moist lock of hair back from her face, his touch lingering.

"Will you wait for me before going downstairs?" he asked.

Serena tipped her head into Brett's caress. For a second, her eyes closed, and she smiled. The course texture of his palm against skin still sensitive from the shower was a heady sensation. She struggled to open her eyes and risked breaking the spell.

It didn't.

Silver orbs smoldered with promise as Brett whispered, "Maybe you better go."

It wasn't his words, but his gaze that conveyed what would happen if she stayed. Serena's pulse raced, and her breath caught. She set the mug down, heedless of the spilled liquid.

"I—okay—I'm going." Unable to break Brett's stare, she backpedaled. "I'll—meet you down there?"

"Mmm-hmm," he purred. "You will."

Beneath that languid glance, Serena caught Brett's grin and felt her lips tug in response.

"Don't look at me like that."

His eyes dipped down her body. "Don't stand there looking like *that*."

Serena's heart hammered.

"Well, all right then—" She retreated. "I'm going now."

Arms crossed, which accented the muscles in his shoulders, Brett rested his hip against the counter and continued to watch her with unabashed desire. Serena had never seen anything look so good in her life.

"I'm going now," she repeated.

"Yeah, you said that."

Serena thought, *It was either get out of here now, or—* "We'll continue this later."

Brett laughed, enjoying the rose tinge to Serena's cheeks, and the smile she tossed over her shoulder before hastening outside.

With her departure, the levity vanished.

Tipping down the last mouthful of coffee, he grimaced in pain as the warm mug scalded his injury.

It was a grim reminder that he had touched something that didn't belong to him.

With the bathroom door shut, his shirt discarded on the floor and his head ducked behind the shower curtain, Brett almost missed the emphatic banging outside. His first thought was that Serena was in trouble. He hastened into the hallway only to find a diminutive silhouette; undoubtedly not Serena's, lurking outside the front door.

"*What?*" Brett barked as he saw Rebecca's animated face glide smugly over his bare chest.

"Well, have I caught you at a bad time?" Rebecca cooed.

"Yes."

Seemingly ignorant of the intrusion, or any lack of decorum, Rebecca crossed her arms and pouted. "Aren't you going to let me in?"

He studied the woman in fake leather slacks and a short suede jacket. Her scarlet curls spiraled erratically in the breeze.

"I'm not exactly dressed for visitors."

Amber eyes converged on that fact. Rebecca all but licked her lips. Brett resisted the urge to drop his hand and fasten the unsnapped rim of his jeans, but he wouldn't give her the satisfaction of knowing that she made him uncomfortable.

"Yes—ah," Rebecca's eyes scaled up his stomach, "I see that, but I'll only take up a minute of your time."

Curiosity and suspicion prompted him to retreat a step and swipe his arm to allow her admission. Closing the door, Brett cursed his sore hand as he lingered near the entryway.

"If you're looking for Serena, she's not here, she's downstairs."

Rebecca cocked an eyebrow and pursed her coral lips. "I know Serena's downstairs, that's why I'm here."

Her wine-colored fingertips dragged along the edge of the dining room table as she sauntered back in his direction. "I wanted to talk to *you*."

Brett folded his arms over his chest and waited.

"What about?"

"Well, I just think it's awfully gallant of you to be looking after Serena like this. I mean," she paused for drama, "there's a strong chance that she murdered your brother, and still you're here every night keeping an eye on—things."

He had no time for games, and if he did, this was not one he wanted to play. "What are you up to, Rebecca?"

One finger was perched by its pointed nail on the edge of the table, till with a snap it released and Rebecca stood before him, head tilted to the side.

"I'm just concerned that she perhaps killed one Murphy brother—what's to stop her from going after the other? I think—" Rebecca stepped even closer, so close he could feel her breath. "I think it's not healthy for you to spend so much time with her."

Brett leaned over so that his gaze was even with Rebecca's. Her head tilted back and her lips went slack.

"And it would probably be best for me to spend some time with you?" He uttered with the ice in his voice going undetected by the redhead.

"Yes," she murmured, closing her eyes.

"What gives you the impression that Serena killed my brother?"

Rebecca seemed annoyed that he had ignored her blatant come on.

"Serena didn't understand Alan," she explained. "He had plans, great plans, and she never supported him on any of them—"

"But *you* did?" His eyebrow inclined as the picture began to unfold. "Were you sleeping with Alan?"

Amber flashed. Rebecca's gaze floundered for the briefest second giving Brett his answer.

"No," she cried, indignant. "Of course not."

Now totally provoked, she continued. "Look, I just came up here to warn you that Serena is the proverbial ice queen. She never put out for her husband and she'll never put out for you."

"But you will." Brett sneered and reached for the doorknob. He had had enough.

"Your concern for my welfare is touching, Miss Sorrenson. It's fortunate I don't have any other brothers for you to rifle through."

"You'll see," Rebecca hissed. "You should leave Victory Cove before you end up out there." Her scarlet mane twitched towards the window and the gray Atlantic beyond.

"Was that a threat, Rebecca?"

Brett yanked the door open and jerked his head to motion her outside. "Because if it was, I'm sure the police would be interested."

Coral lips parted briefly, closed, and then opened again. "Look, I was just trying to be a friend. I thought you could use one in a town full of strangers, and with a woman like that."

He looked her over, and in a deceptively soft voice, asked, "How much do you charge?"

The oath that slipped from Rebecca's mouth as she rushed past him had Brett wincing, or perhaps it was the assault of the blustery November wind.

Contemplating the closed door, Brett stood for a moment, listening to the ocean. He heard the faint cry of spiraling seagulls, and the pounding of blood vessels inside his head.

Victory Cove certainly had its cast of characters.

But the only one he cared about was downstairs. The person who had kissed him last night and opened a door both were afraid to pass through.

CHAPTER XI

"Whew!" Rebecca hustled into the tavern, red hair billowing around her until the door closed and the wind abated. "Serena sweetie, please tell me you put coffee on."

Glancing up from her seat in the booth, Serena smiled. "Would you expect any less of me?"

She returned to a stack of receipts and paid little heed to the woman that flounced into the adjacent seat.

Rebecca cocked her head, and then sighed.

"Something on your mind?" Serena asked without looking up.

Rebecca's fingertips tapped. "How well do you know that Brett Murphy?"

"Excuse me?"

"Let's face it, I'm not blind, I see that he's been up there for the past few nights." Her fingers still tapped. "I'm worried about you. You're very vulnerable right now, and I don't want him taking advantage of that."

Serena sat back and gave Rebecca her full attention.

"I'm not so vulnerable any more, Becky. I'm getting angry more than anything else," she drew in a breath, "and that feels good in a way. Healthy."

"Angry? At what?"

As much as she enjoyed Rebecca's confidence, there was a line to be drawn when speaking about your possibly undead husband who haunted you for the purpose of driving you insane.

"Angry at my—inability to cope." Serena smiled as she drew the conclusion for the first time. "I'm not a babbling idiot anymore that you have to coddle. I'm going to be okay. And as for Brett, he's been a help, that's all there is to it."

Rebecca shoved her hands through her hair in a great show of sentiment, but the gesture barely concealed the tension in her eyes. "That's great, Rena honey." She cast a tentative smile. It's about damn time. Nothing like a man to distract you from your woes."

Frowning, Serena scooped up the stack of receipts and slid out of the booth. "It's nothing like that, I told you, he's just been helping me out, that's all."

"With what?"

"Sorting out some issues Alan hadn't addressed."

Rebecca darted after her. "Business issues?"

Curious, Serena glanced over her shoulder and caught what she thought was a scowl on Rebecca's bright lips. The short woman quickly flounced her hair and grinned mischievously.

"Sorry," Rebecca said, "you know I've always been such a busy body."

"That you have, Becky dear, but it's part of your charm. Don't worry, everything is under control. Right now we just have to concentrate on getting ready for Thursday. How is Simon making out with his preparations? Should I be afraid?"

Rebecca scratched her eyebrow. "Don't worry about Simon. I'm sure he'll surprise us all."

Wind permeated the sun-drenched tavern, terminated by the slam of the door. Two faces looked up. Two conflicting expressions welcomed Brett Murphy as he responded to each in kind.

"Ladies."

"Rena, I gotta go." Rebecca rushed. "We'll talk later, okay?"

Preoccupied, Serena nodded. "What time will you be in this afternoon? I may be running a little late."

"Again?"

The disdainful reply made Serena fumble for an apology. "I—uh—well yes, I've got to wrap some things up at the police station."

Scrounging for a smile, Rebecca managed tightly. "Why? Is anything wrong?"

"No, no, not at all. Just filling out some final paperwork."

"Oh." Rebecca bustled past Brett, stabbing him with her eyes. She tossed a brief farewell over her shoulder.

"How odd." Serena stared at the door seconds after it slammed shut.

Brett rested his elbow on the counter of the bar. "How well do you know Rebecca Sorrenson?"

"I've known her real well for about five years now." Serena dropped her stack of paperwork back into the safe beneath the cash register. She stood and crossed her arms.

"She's had a bad time of it. Her husband left her for another woman, and she had no job, little education and no way to support herself. She came into the restaurant one morning, desperate for work, but still with that Rebecca-ish attitude that screamed 'I'm not going to beg.'"

Smiling at the recollection, Serena continued. "Now she makes a good income with tips here, plus she works at daycare in the morning—she's come a long way."

"Okay," Brett stood up. "But how well do you *know* her?"

"I just answered that."

He wasn't about to mention this morning's interlude. He felt that was best left for another time when Serena might find humor in the tale. He did, however, want to dig at her glowing review of the woman.

"Let me rephrase that." *How well did Rebecca know your husband?* No, he thought, that wasn't the right approach either.

"What are you getting at, Brett?" Serena approached the bar so that only the nicked counter separated them.

"I want to ask you something, and you're going to get angry, but I need to ask it anyway." Brett drew in a deep breath and plunged on. "Do you think Alan was faithful to you?"

With Serena's fingers splayed out on the bar, it was easy to discern them turning white. Other than that one small signal, her expression remained impassive.

"No." Her voice was soft.

Brett nodded before the response registered. His head snapped up. "No?"

"What? You sound so shocked. Do you want me to go on lying like I've been doing? To everyone? To myself? How could I think otherwise?" Serena's pale skin blushed with anger. "Aside from the gaps of time away, and the fact that he seldom touched me, sometimes there was the scent of perfume—"

She turned away and met his reflection in the mirror.

Brett thought he'd never cease being shocked by his brother's lack of propriety, but he still managed a stunned reaction. "I wish it was different between you two, Serena. You deserved better than him."

Her eyes pierced him in the reflective glass.

"Did I?"

"Dammit." He stepped up and reached for her hand. "Of course."

He wasn't going to argue this point to someone who was hell bent on crucifying herself. Someday, when this was well behind them he would show Serena what she deserved. Until then, he had a plan, and he needed her help and courage to execute it.

"Look," he said, "if I asked you to trust me, would you?"

Serena stared at his hand atop hers. Her lips curved into a tired smile. "Not too long ago I trusted so many people." She gently withdrew from his grasp to reach for a dish towel. "I guess I'm seeing what a naïve fool I've been."

Brett knew he was responsible for that enlightenment. "Alright, stupid question."

"No," she continued. "The point I was making is that I *do* trust you, but I've been shown recently that my judge of character has been lacking."

"Well then," Brett managed a grin, which grew when he caught the fact that she slowly mirrored it. "I better not let you down."

"How dare you!" Serena screamed. "Who the hell are you to accuse my husband of sleeping around? You don't know anything about Alan. You've neglected him for ten years, and you're just—you're just bitter."

Brett's face was red as he yanked the front door of the tavern open. "No, maybe it's *you* that neglected him if he needed to look elsewhere."

Straight on Brett's heel, Serena wrapped her fleece jacket around her shoulders and stalked upstairs, yelling back down at him.

"Go back to your goddamn ten thousand dollar a month flat in Manhattan. I don't need your help—your sympathy. Go back to your own kind, you don't belong here."

"Fine," Brett glared up at her. "Can I at least get my bag, *Mrs*. Murphy, or would you prefer to ship it to me?"

Retracing her steps so that she remained one stair above him, Serena's look of utter contempt was clear to anyone who may be watching. After all, that was the idea.

"I'm taking a walk," she said. "When I get back I expect you to be gone."

"You don't have to worry about that, honey." Brett rebuked. "You're a head-case and I don't need to deal with your problems anymore."

"Fine." Serena marched past him.

"Fine." Brett threw back over his shoulder.

Slamming his fist on the roof of the Jeep, Brett drew in a deep breath tinged by salty air. He opened the door and ducked into the vehicle, glancing at his passenger before he hauled the door shut.

"Whew, that was ugly." His head craned to ensure they were alone.

Brett quickly launched the Jeep into reverse and sped down the snaking road towards Victory Cove. For two miles he surveyed the rearview mirror until finally he rolled a shoulder to release some of the tension.

He glanced uneasily at his companion. "Are you okay?"

Serena was looking away from him, her forehead tilted against the window, watching rivulets of water across the glass. "Mmm hmm."

She started when the Jeep came to a halt at a roadside vista. Incredulous, she turned to find Brett with his fists bunched against the steering wheel, his profile strained, with a muscle pumping near his jaw.

"What's the matter?" she asked.

"I hated that."

"It was your idea."

Cloudy eyes converged on her. "I hated it, Serena. Even if it was an act, it was—" Running a hand up into his hair, Brett shook his head. "You know that was an act. You *know* I didn't mean a single word that was said there."

Serena glanced down at the hands resting in her lap and caught sight of her simple gold wedding band. She swiveled it around her finger several times. It was loose, so she started to tug it off.

"Don't." Brett's hand covered hers.

"Why? I want it off, Brett. It—it's cutting off my circulation." Though the ring was loose, what it represented was no better than a tourniquet.

Brett's hand left hers and rose to cup her chin, his thumb sweeping across her cheek.

"Serena, I wish I could have thought of another way. I wish we didn't have to go through that." His voice was quiet and rough at the same time...a gravelly blend as fascinating as the pitch of the surf. "But you're probably right, we're going to hit a dead end with the police. *We* have to take care of this."

Serena turned into his palm, but caught herself and dragged her attention back to the bleak coast. It was mutually agreed that whoever her enemy was—that if by some sordid chance Alan was still alive, the attack against her was impeded by Brett's presence. If this person assumed that she was alone again at night, perhaps he would become brash, not realizing that Brett would be lying in wait. It was simple enough logic, foolhardy perhaps, but it made sense at the time.

Brett merged back onto the road.

"You managed to get a few zingers in there," he forced a chuckle. "Pretty convincing I thought."

She did not respond.

"Did you mean it?" he asked. "That I don't belong here?"

"Did you mean it—that I was a head case?"

Again the Jeep veered to a halt on the shoulder of the road, masked by a fringe of fir trees. Yanking on the emergency brake, Brett reached for Serena's shoulders, his grip demanding.

"No." The denial pounded as hard as the rain. "Goddammit, Serena, *no*."

"Then we don't have a problem."

Air hissed out of Brett's lungs. He fell back against the seat, but he couldn't take his eyes off of her.

Serena turned at that moment and caught his frown. For a spell she just stared at him with that intense focus that made him feel defenseless. But then a timid smile touched her lips. She reached up to dust his forehead with her fingertip, brushing aside a stray lock of hair.

"I think," she whispered softly, "that you would fit in fine around here."

"Oh?" One hand was still fisted casually on Serena's jacket collar. Brett leaned into that grip and brought his head down close to hers. "—and I think," his voice was husky, his lips a breath away from hers, "that you are one of the most stable, beautiful women I've ever met."

The touch was wraithlike. A soft brush against her lips— gone before he could fully savor it. He wanted more, but not now. Not this way.

"And I think," he added. "That I better stop before I do something that's going to make me forget about everything I'm *supposed* to do."

Just looking at Brett made her throat go dry. Serena swallowed, but it didn't help. A moment ago she had felt his soft kiss, as gentle as the rain against her lips. For someone so rugged to exhibit such tenderness, it made her feel cherished. She wanted to lean across the gap in the seat and take more than that ghost of a kiss.

But Brett wasn't hers. He was just a fantasy.

"Okay," her voice wavered and then gained confidence. "We'll run this past the police, just so it goes down in the records that we tried, and then we find out who's trying to drive me insane."

She tossed a pained smile Brett's way. "Sound like a plan?"

The discussion with the police was met with incredulity that both Brett and Serena had anticipated, yet they were not discouraged. Serena returned to O'Flanagans alone. She caught Rebecca's eye as the young woman dodged past with a pen stuck in her hair and a look of determination driving her at full tilt. That brief eye contact caused Rebecca's stride to falter.

"So—how did it go?" she asked. "Get all your paperwork checked out?"

"Yes. Glanced over is more like it." Serena corrected. "Hey, Rebecca, do you have a minute?"

Rebecca shrugged and sidled up to the service bar. "What's up?"

Serena grabbed an apron from a hook on the doorframe and wound it around her waist, while studying her friend. "Is anything bothering you? I mean are things okay at home, do you want to talk about it?"

"What do you mean? I'm fine, you're the one who's not sleeping at nights—or has that been cured?" Rebecca sneered.

Serena inhaled. "See, now that was an implication I don't deserve, and honestly it's not like you. What's wrong Becky?"

"I'm fine." Rebecca rushed. "Busy, that's all."

"You seem different. Something's up."

Rebecca was saved from the inquest by Harriet's boisterous voice.

"Rena, where have you been all day? Hello Sorrenson."

Backpedaling, Rebecca tipped her head and dodged Harriet. Harriet hoisted herself onto a bar stool, nodding agreeably to Serena's offered mug.

"So, where's that Murphy boy tonight? Snooping into something else?"

Hesitating only briefly, Serena brought the mug out from under its spout and set it down before a set of hands that retrieved it so fast the amber liquid sloshed down the side.

"He left."

"Left?" Harriet raised her eyebrows. "Don't like staying at your place anymore—not good enough for 'im?'"

"No," Serena busied herself with a list of drink orders. "He just left. I don't know if he'll be back."

Over a sip of beer, Harriet frowned. "That's odd. He seemed very determined to me. I thought he was hell bent on finding out what happened to his brothah," she took another sip. "Did he just up and lose interest?"

"I don't know, Harriet. Do I look like someone who can analyze men?"

Snorting into her mug, Harriet cackled. "Rena honey, I hate to laugh, but *no*."

Serena's eyebrows narrowed to feign anger, but her smile won. Her laugh was curtailed as she glimpsed over Harriet's shoulder at the dark individual crossing the floor.

With ebony hair drawn back into a loose ponytail and black eyes scanning the patrons warily, John Morse located Serena and targeted on her as he approached the bar. Her quick intake of breath had Harriet rooting around in her seat. She acknowledged Morse with a grunt of disapproval, and then swiveled back.

"What's he doing here? He never comes out in public— kinda like a vampire or something."

"Harriet, could you excuse me for a minute?" Serena was already edging down the bar towards the vacant spot where Morse now rested an elbow, peering disdainfully at the crowd.

A raucous sound drew his gaze into the main dining room where a troop of children in costumes from a Thanksgiving school production circled around the tables to play Pilgrims and Indians. His grunt of disdain was audible as he turned back to glare at Serena.

"Nice place you got here," he scoffed. "Can't imagine why I ever stayed away."

"Probably because you have too much class," she muttered.

To still her nerves, Serena wrapped a towel about her hand, but managed to stare down the man.

"Look," Morse sneered. "For as much as you don't want me here, I don't want to be here." He tapped his thumbs on the bar. "But I need you to know something—something about your husband. You help me out, and I'll tell you what I know."

Cautious, Serena set the rag down. "Suddenly you're a font of knowledge? Yesterday you didn't seem too cooperative. What changed?"

"Are you going to pour me a drink or what?"

"You got money?"

With a snarl, he extracted a five-dollar bill from the frayed pocket of his corduroys and slapped it down on the nicked surface. "Whisky."

Serena poured the shot. She caught Harriet's eye and shook her head to deter the woman from approaching.

"Okay," Serena continued, focusing on Morse. "Go ahead."

Morse tipped his head back and downed the shot in one quick motion. Slamming the glass down, he eyed her for a re-fill. After deliberating a second, Serena complied and then set the bottle aside. She crossed her arms and banked on the knowledge that Brett was just upstairs.

"What are you up to, Morse?"

"Look," he grated. "I've got people coming around, snooping around my place, and I don't like it one bit. There's a group of landowners that stand to be evicted if the Pasamaquoddy suit for land that was legally ours two hundred years ago is passed."

"What's this got to do with Alan?"

"He instigated the lawsuit. Got in bed with the Indians and anyone else who would help out, because he wanted that land. He wanted the profits of a casino. Hell, you're no fool. You know how much money that would bring in."

Serena tried not to flinch at his reference to her husband's promiscuity.

"I know how much money a casino would suck out," she said. "Yes, the people involved in such a scheme might stand to gain, but at the expense of everyone else. Victory Cove is full of lobstermen. They make enough money to live a happy life up here," Serena's eyes scanned the regulars at the bar as she added, "but a casino would strip them of what little extra they have—it's human nature."

Morse tucked his hands into the front pockets of his jeans. "Human nature is to make money. Ask your husband, that's all he cared about."

"My husband is dead, Mr. Morse." Her voice was as cold as the chill in her skin.

"Maybe." He shrugged. "Either way, right now I'm your best bet."

"Best bet for *what*?" Serena reached for the discarded rag again and wrapped it around her hand.

"You give me the contracts and I'll see that the tribe protects you. You keep hiding that paperwork, and you're open game for both irate tribesmen, and even angrier locals."

"If any of this was going down, I'd have heard about it," she challenged. "This is a bar for Christ's sake. A couple drinks and locals are spilling their innermost thoughts out to me. Nobody has talked about a tribal suit—or any land deal that's going to evict them."

Morse shrugged and eyed the bottle she had cast aside.

Ignoring the gesture, Serena continued. "What contracts anyway? I haven't seen any contracts lying around. Alan didn't keep important paperwork at home. I guess he didn't

want me knowing what kind of business he was up to."
Looking away, she spoke to the television as it flashed the
local weather. "I'm *glad* he kept it from me."

The sound of clapping drew Serena's attention. She
caught John Morse applauding her with calloused hands.

"That's good. Real good. Hopefully everyone'll buy it.
Me personally—" He leaned forward. "I think you knew
exactly what your husband was up to. Maybe you turned a
blind eye when necessary, but I think you knew. And I think
you know exactly where he kept the contracts."

Morse splayed his hands on the bar. "You've got a choice,
Mrs. Murphy. You can give them to me and I'll look after
you—cause it seems your brother in-law doesn't want to do it
anymore. Or else you better get used to sleeping with one eye
open."

Blood pumped in her eardrums as Serena sought relief in
the mechanical motion of cleaning dirty glasses. What
contracts was John Morse talking about? And more
importantly, where would Alan have hidden them?

In the midst of rinsing a mug, another troubling thought
occurred to Serena. How did Morse know that Brett was gone?
Morse had entered the bar several minutes after she and
Harriet discussed the matter, so how did he know about the
staged argument?

"Serena, are you done here? I've got to talk to you about
Thursday, I don't know if I'm going to be able to make it."

The words penetrated as she stared aghast at Simon.

"*What*?" she stammered. "But Simon—why? Has
something happened?"

Simon treated holidays as his personal unveiling of
talented coordination and management. He would *never* miss
such an opportunity.

"I've got something to do." Pale eyes flicked towards
Morse. "Look," Simon added angrily, "I'll try my best to get
back before the rush, but it can't be helped—"

Serena's head shook in disbelief as she began to wonder if
the madness that besieged her was slowly ebbing through
Victory Cove. John Morse shows up in O'Flanagans for the
first time to bestow her with threats and promises of
protection. Rebecca's normally bubbling personality is
suddenly edgy and evasive. And lastly, Simon, her rock of
Gibraltar when it came to managing O'Flanagans—a man who
bitched constantly, but thrived in his role—was disappearing on
one of their busiest days.

"Whoah," Serena ran a hand through her hair and took a
deep breath. "Okay, Simon, do the best you can. You've
worked hard and certainly deserve time off," she hesitated,
"just don't expect me to pull off the dove in grape sauce, or
whatever."

Simon dipped his head in acknowledgment and cast
another speculative glance towards Morse before heading to
the dining room podium.

"And as for you," Serena addressed Morse, her distress
evidenced by trembling fingers. "I quite honestly don't know
what the hell you're talking about, and I'm very busy right
now." She pulled his glass off the bar. "So unless you have
something productive to tell me, or unless you want another
drink, I suggest you go home."

With his hand tucked deep into his pocket, Morse
searched for another bill, but only came up with lint. He
shrugged his shoulders. "You're going to wish you had taken
me up on my offer. You're on your own now, Serena."

The door to the bar closed, a cold waft of Atlantic air
besieging Serena as she instinctively turned towards the
thermostat.

"Dammit woman, don't turn that thing up again!" Cooper yelled from three stools away.

"Bittyfield, shut your trap and let Rena do as she pleases. You're damn lucky she lets you in here every night."

"Harriett, why don't you go find yourself a man so that you can stop making my life miserable."

Serena listened to the exchange and her body sagged against the doorframe. She glanced at the cuckoo clock, urging it to move faster, realizing that more than anything she wanted to be with Brett.

Pacing the floor, Brett glanced at the Grandfather clock in anticipation. Anxious to see if anyone bit at the ruse they staged earlier, he stared at the door, willing it to open.

It did.

"Back up." Serena ordered, using her hand to prompt him to retreat.

"Okay, I'm moving." Brett's foot clipped the edge of the carpet as he teetered. "Nothing like a warm welcome."

Wrinkling her nose at him, she switched the lamp closest to the windows off. "I could almost see your silhouette."

"What happened down there?" he asked.

"Craziness," Serena shook her head and sank onto the wooden bench, stretching her legs out as she proceeded to narrate the events of the evening.

"Look," Brett started. "This is way too dangerous now. Hell, I still want to believe that it was just an accident—a stupid accident. But now, Serena, you're in danger, and by pretending that you're up here alone, I've opened the door for whoever is behind this." He hesitated, "I've risked your life."

Serena waved away the concern. "I was alone only a week ago, Brett. I would have sat here and slowly gone insane. After all, that seemed to be the plan I guess." Her head cocked. "Yeah, let's make Serena go mad. Then, all we have to do is sneak up to her loft. Don't worry, she'll be a basket case and won't bother us." She looked at him. "Is that how you'd rather it went?"

"No." Brett advanced. "I'd rather a lot of things were different, but we're left to deal with the current situation."

Extending his hand, he stared long and hard at Serena's fingers entwined in his and finally used that grip to draw her upright, thinking that if he pulled hard enough, he could draw her into his arms.

And God, he wanted her there.

"I think we should go downstairs and start searching your old apartment." His voice was hoarse. "Those contracts have to be around here somewhere."

"Umm," Serena trailed, their hands still linked. "I was afraid you were going to suggest that."

"I would let you stay up here, but I don't want to leave you alone." Brett glanced over his shoulder at her. "Are you sure you're up to this?"

Staring down the dark stairwell, Serena murmured, "You won't be able to find anything down there without me. And besides, I don't want *you* going down there alone."

Brett's quick grin was lost as they descended into obscurity. At the base of the steps he flicked on the heavy metal flashlight. Moonlight infiltrated the windows, enabling them to make their way across the living room floor, dodging ghostly mounds of furniture.

The room was frigid, the warmth of the fire upstairs long forgotten. Brett was conscious of Serena's fingers entwined with his as she guided them past the bank of windows into a short hall flanked by blackened chambers.

Doorways to the unknown.

In a whisper, she chronicled what each quarter represented.

"This is the den to the right, and on the left is a guest room, and towards the far end there, was—the bedroom."

Brett felt a stab of shame for resenting the happiness his brother once had, but Alan was foolish enough to damage a good thing.

Flashlight held aloft, Brett slipped ahead of Serena into the den. Erratic sweeps of the light dissected the darkness. In its scope, the flare encompassed bookshelves with threadlike cobwebs linked to the recessed ceiling. He swept the light over a wooden desk adorned with a blotter, brass lamp, and photo of Serena and Alan. Brett scooped up the framed picture and heard Serena's startled gasp behind him. She too saw that the glass had been shattered, their faces obscured behind a web of jagged shards.

"Any strong breezes in here?" Brett inquired cynically.

"No."

He rested the frame down flat on the desktop, out of Serena's view, and then began to open drawers. Shining the flashlight on their contents, he paused as Serena grabbed his arm and nudged her way forward.

"What's that?" She was already in front of him, retrieving an envelope with Alan's name written in elaborate cursive.

Unsealed, Serena extracted the handwritten script.

Dearest Alan,

It makes me crazy that I can't be with you. Why you choose to go away and leave me here with this depressing ensemble is beyond me. We were meant to be together. Last night is testimony to that fact. I know you've told me to be patient—that as soon as your deal comes together we can go away, but I ache till that time comes.

Please Alan, see me tonight.

It was unsigned. Serena folded it back up with only a slight tremor in her fingers.

Brett cleared his throat. "I'm guessing that the letter wasn't from you."

"That would be correct."

"If this was your house, why would he leave that sitting right in the top drawer in such plain view?"

"He never kept anything of importance around." Serena said. "I know he must have had an office somewhere else, but this room was where he spent most of his time, so I never bothered with it. All my paperwork—receipts, accounting, taxes, are stored downstairs behind the bar in one of the safes. I really had no need to ever look in here." She sighed. "Maybe if I did—"

Brett touched her shoulder. "I'm sorry, Serena."

"About what?" Her voice peaked. "You have nothing to do with me being a blind fool. Heck, I deserve this. I should have listened to everyone's advice. But I didn't."

"Stop that, okay? Just stop it." Brett's fingers gently squeezed. "Nobody deserves to be treated like that. Look," he said, "Alan is a man of very few morals. So now this accident seems less and less innocent."

A sweep of the shadows failed to offer Brett insight. "The question becomes," he pointed out, "is Alan still alive? Is he in hiding? Or has someone killed him? And then, *who* out of the growing list of people with incentive?"

"And who wrote that letter?" Serena tried not to disclose the pain in her voice.

"I have my ideas." He sifted through the rest of the manila folders stacked in the cedar drawers, all of them empty.

There were no further clues to be found in the rank den. No traces of a man that lead a secretive life. A life that now exposed infidelity and corruption.

Suddenly Brett switched off the flashlight and his arm snaked around Serena's waist to haul her behind the door.

"Shhh," he whispered.

Straining to listen, Serena heard it. The gentle scrape of a shoe. Beyond the door, a slice of light danced around the living room, like a heat-seeking laser. Instinctively, she shrank back against Brett, his arm a protective barrier across her stomach.

Someone was very close, ambling past the huge casement windows, pausing to draw a sheet off a piece of furniture. The resultant whoosh of air floated into the den, rustling the papers Brett left out on the desk. Serena held her breath, certain the noise would expose them, but it sounded as if the visitor simply sat down, the subsequent clip of a beer cap and silence of intake confirming this.

Anger at this intruder streamed through Serena. *How dare he make himself at home here.*

But the realistic possibility that it was Alan in that room quickly doused the rage, replacing it with a glacial chill.

The unwanted guest shifted as they heard papers ruffle, and then both Brett and Serena started as the figure abruptly rose and slashed the shadows of the den with the flashlight beam.

When she would have bolted, Brett clamped down, locking her against him. The glow receded and the intruder moved into the kitchen. Drawers opened and closed, followed by a loud smack on the counter that nearly jolted them into revealing themselves. Several anxious moments ticked by before the stairwell door swung open on corroded hinges.

Only a hollow silence remained.

They waited interminably, with no indication that the intruder was present. On instinct, Serena burrowed back against Brett's warmth, wanting to hide inside him—wanting to disappear within his refuge. She strained to distinguish any hint of the trespasser, but heard only the beating of her own heart.

"*Serena*," Brett murmured in her ear, the sound husky and emphatic. "Stop wiggling—you're killing me."

Freezing at the tone, she was suddenly aware of her position and the impromptu embrace. The exact effect she had on Brett became very evident.

Sheltered in his embrace and excited by the intimate contact, she instinctively rubbed against him. His grip tightened in response and she bowed into that desire.

The hand that had been fisted against her waist now splayed across her abdomen, its counterpart grasping her hip and drawing it hard against him. Serena's breath rushed out. She felt Brett's lips brush her neck and arched her head back into him.

"What are you doing to me?" Brett hissed, but his mouth continued to feast on the curve of her throat.

"Brett," Her plaintive whisper was full of hunger as Serena tried to spin around in Brett's arms, but was held firmly in place by strong hands that nestled her against him. She felt the nudge of his hips and heard her own muffled groan deep in her throat.

Above, the methodic tread of footsteps invaded their rapture. Brett wrenched away and immediately Serena missed his warmth. Even in the dark she could distinguish him glaring at the ceiling.

"Jesus, he's probably waiting for you to get home from the restaurant." Brett's grip altered from passion to protection. "Dammit, Serena, if you were up there alone—"

Furious and anxious, Brett switched on his flashlight and exchanged positions so that Serena flanked him. "That's it. This is going to stop now."

She reached for his arm. "Brett, don't go up there—he's probably armed. Or just plain crazy."

In the glow of the flashlight, Brett looked at her and brushed the tip of his finger along her jaw.

"Exactly," he whispered. "Meaning he's waiting to hurt you. Stay down here, *please*."

The hoarse emphasis of his voice played with Serena's emotions, but she nodded, knowing all along that she had no intention of obeying.

Brett was swift. She had to dash up the stairs to keep up with him. At the top she found him circling the living room, a flow of curses streaming from his mouth.

"Dammit," Brett grabbed the back of his neck, "he's gone."

Serena moved to the window for a glimpse. The stairwell and deck were vacant, but as the moon emerged from a cloudbank to illuminate the cliffs of Victory Cove, she caught a lone silhouette climbing grassy knolls, hastening towards the nearest building. *The lighthouse.* Serena could see the shadow slip several times, but the destination was obvious.

She drew her mouth open, prepared to shout her findings, but the outburst died on her lips as she turned towards Brett.

He cased the loft like a predatory creature, searching the room, stopping to look out the front window, while muttering a subdued oath that didn't threaten Serena—instead it warmed her.

As if Brett sensed that he was being watched, he dropped the curtains back in place and met her gaze.

"What?"

Serena looked at him. He was a tall man with a stalwart build and dark hair, nearly black, disheveled enough to make him endearing. He had eyes the color of a winter's strongest gale, and delving into those eyes was like tossing yourself to the whim of the ocean—but the water was warm.

As impossible as the situation was, Serena knew that she was falling in love with Brett. Acknowledging that bittersweet fact, she could not allow him to go into the night and battle her demons.

This was something that she must do alone.

"Serena?"

"It's been a hell of a day," she yawned. "I think I'm going to bed."

Skeptical, Brett nodded. "Go on and get some rest. I'll watch things out here for awhile."

Panicked, she struggled for another strategy to preoccupy Brett while she made good on her escape.

"Actually you look tired, Brett." She touched his arm, just the softest nudge towards the hallway. "Why don't you go get some rest and I'll just finish cleaning up here?"

Brett's eyes narrowed. "What are you up to, Serena?"

"I'm not up to anything. I feel bad that you've basically exhausted yourself at my expense—you probably haven't had a good night's sleep in a week. I'm fine. I'll turn in shortly."

Arms crossed and eyebrow arched, Brett stated mildly, "Someone was just in your house, kicking back, having a beer, searching through your stuff, and you want to stand there and tell me that you're fine?"

Serena strived for an impish grin, but it appeared more painful than anything. "Resilient?" she managed weakly.

"Resilient, my ass. Go to bed." he ordered.

CHAPTER XII

Serena stood before the dormer window waiting for Brett's pacing to end. She added another half hour to ensure he was fast asleep before she dragged on a heavy down jacket. Thrusting her hands into a pair of insulated gloves, she yanked a blue knit cap over her head, frowning at the reflection in the pane of glass. For a moment in this dark light, she caught a glimpse of herself as a teenager. A tomboy, sneaking out to climb the cliffs at night.

With a steadying breath, Serena convinced herself that it was fifteen years ago—and that the adventure she was about to embark upon was as innocent as it had been then.

Cringing as her door squealed, Serena opened it just enough to slip through. She peeked around the corner and located Brett sprawled across the loveseat, one leg hooked over the armrest, one arm crooked over his forehead. She stood at his feet, waiting for his eyes to open and put an end to her endeavor, but he just shifted, mumbled, and settled back into slumber.

Unable to resist, she bent to pick up the folded blanket and draped it across him. She lingered, mesmerized by Brett's features. Even in slumber, he was awe-inspiring. So strong this man was. Her protector.

But it was time for her to step up and defend them both.

At the front door, Serena cursed the frigid Atlantic blast that lashed past her to penetrate the loft. She expected the cold to wake Brett, yet miraculously he slept on. Closing the door, she faced the ocean and black cliffs, wondering if she truly had lost her sanity.

Serena zipped the jacket all the way up so that her chin disappeared into the collar. Hurrying down the steps, she broke into a swift jog. Her destination was the menacing silhouette projected over the sea cliff. From this perspective, Victory Cove's lighthouse looked like a tall gravestone.

And she was about to walk across its grave.

A brisk ascent up the incline did little to keep the cold air at bay. Serena's breath clouded her sight. She moved instinctively, traveling a path she had trekked since childhood, when the lighthouse was once operational. Extinguished more than fifteen years ago, replaced by the modern, high-tech model further down shore, this empty beacon stood as a lofty symbol of Victory Cove's romantic past.

As the outline drew close, Serena's pace stalled. She circled the tall edifice. The aid of moonlight came and went as the fickle north Atlantic current forced along a patchy cloudbank. She took advantage of the brief moments of clarity to discern the single stone building at the base of the tower. In the past, gale force winds had lashed the waves high enough to mount the cliffs and engulf the tiny abode. Nonetheless, it survived through the years—a testimony to the hand-laid rock walls.

She hoped the underground shed still offered the same access it had when she was a child.

Serena's feet crunched over the frozen turf. Air billowed from her mouth as her eyes began to tear from the wind. She tucked her chin even deeper into the down collar. Seeking relief by walking backwards against the wind, she focused on the floodlights illuminating the tavern's deck. From this perspective, O'Flanagans represented a warm and inviting symbol of hope, the lights on the third floor reminding her that Brett lay safe and asleep.

Most importantly, safe.

Turning back into the blustery weather, sounds came to Serena in muffled echoes within the cocoon of the jacket hiked around her ears. She nearly missed the grinding tread to her right.

Instinctively, she crouched, cursing the open knolls that lead to the lighthouse. She prayed for cloud cover—any form of camouflage, but the moon glimmered across the fresh snow.

Spinning about, she studied the dirt path that led to the light keeper's house like a black vein scarring white marble.

The path was empty. She was alone.

Hastening into a jog, she felt the tears of windburn on her face, and cursed when her boot skidded on a slick rock, pitching her into a heap. In frustration, she smacked her clenched fist on the rigid dirt and yelled at the pain.

Unsure whether to laugh or cry, Serena tipped her head back and stared up at the bright orb, searching its wizened face for insight.

"Sunning yourself?"

Her head snapped down so fast that her teeth rattled. She shrunk in fear from the tall silhouette.

The voice finally registered.

"What are you doing out here?" She struggled upright.

Brett's laugh was lost in the wind. "Taking a stroll. Seeing the sights, wondering what you're up to."

"You followed me?"

Concerned by the way Serena's body shook, and freezing himself, Brett extracted his bare hand from the sheepskin pocket and reached for her shoulder. He used his grip to steer Serena towards the stone building, but she shrugged out of his grasp.

Deferring to her superior knowledge of the lighthouse, Brett trailed a step behind. His eyes roved the bleak terrain as a grim apprehension began to steal over him. Something felt drastically wrong. Granted, he'd never been here before in his life, but the stillness—the abrupt cessation of wind put him on edge.

Locating the pair of rusted panels lodged in the frozen earth, Serena forcefully tugged one of the handles. In a graceless move, she ended up on her rear, the curved metal protrusion still clutched in her palm. Belligerent eyes flashed up at Brett from beneath her knit cap. There was a challenge in her glare, but Brett disregarded it and stooped over to give the second panel a quick jerk. He felt it give way. Using both hands this time, he was able to hoist the door fully open. He dropped it onto its back and looked down into the black hole, which even in this strong current produced the foul smell of trapped air.

"That's great." he said. "We're going in there?"

Serena seemed to battle the desire to smile at his reluctance. A frown wove between her eyebrows though as she studied his silhouette. She surged to her feet and grabbed for the flashlight protruding from the back pocket of his pants and used its scope to test the first step down into the weather cellar.

"Hey, anytime you want to cop a feel, just ask, okay?" Brett grabbed her around the waist and hoisted her out of the pit.

"What the hell—"

"Give me that thing." he uttered, taking the flashlight from her hand. "Now stay right behind me."

"You don't know your way around down there."

"You're going to show me then, aren't you?"

Flashing the light down the wooden stairs—stairs that looked like they could barely support a rat, Brett shook his head and questioned his common sense.

"There's no need for you to be macho, Brett. I grew up here. I can handle this. You should have stayed back in the loft."

Brett tested the first step, flinching as he felt it give under his weight.

"Let me ask you this logical question." He dared the second step, ready to leap up to safety if the ancient wood collapsed. "What the hell has you out here at this godforsaken hour by yourself?"

Serena crossed her arms. "I saw someone out here—from the window—after we came upstairs." Her teeth began to chatter. She hugged her arms tighter.

Brett's head tipped back in frustration. "And you didn't tell me because—?"

"Because it's my problem," she retorted.

"Dammit, Serena!"

He negotiated a careful retreat so that he could stand before her. "*You're* my problem."

Gently, he traced the back of his knuckle down her cheek.

"Look," he said. "I'm not about to get into this with you right now because I'm freezing, I'm tired, I want you, and there's a murderer potentially waiting for us in that lighthouse—if we don't kill ourselves on these damn stairs first." Brett took a deep breath. "So please—just stay close behind me and let me know when I'm about to make a wrong turn. *Okay*?"

Mouth agape, Serena managed a concise, "*okay*" before her jaw snapped shut.

With Serena's feral grip on his arm for support, Brett navigated the steps. He was cautious not to let the beam of light stray from the decaying planks. Several boards were missing. With an awkward gate, they dodged these obstacles to reach solid ground. A rank scent of mildew pervaded the stale air as the arc of light glanced across a rusted generator. Unmarked crates, looking like they dated back to the battle of the colonies, were strewn in the corner. Flicking the flashlight above them, Brett found that the worn beams of the ceiling barely accommodated his height and looked like they might give way at any moment, allowing the earth above to tumble down on them.

"And I used to come here for fun." Serena mused quietly.

Running the light over the solid clay floor, Brett couldn't tell if anyone had recently tramped across it, but assumed the worst. His muscles tensed.

Serena's whisper sounded like a gale force wind in the stillness of the crypt as she tugged on his arm. "To the right, there should be a door leading up the light keeper's house."

Brett veered in that direction, noting with dismay that the shaft of light was losing its intensity. An orange glow. That's all he got.

He searched for the portal and cursed as his hand scaled over wood, coming away with a splinter. "Yeah, I found it," he grumbled.

The light keeper's house consisted of a single chamber that had once been divided by a bed to represent the sleeping quarters, a coal stove and table to symbolize the kitchen, and a spacious roll top desk, overlooking the Atlantic to signify the office. Now all that was left was the sagging metal bed frame, the coal stove with its door hung askew, and the roll top desk engulfed in years worth of grime. Drawers were removed from the desk and upturned on the floor.

The moon crept behind a cloud, turning the windows into impenetrable black panes which concealed an ocean detected only by its steady rumble.

Brett stooped down and trained the beam of light on the overturned drawers. With a grunt, he noticed that the handles had fresh trails lancing the thick layers of dust.

"Someone's been here recently."

Serena crouched down beside him. "There's nothing here. They either got what they were looking for, or someone beat them to it."

"Mmmm—" Brett stood up, drawing Serena with him. "They've rifled through here—come up empty, so they decide that whatever they're looking for is in your house—and create some elaborate scheme to scare you out of there so that they can search the premises?" his voice trailed off . "No, something's missing—we're missing some critical detail."

"Yeah—*who?* Who is doing this?"

Brett arced the beam of light around the room and trained it on a doorway tucked behind the rusted coils of the bed frame. "Does that go to the lighthouse?"

"Yes." Serena's voice sounded distracted as Brett found her leaning over the roll-top desk, peering into the night.

"Can you actually see something out there?"

Her head shook and she withdrew to join him by the door. "I don't know. For a second when the moon came out—I swear there was something down on the cliffs—"

"We'll check it out. First, let's take a look and see what your old lighthouse is hiding."

The door was unlocked. Wary, Brett proceeded with the flashlight. He entered the cylindrical edifice, scaling the beam up a spiral staircase, past the network of cobwebs, into obscure shadows that tortured the soul with unlimited possibilities of danger.

If one believed in ghosts, this place seemed like a potential breeding ground for them.

Brett flinched against the chain of echoes. Their footfalls resonated with chilling clarity while the waves that crashed below sounded as if they would tow the precarious structure off its moorings and out to sea.

"And this is where you would come to play?" he asked of the dark.

"It was beautiful then," Serena whispered. "So big—fascinating. An adventure."

"Yeah, yeah, I get the picture. Suddenly I'm not big on the adventure part." Brett reached for Serena's hand to ensure she was still behind him. "How trustworthy are these stairs?"

"They supported me fifteen years ago."

"That's just great, Serena." Turning, he held the flashlight so that both their faces were illuminated.

"Look, let me go up there." she said. "I'm lighter. I know the layout—"

"No," Brett commanded. "I'll test a few first. If someone hid something up there, I'd venture the stairs are still pretty reliable."

"And if someone didn't?"

"Catch me."

Brett made it exactly three stairs before the fourth caved in under his weight. Grabbing the railing and gaining his footing on the frame of the stairwell, he continued climbing and used the rail in the fashion of a ladder.

"Brett, stop. Nobody would go through that much trouble to hide anything."

"This is Alan we're talking about." he grunted from above.

He had a point, Serena thought. Nevertheless she was certain this was futile.

As he passed the first bend, Serena called out, "Brett, come on down. This is just silly. We're not going to find anything here. Let's call it a night."

"But you saw someone—they had to be here for a reason."

"Yeah, making as big a fool out of themselves as we are. I wish you never followed me."

Rather than picking his way back down, Brett let go of the rail and dropped down to her side, grimacing as his feet struck the earth.

"And miss out on the adventure of climbing a dilapidated lighthouse at two in the morning?" He winked at her, and then his eyes spanned the circumference of the room. "There's got to be an easier way out of here than that godforsaken cellar."

Brett tested a recessed doorway and it yielded as he used his shoulder to manipulate it fully open. The sudden assault of gusting wind made Serena burrow down into her collar, yanking the knit hat deep over her ears. Brett lunged the beam of light out onto the cliffs as it pitched a feeble glow for a yard or two and then drifted ineffectually to darkness.

"Come on," he said. "Let's get back to the loft."

Brett's words were nearly stolen by the blustery gusts, but his nod of encouragement was sufficient translation. Serena plummeted into the night, her head pitched against the wind as she caught a brief and welcome glimpse of the lights of O'Flanagans.

One hand aimed forward with the unproductive flashlight, Brett extended the other backwards, seeking her fingers. Serena reached for it, but at that second, she detected a blaze of color in a world that was black and white.

Black were the cliffs, as distended white waves billowed against them like sheets on a clothesline. Black was the ocean until the radiant moonlight bathed the surface with white diamonds. And in the midst of night, a slash of red spilled like blood across the rock face.

"Brett!" Serena yelled against the wind, tugging him to a halt.

"What?" As short as Brett's hair was, it whipped frenziedly atop his head.

"I—I see something. Down there—down below on the cliffs."

Cursing as the moon disappeared behind a full cloud, Serena watched listlessly as a patch of shoreline further down the coast benefited from its glow. With the current as strong as it was, it did not take long for the clouds to disperse and the slice of color to become visible again. Inching close to the edge for a better view, Serena felt Brett's hand fist around her down jacket.

"Careful, dammit."

"Don't you see it?" she called over her shoulder, leaning forward to discern the strip of crimson lodged between fissures of rock and churning surf a hundred feet below.

Still with a protective grip on Serena's arm, Brett squinted against the wind and caught sight of the object.

Something wrenched deep in his gut, but he managed a controlled voice. "I'll go down and check it out."

"Are you crazy?" Serena's voice was loud. "Brett, there's no way you can scale those rocks. For God's sake, let *me* go then, I've been down there before."

"Serena, we're not going to argue over this." Brett flicked off the flashlight to conserve it for a time when he would really need it. For now the moon was sufficient enough to guide him down the treacherous course. A cloudbank coming in from the east warned him that he had to move fast though.

"Look," he said. "The path is pretty clear most of the way, and by the time it turns dicey I should be able to get a good glimpse of what's down there. It's probably garbage from a passing ship."

Brett thrust the long end of the flashlight into the back pocket of his jeans so that his hands would be free for negotiation.

"No, I won't let you go." Serena yanked on his arms so that he was forced to face her.

"You don't know what it's like," she pleaded. "A wave can erupt from out of nowhere. A path that looks so innocent, so simple to read, can get wiped out with one quick surge of water. It could draw you out and I'd never be able to reach you." Her fingers bit into his arms. "Brett please, I don't want anything to happen to you."

Wind lashed at their faces, stinging their eyes. Brett thought this might account for the tears in Serena's. He reached for her collar and gently drew her closer, into his arms.

Into his heart.

For an instant, Brett shared Serena's warmth in an embrace that did little to console her.

"*No*," she read into the finality of the gesture. "Just let it be. It's probably some old rag wrapped around the rocks—it's not worth it."

Convinced otherwise in the brief glimpse he had, Brett grazed her cheek with the back of his knuckles.

"I'll be right back," he smiled gently. "And then on the walk home you can go into great detail why you don't want to see anything happen to me."

The taunt did little to goad her. Dread overwhelmed Serena as she watched Brett begin his descent. It was madness she thought, madness to negotiate that trail in the dead of night, under a moon that made wraithlike appearances. Irrationally, she believed that yet another ghost would besiege her if Brett ever reached the bottom. Shouting to him, her words lashed back in her face, a sarcastic slap from the Atlantic's blustery hand.

With Brett's tall frame already engulfed in the impenetrable shadows of the sea cliff, Serena strained to hear whether he slipped or called out. Frothing waves ebbed in a constant stream, while the piercing scream of the wind droned in her ear until she thought she would go mad. In the distance, the solemn bell of a buoy clanged its alert that the seas were choppy.

Serena clutched her arms about her and prayed.

Listlessly pacing the overhang, unable to stand by any longer, she finally hoisted down the erratic trail carved out by the elements.

Nature's spiral staircase.

Gloved hands grasped ineffectively at the bedrock as Serena scaled downhill, cringing with each furious wave that broke below to shower her in an arctic mist. Hugging the cliffside, repeating Brett's name in a mantra that went unheard, she continued until the path became nothing more than a checkerboard of gleaming rocks. She hurdled onto the nearest ledge, praying that the slick surface would support her. With a hand held over her eyes to deter the spray, she assessed the immediate area.

Unaided by the moon, she was trapped in the shadow of the headlands and balanced only by a well-placed foothold. Serena screamed out Brett's name.

The hiss of the tide answered her.

Moonlight freed from the clouds gravitated towards the coast, illuminating the crags on which she now clung. Risking another leap, Serena landed on the sheared end of a rock, her leg slipping and plunging into the frigid water. She shrieked.

"Serena!"

Scrambling onto her knees, Serena's sodden gloves encased useless fingers as she tried to regain stability. Her head snapped up, swearing she heard her name on the wind. Madly, she thought it was Alan finally coming to claim her and draw her out to sea.

She swallowed a sob and fought against the obsession. Hoisting herself upright, she focused through the mist. There he was, coming towards her, a soaked creature that looked as miserable as she felt. She struggled to keep the weakness out of her knees at the sight of Brett.

"Serena."

She saw his mouth move rather than hear the word, but not until he negotiated the last rock that separated them did she hear her name and reached for him. Brett enveloped her in his arms, using his back as a shield against the next spray of an errant wave. He dipped his face against her ear and admonished with pain in his hoarse voice.

"Of all the stupid things to do, woman. Why on earth did you follow me?"

"You—you—" Her teeth were chattering so much it was hard to speak.

Brett pointed back up towards the lighthouse.

Serena's head swayed in denial. "Did—did you find it?"

It was dark again, but not enough to conceal the desolate steel of Brett's eyes. "Just get back up there before the tide gets any higher."

Wrenching out of his embrace, dread possessed Serena. Something in Brett's eyes—something in the tightness around his mouth and the gruffness of his voice, had her surging past him, grappling for a foothold on the next rock.

"Serena, *no*!"

There, trapped between the jagged channels was a strip of scarlet fabric, bobbing erratically in the surf. It was belligerent in its struggle to reach shore. She peered up and waited for the moon to emerge from a bank of clouds. Blindly, she inched forward until nature threw on the lights and the bright globe burst free.

Serena's scream nearly doubled Brett over in pain. He reached her a second too late and spun her about, collapsing her against his chest, containing her despite the fists that pummeled his body.

"Let me go, dammit." Serena's muffled voice sounded from inside his jacket. "I've got to see him. Brett I have to see—I have to know—"

This was something he could not protect her from. Brett relaxed his grip and felt her tear away.

Serena dropped down into a half crouch, one palm flat against the freezing granite to keep her balance, the other thrown across her mouth, trying to keep from being sick. Several feet away, a body bobbed up and down, ensnared by a shackle of serrated rocks, battered by the oncoming waves. The surf's frothy maelstrom roared into the alcove, momentarily shrouding the crimson jacket.

When the tide finally retreated, she was left to stare into the lifeless eyes of her husband.

Instinctively, Serena recoiled, the moon clipping those dead black eyes, animating them for one horrifying moment as she expected Alan to rear up from the ocean and draw her in. Instead, the red vinyl jacket billowed about the twitching corpse still snagged on a barbed rock.

The moon once again vanished behind a fog dense enough to matt the sky black, leaving Serena to gaze into darkness. Listening to the ebbing surf and the haunting buoy, knowing that Alan was only a hand stroke away, but unable to see him, she wondered frantically if it had all been a cruel hallucination.

Like a strobe light, the moon erupted from the clouds to expose his body again. Serena gasped at the lifeless eyes and dark hair matted against pale skin, like blades of seaweed. Several emotions vied for dominance, numbing her against the frigid water as she stared at Alan. Even in death she still feared the hateful glare in his eyes.

A persistent wave surged through the maze of crags to collapse into his corpse, rocking it on its side so that an arm lobbed to the surface, dead fingers extending towards her.

Serena choked on a scream.

"Enough." Brett called in a hoarse voice.

He reached for Serena's shoulders to hoist her away from the sight. "We've got to get back and call the police."

Noting the vacuous gaze with a lump of dread, Brett cupped her chin. "Serena, you're going to freeze to death out here."

Another frothy surge crashed atop the broad rock, swirling about their feet with a hearty tug. "We'll be lucky if we can even make it back up those cliffs, the tide is coming in."

"But—but—" she pointed.

Brett was certain that Alan would forever haunt her now.

"The body hasn't moved in almost a month." He needed to refer to it as an object because if he stopped to acknowledge that the bloated corpse belonged to his brother, he would risk his own safety to haul up the remains. Right now it was more important to worry about the living.

"Serena, look at me. No, look at *me*. We have to get out of here." Shaking her, Brett yelled above the din of the Atlantic. "Do you want to drown out here with him, is that it?"

Serena blinked against the saltwater clawing at her eyes. *No*, her mind cried in anger, but not loud enough to pass her trembling lips. She felt Brett's grip on her arms, stable, alive, and again she screamed *no*. He seemed not to hear as his gaze grew increasingly frantic.

Brett. Suddenly Serena was obsessed with the need to protect him, to keep him alive at all costs.

No more ghosts.

Hands that had refused to cooperate now rose to clasp Brett's forearms. Serena would have shoved him back up the path were it not for the icy tendril of water that ensnared her ankle. Manacles from the deep wrapped around her boots, as the suction of the tide yanked her from his grasp. Serena screamed in terror, positive it was Alan drawing her back in.

Brett lunged forward to catch Serena's hand just as it slipped off the rim of the rock and submerged beneath the surf. With only her arm visible, he held on and climbed up her jacket until she surfaced with a wheeze. She struggled against the current, her free hand uselessly scrambling to grip the slick surface, but he connected with her fingers, and with one strong lurch, plucked her from the sea.

Wasting no time, Brett wrapped his arm around Serena, and urged her up the cliff, sensing the dogged vines of water that sought to haul them back to hell.

CHAPTER XIII

Racked with chills, Serena stumbled into the loft. She could not speak. Her jaw was locked. Still functional, her eyes skewed frantically until she located Brett behind her, his hands red and shaking. He quickly shrugged out of his suede jacket and reached to haul off the sodden mass of down that trapped cold seawater around her like an icy shroud. Trembling in place, her feet felt like they weighed a hundred pounds each, making it impossible to inch closer to the fire that was a haunting afterthought of glowing embers.

"Y-you got to g-get out of those clothes." Brett's hands seemed uncooperative as he tried to draw the sweatshirt up her arms, which gradually lifted at his prompting. "The boots— you have to take off the boots."

Serena stared down at the soaked hiking boots as if they were a million miles away. Distantly, she acknowledged that if she did not remove them, the damage could become irreparable. She made a valiant effort to bend over and reach the laces. Realizing that her gloves were still on, accounting for the numbness in her fingers, she tried to peel them off and cried out in frustration when her hands would not cooperate.

Brett managed to strip to the waist, lugging off his own shoes, stoking the fire so that he could return to her.

"Okay. It's okay." He soothed as he stripped the sodden material from her white hands, and then stooped to attack the stiff laces.

Numbly, Serena obeyed as Brett asked her to lift one leg, then the other. Equally as dazed, she responded mechanically when he hoisted the turtleneck over her head. Lastly, she stepped out of drenched jeans after he yanked them down to her ankles.

Brett moved fast, reaching for the quilt draped across the loveseat, wrapping it around her, moving her closer to the fire.

Uneasy, he watched Serena, noticing that her hands still shook. Her cheeks, however, had begun to develop a healthy blush—a much welcome change from the ashen shade of hypothermia.

Shedding his jeans, he disappeared into the guest room to yank the spread off his bed. He draped it across his shoulders and returned to draw Serena down onto the loveseat where he wrapped them both beneath the queen-sized quilt. He pulled the knit cap off her head and rubbed at her hair with the edge of the spread, and then brusquely tried to dry his own.

Everything smelled of the ocean.

Serena burrowed closer, and he touched her tangled hair, drawing in the scent of the sea that could have so easily claimed her. Trying to dispel that morbid thought, he waited until her trembles subsided and her cold flesh began to warm against his.

With Serena's head tucked beneath his chin, her soft breath tickling his throat, Brett finally opened himself up to the memory of his brother's lifeless face.

Their youth in Boston passed by seemingly straightforward, yet it was not without hostility. Many of the ruthless experiences Brett managed to withhold from his parents. Alan seemed to be their wonder child, born late in life to a couple in their late forties who hadn't expected this belated marvel. That should have been Brett's first warning, but he paid it no heed.

As they grew older, it seemed the more Brett concealed from his parents to protect Alan, the more Alan tried to get away with. Only when he reached his teenage years did Brett begin to recognize that his younger sibling bore true signs of malice.

Now sitting in this secure loft, holding his brother's widow in his arms, Brett contemplated his emotions. There was grief, as there should be when a family member is taken. There was also anger. Anger at Alan, and anger at all the things Brett felt he should have handled differently.

And lastly, there was hope. Hope that Alan might have finally found peace.

"Oh God," Serena sobbed.

Brett tensed, holding her. Her body grew restless in his arms.

"Oh, oh, oh," She rocked against the grief.

"I'm sorry baby," he whispered. "I'm so sorry. I wish you didn't have to see that."

Closing his eyes, feeling Serena's pain—immersed in his own, Brett tried not to think of what his brother's last moments on earth were like. To have fallen into such a quandary that someone would murder him for it, was initially incomprehensible. But that was grief doing the talking. There was still no concrete proof of murder. Although, if Brett were to recite all that he had already learned about his brother's time in Victory Cove, he knew that Alan was capable of inciting such rage.

"H-he's still down there. We just left him there."

"I know," Brett touched her hair. "But I didn't want to sacrifice *you* just to bring his body up here." In a husky voice, he added, "We'll call the police first thing in the morning."

Serena lifted her head and stared into the fire. Brett watched her study the twitching flames—flames that cast spasmodic shadows—writhing figures on the wall which reminded him of hell.

"Brett," she whispered. "Can the cold make you so numb you don't feel anything emotionally?"

Brett explored the shadows on her face. "Yes, yes it can."

"I should be feeling something more," she choked. "I—I was married to him for ten years. Am I so cold that I can't feel anything for Alan?"

Serena shook her head before he could respond. "There's pain—oh God, the pain, but I don't think it's from seeing him dead, I think it—" she hesitated, "it's so much more."

Grappling to find the words, Serena tried to pull free of Brett's hold. His eyes remained closed, but his embrace was steadfast.

He spoke solemnly. "I want you to do something for me, Serena."

In his arms, Brett felt her go still. Her lips parted and dark green eyes rounded in horror. "Brett, oh I'm so sorry, he was your brother, oh baby, I'm so sorry."

For a second, Brett almost smiled at the endearment. He persisted. "Serena,"

No, don't smell her, he thought, *don't feel her warmth seeping into your cold body. Just ask her.*

"Tell me what happened out on the boat that day—that day you lost—" Okay, he couldn't finish the sentence, but he sensed from her stiffness that she understood.

For a time, Serena sat in silence, staring blindly at the fire, and he presumed that she would not respond.

"I was so happy about the baby when I found out I was pregnant," she hesitated, "but I guess, in retrospect, it was for all the wrong reasons."

It was painful. Painful to dig up the memories. But this was Brett, Serena thought. The man who had been there for her. The man who deserved answers. The man she was falling in love with.

"I guess I was happy because for once I wasn't going to be alone," she said. "Yeah, I duped myself into believing that this would somehow mend a relationship that was un-healable."

The mantle over the fire was an afterthought, the dark of night, absent. That left only the haunting memory of bright sunshine and optimism on that fateful day.

"—but the bottom line was that I wouldn't feel deserted. I'd have someone with me, someone to love me. Needless to say Alan was not pleased with the news—" Serena breathed in, because encapsulating that statement cost her dearly.

In dire tones she proceeded to recite the events leading up to this moment, until a gloomy silence descended upon her snug loft.

It was a night that Brett would carry with him forever. A night he discovered his brother's body. A night he grieved his loss. A night he confirmed the disease that possessed his sibling's mind. And a night that he would bring his feelings for Serena to a higher level, a level that might cause them both pain.

And when it was over, when dawn approached to envelop the living room in an unearthly radiance, Brett bent to kiss the soft crown of Serena's hair. He left her sleeping prone on the couch and made phone calls that were both distressing and necessary.

"Brett!"

The plaintive call reached Brett's ear. In haste, he spun the faucets and sprang out of the stall. Swathing a towel around his hips, he hoisted the door open and surged into the hallway.

"Are you okay?" His eyes sliced the living room in search of danger.

Serena glanced up at him, wide-eyed from the heap of blankets she had furrowed into. Only her face and the tips of her fingers were visible from inside the fluffy mass. Green eyes roamed the length of his body, lingering on his chest, which he felt heave as her glance dipped down to the rim of the towel.

Brett shifted awkwardly, water dripping from his hair. He swiped a hand through it while trying to determine the source of Serena's panic.

"I woke up" she explained, "and you weren't here. I thought you left."

Breathing easier, Brett nodded and held up a finger. "Hold on a sec."

He disappeared into the bathroom and re-emerged a moment later in jeans, rubbing vigorously at his hair with the towel. On bare feet, he crossed the wooden floor and settled on the edge of the loveseat.

"I'm not going anywhere without telling you first." He vowed in a sober voice.

"Serena," he began. "I'm sorry, but you're going to have to get up. The police will be here soon. I called them."

Serena coughed. Now she remembered why she had called out to Brett. When she woke, she felt the warmth of the sun streak through the windows across her face and experienced a moment of surreal tranquility. Then, the night came crashing back in waves more vicious than those of the sea. She could not rid her mind of the sight of Alan's lifeless eyes.

She gazed out the window, scarred by the knowledge that Alan's body was still out there. All along she had been seeking this closure—seeking confirmation about Alan's fate, and now that she had the answers, she was more afraid than ever.

"I know." She drew her legs down off the sofa.

"Just get through this and—" Brett began.

"—and wait for Alan's murderer." She finished.

"Dammit, Serena." His fist clenched. "You don't know that he was murdered. Anything could have happened. He could have hit his head—"

"I'm sure that's what the police will tell us. I told you Brett, they've written it off, especially now that they have a toe to put a tag on." Serena winced at her analogy.

Brett leaned forward, steeping his head into his cupped hands.

"You've found what it is you came here for, Brett. Confirmation on your brother's fate."

He sat up, eyeing her incredulously. Her quick hand signal kept him from interrupting.

"You probably want to get back to Boston," she continued. "Surely, you've neglected your business. The market's been wild. I hope for your sake you aren't heavy into technology stocks."

Noticing that his scowl intensified, Serena rushed on. "You've shown me that I have no real ghosts, and I'm not afraid to climb the stairs at night thanks to you. I—I don't even know where to begin to thank you, but I just want you to know that if you have to leave, I understand—"

Brett reclined in his seat and hoisted an ankle over his knee. He studied her and waited. "Are you through?"

She clutched the blanket beneath her chin. "Ummm hmmm."

"First," he began, "I am capable of making my own decisions. Second, neither of us have a clue as to what Alan's fate actually was. Yeah, sure we saw the outcome, but we need to find out why. Serena, if we don't find out *why,* you may end up just like him, and I'll be damned if I'm going to let that happen." He leaned forward. "Do you want to spend the rest of your life looking over your shoulder? Do you really feel safe right now?"

His voice turned tender. "Are you trying to push me out the door? Is that what this is all about? Because if so, just say the word and I'll be gone. I'll try to protect you from a distance, but if you don't want me around, if I remind you of—"

Serena reached forward and touched the tips of her fingers to his lips.

"For God's sake," her glance lingered on his mouth, "shut up."

Brett wondered if she was even aware of how she looked at him. Sometimes like a frightened child—more times like a hungry woman. One moment those sultry eyes were wide and innocent. Then without knowing it, they darkened with the promise of passion.

He wanted her.

God damn, he wanted her.

Serena looked at him. "Brett," she whispered. "Please don't go."

His foot slipped off his knee. He stood and approached her, and for a moment, he just touched her with his eyes and watched her cheeks burn under the scrutiny.

Finally, his hand lifted to stroke her blushed cheek, and then slipped further back into her hair.

"Honey," he smiled. "I'm not going anywhere."

"How do I explain you being here?" From the recesses of a gable window, Serena watched the white cruiser approach. It lumbered over a pothole as a spray of muddy water coated the fender.

Serena turned around and crossed her arms.

"You were right," she affirmed. "I don't want to be looking over my shoulder for the rest of my life. If we're going to catch this guy, I'm the only bait we have, and he isn't going to bite if he thinks you're hanging around."

Brett joined her at the window, his frame filling the alcove.

"As far as everyone knows," he said, "despite our differences, he was my brother. Naturally you called me when you found him." He looked at her, "But tonight you'll be alone—" he paused, "—in theory."

Watching the officers approach, Serena pushed herself off the wall and started towards the door. Her progress was halted by Brett's grip on her arm.

"*In theory*," he emphasized.

Serena stared down at Brett's hand as if it was a magical source of heat that infused whatever it touched.

"I know I have a role to play," False conviction thickened her voice. "I mean, portraying that you are nothing but a pain in my ass and all." Her valiant effort to smile failed. "But just for the next few hours, please don't leave me. I—I'm still afraid of him, if that makes any sense?"

"I won't leave," Brett vowed. "And he won't hurt you anymore."

Serena started towards the door with Brett trailing a few steps behind. Just before she responded to the emphatic knock, he added, "but I'll play the role of *pain in the ass* with great eloquence."

Officer Juenger frowned when Serena swung the door open.

The grin that tickled her lips fell as the sight of this officer was just another sobering dose of reality. A reminder that last night was not a horrible nightmare that she would wake up from. She cleared her throat.

"Mrs. Murphy." Office Juenger tipped the edge of his hat by reflex and twitched his head in the direction of his stout partner. "This is Officer Hennessy. Ah, we understand you have located your husband's—you found your husband?"

Serena's voice hitched for a second. She nodded and stepped back to admit them. "Y-yes. That's right. I called my brother in-law over. He's been very concerned about his brother."

Officer Juenger gestured towards Brett. "Yes, he's been in the station several times. Can you take us to the bod—Mr. Murphy?"

Brett stepped forward to inject, "Yes, I will. Mrs. Murphy doesn't need to see this again."

"Yes, Mrs. Murphy *does* need to see this again." Serena inserted. In part to convince herself, and also to play their role of staged hostility.

Officer Jeunger's winged eyebrow inclined, but he was already motioning his partner back down the stairs, apparently eager for this matter to conclude.

Serena sat on a stool, her arms folded atop the bar, her head resting in the cradle they fashioned. One eye was exposed and she used it to peer at the clock. Ten-thirty. It was amazing how much could transpire in a few short hours of daylight.

After having confirmed Alan's location, a team was called in to haul up the corpse. Serena was asked to accompany them to the morgue where she officially identified the body, a recollection that now had her one eye piercing the thermostat. She had to keep reminding herself that others did not share the coldness she felt.

Funeral arrangements were made, with Brett handling most of the details. And finally, about a half hour ago, with all paperwork signed, the matter was considered *closed* by Victory Cove's finest.

Tucking her head into the shelter of her arms, Serena allowed for the tears that pooled onto the wooden counter. The spell was brief. She sat up, swiped the tips of her fingers beneath her eyes, and stared at her reflection in the mirror behind the bar.

Where was the young O'Flanagan girl that used to run around the tavern, singing loud and off key while doing her parents bidding? The woman in the mirror seemed like an aged flower, trapped in the ground, waiting for a spring that would never come.

The front door of the restaurant opened as Serena jolted and whirled to find Simon sauntering in, fluffing freshly fallen snow out of his hair. Catching her gaze, he paused and defensively glanced around him.

"What?"

"Nothing," she stammered. "You're early."

"I told you I'd be late tomorrow, I'm trying to make up some of the time."

"You don't punch a clock here, Simon. Come in when you can, there's no such thing as making up hours."

Alighting from the stool, Serena slipped a strand of hair behind her ear. It was time to prepare for the lunch crowd.

"What's the matter with you?" Simon simpered. "You look like crap." He shrugged out of his black leather jacket and added. "No offense."

"None taken." Serena pursed her lips as she lurched through the service panel.

Simon followed; extracting a hanger from the closet and meticulously draping his jacket around it.

"So, I repeat, what's up? Is it that your delicious brother in-law won't talk to you anymore?"

Heat infused the back of her neck, but Serena did not respond to the taunt.

Rambling after her into the kitchen, Simon persisted. "Did you and Becky have a fight?"

Rooted in the midst of aluminum shelves and crates of potatoes, Serena rested one hand on a stack of lobster cages and used the other to press at a pain above her left eyebrow.

"We found Alan's body." It hurt to say that.

Composure being Simon's middle name, when he lost it, the affect was discomforting, like watching a child become disillusioned with their television hero. Puzzled by what Serena deemed an expression of pain and sorrow, she said, "Simon?"

"Where?"

"At the base of the cliffs," she explained. "Beneath the lighthouse."

"What do the police think happened?"

"Th-they say it was an accident at sea. They've pronounced the case closed."

Rolling his head around atop his neck until a satisfying crack sounded, Simon watched her.

"Closed," he repeated. "So there you go. Now you can get on with your life, Serena."

"Rena! Where the hell is my lunch?"

Cooper. Serena expelled her withheld breath.

"That damn old bigot." Simon snarled. "His wife sure as hell doesn't want him eating lunch at home, so she pawns him off on us. I can't wait till the spring when he sets back out to sea."

"Excuse me, Simon. I better get out there," Serena attempted to brush past him, but he stopped her with his voice.

"I'm sorry about Alan, Serena."

Not affording to look at his face, Serena nodded and plunged back into the tavern.

CHAPTER XIX

Unable to stand the subdued current running rampant through the tavern, Serena stepped out front. She appreciated the shock of arctic air. All night she listened to hushed conversations as patrons cast furtive glances in her direction. Alan's name was dropped, typically with enhanced tales of resentment and exploitation, but the affect was unanimous— no one seemed to care that Alan Murphy was dead, and all feebly sought to hide their views from the proprietor of O'Flanagans.

Stepping out from under the awning, Serena tilted her head up into the wind and felt tiny pinches of ice settle on her cheeks. In the wake of the swinging lantern she could see that the flurries were picking up in volume. The peaceful quiet of snowfall blanketed her–a welcome change from the din inside. Yet, something in the serene background was disturbing.

Serena peered into the darkness beyond the sweeping glow of O'Flanagans, and scanned the row of parked cars on the opposite side of the street. At the end of the road, beyond the reach of the streetlight, she spotted John Morse's pickup truck and felt her chest constrict.

In reflex, her head inclined towards the third story windows where drawn shades muted the glow from within. Serena had left the inside stairwell unlocked so that Brett could enter unseen, and now she worried who else might creep up her stairs tonight. Fearing for Brett, and eager to be up there with him, she rushed back inside. The shock of the noise made her hesitate in the doorway as she motioned Rebecca over.

"What's up?" Rebecca blew a dangling red curl away from her eyes. Her hands were occupied by a loaded tray in one, a pitcher of beer in the other.

"I—I don't feel well," Serena improvised. "I'm sorry, I've got to run upstairs."

"Yeah, well I don't feel well either, but I've got to make a living."

Serena jolted at the spite in her waitress's voice. "You should have told me you were sick. Go home, Becky, we'll manage."

Rebecca pursed her scarlet lips and set the pitcher down on the closest table as the seated party eyed up the beer they did not order.

"Oh, don't play the role of benevolent boss with me." Rebecca attacked. "Everything always goes your way, and now you expect everyone to wallow in misery for you because you lost a husband you didn't even love."

Recovering from the shock, Serena felt heat rise to her cheeks. She reached for Rebecca's arm, hauling her into the foyer to conceal them from the inquisitive customers.

"Okay, let's have it, Rebecca. What the hell has been up your ass the last few days?"

Scarlet eyebrows inclined. Rebecca dropped the heavy tray down atop the gumball machine and planted her hands on her hips.

"Did you ever stop to think that maybe *I'm* grieving, that maybe *I'm* in pain? Come on Serena, I know you're not as naïve as you like to portray—you saw it all along, didn't you?"

Yes. Yes she had seen it all along. And only years of practiced ignorance had kept her from acknowledging the treachery. Wasn't the smoldering scent of violet lingering in the tight entrance the same perfume that had filtered through her bedroom on several occasions?

Hadn't she always sensed Rebecca's defense of Alan, her furtive glances at their photos? And the final assault—hadn't Rebecca been visiting relatives during Alan's last two month stint away?

Yes. She had known all along, and in the end, could she blame Rebecca for acting upon something that she did not dissuade?

"You're right, I'm not as ignorant as some would choose to believe, Becky," Serena's voice turned cold. "I suppose if you were a closer friend I would have gotten around to warning you about him, but I can only assume that your grief isn't over Alan's death, but the fact that you were robbed the opportunity to make him suffer for the pain he caused you."

Bright red lips trembled, though Serena was unable to decide whether the woman was close to tears or ready to snarl. Reading the molten amber eyes, Serena concluded it was the latter of the two and fleetingly wondered if Rebecca had been robbed that opportunity after all.

With this realization, Serena's posture changed. It grew rigid. An eerie calmness possessed her as she whispered, "*It was you.*"

"I beg your pardon?"

"It was you," she repeated. "You were in my house—you smashed the picture on the desk—you, you knew what he liked to drink, you knew what he liked to eat—you—"

"Ladies, do you mind breaking up this coffee klatch," Simon huffed as he approached, "We've got business to attend to, and the natives are getting restless." His head tilted to indicate three tables loaded with intoxicated fishermen.

Assessing the two females engaged in a stare down, Simon tapped a finger against his wristwatch. "Tick, tick, tick. Come on, *let's go.*"

Rebecca blinked and glanced his way. "Go to hell, Simon." She hoisted the tray back onto her shoulder and skewed Serena with one final disparaging look. Rebecca turned to retrieve the discarded pitcher and found with slight surprise that it was empty.

"Brett?"

Serena kept her voice low as she crossed the living room floor, sweeping her gaze into the kitchen. Empty. Continuing down the hall, she repeated with hushed emphasis, "Brett?"

"In here." Came the muted reply.

Serena turned into his bedroom and located the tall silhouette against the window. She gave a secret sigh of relief. Brett had turned out the lights and drawn up the shade as she joined him with a muffled yelp of surprise.

"What?" he asked.

"John Morse's pickup was just parked out there."

"I know, I saw it."

"Did you see *him?*" Serena craned her neck to peek up the far end of the street, but both night and the thickening curtain of snowfall obscured it.

Brett reached for the back of his neck, massaging it. "No." he paused and frowned. "Hey, what are you doing up here this early? The bar doesn't close for another hour or two, right?"

"I—I was worried."

"About what?"

"I knew the stairwell door was unlocked," she said. "And I saw Morse's pickup—and I knew you were up here—"

Brett smiled, the first indication since she walked in that he had relaxed somewhat. "You were worried about me?"

Witnessing the smug male expression, Serena crossed her arms.

"Don't go getting all full of yourself, Brett Murphy. Just because I might have felt a little pang of concern doesn't mean that—"

"You care about me?" he smiled, boosting himself off the wall.

Serena drew in a swift breath when Brett strode up to her, and then expelled it irritably as he passed right by.

"We both know there's a killer still on the loose," she addressed his receding back. "Obviously I'm going to be anxious that I've left my loft unlocked. Hell, I should have just put a welcome sign out."

Nearly charging into him when Brett stopped in the hallway, Serena found his brazen grin sexy and felt heat rise to her cheeks.

"You care about me." he repeated with confidence, and then strolled into the kitchen, a soft whistle on his lips.

"Listen," she snapped. "If your head hasn't swollen up enough to block your hearing—" Ignoring his quiet chuckle, Serena proceeded. "I confronted Rebecca downstairs. I told her that I knew about her and Alan."

That drew the complacent look from Brett's face. He laid his palms down flat on the counter and offered her his full attention.

Satisfied, Serena nonetheless sobered at the recollection. She could read Brett's stormy eyes well enough to see he mirrored her unease.

"It gets worse," she continued. "I accused her of killing Alan."

"Whoa, and I have to stay in hiding up here and miss all the action."

Serena could tell that the joke was strained.

"How did she respond?" Brett asked.

"Simon interrupted us and she ran off. I wanted to get up here to tell you about this, *not* because I was worried about you."

Only the pale light from a lamp in the living room kept the dark at bay. *Her trusty nightlight.* The day it was finally extinguished would be the day she recognized an end to her fears.

"Okay, so Rebecca has motive." Brett reasoned. "Do you think she's capable of terrorizing you?"

Serena cocked her head and drummed her fingers anxiously against her arm. "The crying child—that strikes me as a woman's touch."

"Mmmm, perhaps," he murmured. "But what about the guy you saw last night, the one heading to the lighthouse?"

"It was a figure, not necessarily a male figure."

"But was it only five feet tall?" Brett asked over his shoulder as he stoked the fire.

Serena wanted to recall that one small fact, but try as she might to doctor up the image, she knew in her heart it was not Rebecca hiking up to the old lighthouse last night.

"No, no it wasn't." She stooped to adjust a doily on the end table that was already smooth and neatly situated. "But hey, that could have been anybody out there. Someone out for a walk perhaps?"

Brett turned around and gave her a *come on now* arch of the eyebrow.

"So let's recap. We have John Morse's pickup parked out front, yet he's nowhere in sight. Rebecca has admitted to her affair with Alan—" Brett cleared his throat, noticing the pain lance Serena's face, "sorry bout that."

Serena waved, shaking her head. "And Simon."

"Simon?" Brett came alert.

Listening to Serena describe the encounter in the kitchen, Brett's fist clenched as he began to pace before the mantle. "That guy gives me the creeps."

"Why, because he likes you?" Emerald eyes glinted in the firelight.

Brett's body shook in a staged chill, but he ignored the taunt.

"Okay, so that's three possible suspects right there, not to mention half a dozen local tribesmen I've talked to that have it out for Alan."

"Most everyone in this town had it out for Alan."

Brett heard the gloomy tone to Serena's voice, but decided not to pursue it. Right now he was more concerned with the fact that the Grandfather clock had struck midnight, and wondered if their downstairs visitor would return.

Brett wrenched a hand through his hair. He felt the heat of the fire on his back and inhaled the scent of charred embers mixed with the fragrance of Serena's honeysuckle shampoo. His forehead knotted.

"You think he's going to come back tonight, don't you?" Serena prodded.

"Yes. I wish I thought otherwise."

"Well," Edgy, she glanced around the loft, "at least all the lights are off." She crossed her arms. "He'll probably have assumed I went to bed by now, and that I'm alone."

Stating this didn't make it any less frightening when a grating noise emanated from behind the inner stairwell door. Serena's eyes flared. Her hand reached out and connected with Brett's arm.

"In there," he urged quietly.

Brett pushed Serena down into a crouch behind the kitchen counter. He stooped beside her and ordered in a hushed voice. "Stay here."

When he would have risen, Serena's fingers captured his. She pleaded. "Brett?"

He crouched again and touched her cheek. "Shh. Please baby, please stay here."

He didn't wait for a reply. Instead Brett inched out to the living room, trying to conceal his tread on the worn planks.

A smoldering log popped aloud. The noise made Serena's body spasm as she hung to the handle of a cabinet door with a grip that cut off her circulation. Brett rounded the corner into the hallway, out of view. She squeezed her eyes shut and listened to the revealing tales of the old inn, but today its silence only enhanced the rasping sound of the doorknob.

Fearing for Brett's life, she leaned forward to peer into the hall. She found him; a menacing silhouette crouched behind an open doorway, a fierce creature waiting to pounce on its prey.

With a groan, the stairwell door swung ajar as a shadow emerged within the two-inch gap. Brett tensed, his muscles twitching with the need to ambush. But he waited—waited until the door gaped open completely and the stranger took his first step. All Brett could make out was a leather-gloved hand wrapped around the doorframe, followed by a black boot, broaching the hall.

With his weight behind his shoulder, Brett launched at the roving shadow, plowing into the stranger and pitching him forward. The momentum forced him down on top of the figure as the two men grappled for dominance. Brett's fist landed a forceful blow, followed by a whoosh of air heaving from the assailant's body. Struggling to right himself, the momentary pause cost Brett as a heavy boot clipped him under the chin, knocking his head back and his balance off.

In a fog, Brett heard the squeal of rubber heels against polished wood. Scrambling to his feet, he watched the living room spin around before it wobbled back into place. The squeal drew Brett's attention again as he discovered the shadow vaulting towards the front door. He launched after it.

Brett managed to seize the hem of a dark raincoat, hauling with all his might, until gradually he felt the impetus swing in his direction. A muffled curse sounded as the door swung open, but the shadow was slowly drawn back from freedom.

Bitter wind and stinging snow blinded Brett. He sensed the upward swing of an arm and ducked against its descent. The maneuver was too late. Unable to dodge the blunt object that cracked against the side of his head, Brett was knocked to the ground and into a black chasm, where only the roaring sound of the surf penetrated.

"Brett?"

Brett cringed and then growled at the pain. Gingerly, he touched his fingers to his temple, wincing at the contact.

"Brett?"

"Not so loud please."

"Well, then answer me when I call you." Serena whispered above him, anxious.

Thankful that the light was still dim, Brett forced his eyes open and witnessed the veil of cinnamon caressing his chest.

"Ummmm." The sound came from deep in his throat.

"Are you okay? Can you see?"

"Feeling better," he muttered as he struggled to sit up. "Wh-what happened?"

"He hit you and got away." Serena's voice was strained. "By the time I got to the door he was gone. I couldn't see him anywhere, but I wasn't about to leave you."

"Good girl," Brett tried to smile. "The last thing in the world I want is for you to be out there with some maniac."

Brett tested the wound again and grimaced at the touch, but found he was beginning to control the pain. "Christ, he thought you were up here alone—he would have—" He didn't dare finish the thought.

"So you care about me?" Serena teased softly, although her mouth was pinched with concern.

Brett tried to stand up. Reaching out towards the table for support, he missed it as Serena surged under his arm, awkwardly steering him to the sofa.

"What the hell did he hit me with, an anvil?" His hand reached for his head.

Serena gasped.

"What?" Brett cringed.

"Don't move." She ordered and disappeared into the bathroom.

When Serena returned, it took too much effort to open his eyes, so Brett listened to her settle on the floor by his side. Next, he heard the sound of a cap being extracted from a bottle, followed by a toxic scent.

"This may hurt," she warned one second before administering the peroxide.

"Jesus, woman. I stood a better shot with the other guy."

Serena replaced the medicinal cloth with a towel. Brett heard her rest back on her heels and he sensed her eyes on him.

"It's starting to clog." She proclaimed, as he felt her hand begin to quiver.

"It's okay," He heard the fear and anxiety in her tone. "I almost had him too—I didn't count on the anvil. Next time I'll be prepared."

"Dammit Brett, I don't want there to be a next time. This is getting out of hand. What if the *anvil* was a gun? What do they want? I wish to God I knew what they wanted. I'd just give it to them."

Cautious, Brett opened his eyes into a squint and then once he acclimated, slanted a cunning look.

"We're going to have to set a trap," he declared.

"But I thought *I* was the trap. I thought pretending that you weren't here anymore was going to lure this person, which it did."

Trying to shake his head and suffering for it, Brett frowned.

"No, not enough. We're going to have to have another performance tomorrow to convince our *friend* that you are here alone again. He was surprised to see me, and that'll make him cautious next time. We don't want that. We want him to think that you're vulnerable. Tomorrow we have to make a good show of it, maybe drop a hint that we found something, some vital papers—"

"But—but, okay so sure, that will bring him back, but what are we going to do when he *does* come back?" Frustration boosted Serena's voice. "He has a gun, and you're in no shape to fight him. What can I do, clobber him over the head with a beer pitcher?"

Brett struggled to sit up, dropping his legs down on the carpet, while still holding the damp towel to his head. "I'll be fine by then, nothing a few aspirin can't fix. I've survived worse headaches in the stock market."

"But—"

"No more buts, Serena. We've got to deal with this."

"It's a matter for the police."

Brett snorted. "Yeah, a lot of help they'll be."

He took the towel away from his head so he could look at her. "I know you're scared. You know I'll do everything in my power to keep you safe, but I need you to go through with this hoax tomorrow if we ever hope for this to be over."

Brett's knees were parted as Serena knelt between them and placed her hands on his forearms, squeezing for emphasis.

"He could have killed you tonight. Do you know how much that terrifies me?"

"Ah," Brett's husky voice rumbled. "So, you do admit you care about me?"

A brief growl and she released her grip. "You're my brother in-law. Of course I care about you."

Brett's free hand reached out to snag her by the waist. He hoisted her between his legs so that their faces loomed close together.

"Well, I don't feel very brotherly to you, Serena. I've been holding back out of respect to our mutual loss, but that's not going to last." His gray eyes smoldered. "So if you don't feel the same—if you don't want this—you better run, Serena. Run as fast as you can. Because when this is over, I'm going to chase you," he leaned in, "and baby, I'll break every record to get you."

Serena's breath hitched in her throat and then burst out to fan his lips. She wondered at God's logic for giving a man such stunning eyes. Half of her wanted to flee, to run as fast as Brett warned. The other half wanted to lean into his embrace and sate the desire making her heart beat in triple time.

"Brett—"

"So," he gently set her back on her heels, "for now we have to seriously consider our list of possible suspects. I couldn't get a good look at the guy, but I know without a doubt he was male and about six feet tall. That ought to narrow things down. Did you catch a glimpse of him at all?"

Flustered, she shook her head and shot to her feet. She looked down at him with arms crossed. If he could dismiss the subject so easily, so could she.

"No. You shoved me behind the counter, remember?"

"I'd rather an anvil rammed into *my* skull than yours. I've got a hard head, I can take it."

Serena jolted as another log cracked in the fire. "Well," she breathed. "I'm not as soft as you'd like to portray me."

Brett relied heavily on the arm of the loveseat to inch upright, and then managed a grin.

"Honey, I've never accused you of being soft. You're stubborn, you're proud, and you're beautiful." He looked into her eyes. "Quite a deadly combination."

"Damn." Serena smiled.
"Damn." Brett echoed.

CHAPTER XX

With a ballpoint pen lodged behind her ear and a turkey feather blown free from the copious décor nestled in her hair, Serena moved through the dining room, adjusting napkins and autumn-patterned placemats. In the center of each table was a woven ring of foliage that flanked an ocher candle, as yet unlit, but still effervescing the scent of maple.

Faux candles dangled from the ceiling to provide intimate lighting over booths lined with Thanksgiving cutouts. Brown and orange streamers awaited the festive crowd that would soon bustle in from the annual rivalry against Victory Cove's neighboring football team.

Standing beside the longest table, a link of three smaller ones, Serena tapped her fingers against the sleeve of her sweater, and then swooped down mechanically to smooth unseen wrinkles in her knit, calf-length skirt. She dusted some imaginary crumbs off the nearest table and smiled at her domain.

Perhaps the décor was a bit tacky. Perhaps the shadows chosen for atmosphere conveniently hid layers of dust she couldn't reach on the beams. All in all, O'Flanagans represented home, and Serena needed that feeling. She needed the warmth of friends, and in return, would show them that Thanksgiving in her home would be the best damn meal they ever had.

Two hours later, Serena's face was flushed. A speck of mashed potatoes clung to her glossy hair, while the sleeves of her sweater were hiked well above her elbows.

"More gravy!"

"Coming," She muttered, ladling the creamy liquid into a ceramic turkey. She handed the bowl off to one of Harriett's great nephews and resisted the impulse to muss her fingers through his unruly hair. She flashed him a smile that had the eleven year old blushing as he hastened back out of the kitchen.

Straightening her own haphazard mane before plunging out into the crowd, Serena felt a rush of warmth and listened to the harmonious clamor.

"When the hell is Simon getting here?" Rebecca muttered nearby, breaking the positive meditation.

"In about an hour. Don't worry" Serena said, "everything's under control."

She tried her best to stave the disdain in her voice. She did not want to face Rebecca's betrayal until after the holiday was over.

"Easy for you to say. You haven't been behind the bar taking the sixteen thousand orders I've had to fill." Rebecca snorted.

Not about to argue that she was busy in the kitchen throwing sixteen thousand rolls into the oven, nor eager to point out that she had placed a pitcher of iced tea along with a carafe of wine on each table simply to prevent Rebecca from having to take many drink orders, Serena swallowed her sigh and shouldered her way back into the crowd.

"Rena, honey, you've outdone yourself this time," Harriet reached out to grab her as she hastened by. "But I've got to ask—what's this here stuff?"

Dressed in her best corduroy jacket, the shopkeeper sniffed her nose at a bowl full of unidentified liquid.

"Dove sauce?" Serena attempted.

"Dove sauce? What the hell is dove sauce?"

One of Harriet's elder daughters quietly admonished her mother for her language, but Harriett shrugged it off.

"I don't know." Serena said. "Ask Simon when he comes in. It was his masterpiece."

"I'm gonna pass. Just keep bringing out the mashed potatoes dear—and some more of those dinnah rolls if you will?"

Serena pirouetted back to the kitchen and caught sight of Simon entering through the back door. She summoned up a smile.

"Happy Thanksgiving, Simon."

Simon shook the snow off his black leather jacket and glanced over his shoulder. "Huh, uh yeah, you too. How bad is it out there?"

"Not bad at all, everyone's enjoying themselves. They've even commented on your—your sauce."

A glint of interest pierced the cerulean eyes. "Really, what did they say?"

"They, ah, they wanted to know all about it. Nobody asked about my gravy as much as they've asked about your sauce."

Seemingly pleased, Simon tucked his black necktie into the waistline of his sleek black trousers, and then tested the cuffs of his starched white shirt. He reached up to run a hand through his hair.

"Well alright then, I guess I'll get started."

It was impossible to ignore the subtle underscore of conversation about the discovery of Alan's body, but Serena managed to disregard it along with the accompanying sympathetic glances. She moved through the crowd, pausing to touch people on the shoulder while sharing a familiar tale, and even managed an opportunity to test a slice or two of the tender, golden meat.

That brief amount of food now churned uneasily in her stomach as the door opened and Brett walked in, smirking at the hush that befell O'Flanagans. He did not so much as glance in her direction as he strolled up to the bar and asked Rebecca for a beer.

"So, you decided to join this festive event?" Rebecca drawled as she handed Brett the frosted mug, letting her fingers linger for a second against his.

"Well, Thanksgiving is supposed to be for sharing with your family—" Brett tipped back the beer and set it down forcefully enough to draw attention. "And my family is lying in the morgue right now."

Conversation halted completely as all eyes in the restaurant swung back and forth between the outsider and Serena.

Serena's hand, which had been casually resting on Cooper's shoulder, now clenched. He winced and pried her fingers loose. She gathered herself, remembering this had to be done—grateful that the act came after dinner was complete.

She approached the bar.

"Would you like some turkey, Brett?"

With a derisive grin, Brett hoisted an eyebrow. "Ever the hostess, aren't you, Mrs. Murphy?"

"It's Thanksgiving," she managed. "Can we at least keep peace for a couple more hours?"

Brett tipped back another sip and watched Serena over the rim of the glass. Outwardly his stance appeared relaxed, one shoe hiked on the brass foot rail, one elbow atop the counter. Serena could tell that his muscles were tense, and by the faint twinge in his glaring eye, she sensed the pain pulsing behind it.

He managed an irreverent snort. "I'm at peace, right Rebecca?"

"Anything you say, sugar."

"Serena, we have to get going, uh, it was a lovely dinner. You outdid yourself as usual."

Serena flinched and turned to find Lois Goodall fidgeting with the collar of her coat before her husband rescued her and secured the garment over his wife's shoulders, blatantly ushering her towards the door.

"Oh, I understand," Serena stammered, "yes it's late. Please take home some of the leftovers."

Lois made a theatrical rub over her abdomen and rolled her eyes, yanking against her spouse's insistent pull. "We won't eat for days, we're so full. Thanks again."

And just like that, Serena watched as families begged their excuses and friends glanced worriedly at their watches. Next thing she knew, she stood within a silence so substantial compared to the clamor only moments ago, that she had to clutch the back of a chair for bearing.

"Wow, you know how to clear a room." Rebecca leaned across the bar. The pose pushed her breasts up, a gesture she had practiced in front of the mirror. "I wish I could have done that hours ago."

Brett merely cocked an eyebrow and raised the mug to his lips.

Simon thrust open the swivel door from the kitchen with his one free hand, the other hoisted over his head, supporting a tray of sliced cake. He halted so abruptly that gravity nearly toppled the plates off one end. Mouth agape, he gazed into the empty dining room, where dirty dishes lay scattered across stained tablecloths. Balloons dislodged by playful children now bobbed lifelessly through the aisles.

"What the hell—?"

Aiming his question at the few remaining inhabitants, Simon's cool blue gaze alighted on Brett and tapered suspiciously. "What did you do?"

Brett shrugged his shoulder and took a step closer to Serena. "Hey, somebody said cake and they all high-tailed it out of here."

Simon glared and dropped the tray into the nearest booth. "Who the hell invited you?"

"Didn't know it was on an invitation basis."

"Well, he's leaving now," Serena stepped forward, reaching for a dishcloth to wrap around her fingers. "The party's over."

Rebecca's hand shot across the bar to grab Brett's wrist. She cocked her head and simpered. "You can come home with me. I've got some Thanksgiving food of my own in the kitchen."

Serena's grip on the towel was so tight it cut off her circulation. She envisioned wrapping the cloth around Rebecca's thin neck and twisting with equal force.

Cheeks aglow, Serena's eyes flashed a challenge as she approached the bar. "Get out."

The initial order was directed at a woman she had blindly considered a friend—a woman, who if she didn't take her hand off Brett in one second, Serena was going to reach for the nearest meat tenderizer and forcibly remove it. The mad rush of jealousy was a shock to her system, a system that was already reeling from so many jolts. "All of you—please get out."

"Easy now *sis*," Brett placated, "don't go getting all riled. I think we should have a nightcap, a toast to my deceased brother."

Serena could tell that Brett detected her trembling hand, so she yanked it behind her back.

Well, all right, she fumed. If Brett wanted a performance, he damn well was going to get one, and she was sure to be loud enough for any straining ears within a half-mile radius to hear.

"I don't think a toast is in order to mourn your brother. I think what would be more appropriate is for you to get your 'holier than thou' ass out of this town before Rebecca here stakes claim on yet another Murphy man. And as for you, Ms. Sorrenson, this establishment no longer employs you. Out of some perverse reminiscence of good times we once shared, as deceitful as they must have been, I will offer you an excellent severance pay—but I don't care to see you again."

"On what grounds are you firing her?" Brett challenged.

"She slept with Serena's husband." Simon injected, fueled by the lynch mob frenzy.

Rebecca stood upright, spoiling the effect of her deceptively voluptuous chest. "So," she shrugged, "who hasn't?"

Brett's eyes shot to meet Serena's, but it was Simon who roared a comeback. "You're fired remember? Get your white trash, used body out of here."

"What the—" Rebecca charged out from behind the bar to thrust her pointer finger against Simon's chest. Her face was as red as her hair as she spoke and jabbed simultaneously.

"Who the hell do you think you are, you goddamn two-faced—"

"Don't you say it." Simon's fingers wrapped around Rebecca's wrist. "Don't you dare say it."

Rebecca wrenched from his grip and rubbed her hand. "How many nights did you stand here by the bar with me and say that you thought Serena was frigid, and that it was no wonder Alan was looking for someone else?"

"Well you sure as hell jumped in with your legs wide open, didn't you?"

"Stop it!" Serena screamed, certain that she would lose her mind if she heard any more. "All of you. *Get out now.*"

Rebecca tossed her coiled hair and reached in the closet for her coat, ignoring Simon as he simultaneously grabbed for his. She held out the fake leather towards Brett, but to her dismay it took him a second to acknowledge her expectation.

He lugged the jacket up both her arms and watched as she turned around.

Rebecca's hands came to rest against Brett's chest, her head tilted back as she murmured, "Forget about all of this. Come home with me. I've got a nice bottle of Chardonnay with your name on it."

"What I need to do right now," he said, "is to go pack, so I can get my 'holier than thou' ass out of town."

Anyone else watching would have seen Brett's sneer and heard the disdain in his voice, but only Serena caught the quick flash of mirth in his eyes. "Maybe after that, I'll take you up on your offer."

"Don't wait too long," Rebecca tried to conceal her disappointment that she couldn't make a dramatic exit with Brett Murphy in tow.

Skewing her boss a caustic look, Rebecca reached up onto the pointed toes of her knee-high boots and aimed her glossy lips at Brett. She landed a slight graze to his jaw, Brett tipping his head at the last second to avoid her intent.

Serena reached the back door to the tavern and wrenched it open, heedless of the wind that whipped the Thanksgiving décor into a cyclone at the center of the room. Tilting her head into that frigid stream, she relished the bitter bite against her hot skin. With strained patience she waited for everyone to shuffle out.

Simon charged by without a word, loose blond hairs corkscrewing over his head as he vanished into the night. Serena waited for Rebecca to follow and turned to find the woman with her hands on Brett again. She wanted to hurl Rebecca outside by her long auburn mane.

"Rebecca."

There was a stony calmness to Serena's voice that Rebecca merely wrinkled her nose at. Blowing Brett a kiss, the redhead stalked clumsily over the grouted deck.

After the diminutive figure disappeared into the shadows, Serena kept the door open, turning in Brett's direction. When he did not move, she cocked her head to prompt him outside. Brett crossed his arms and leaned back against the bar, watching her with steady gray eyes.

"Aren't you going after her?"

"No." He replied quietly.

Serena slammed the door shut. She ignored Brett and stooped to gather up the spoiled streamers. Behind her, she heard him rustling with dishes. With her hands full of autumn colored ribbons, she blew the bangs out of her face, exasperated.

"What are you doing?" she challenged.

"Cleaning up."

"If you're going to play the role of the angry brother in-law, that doesn't involve janitorial duty."

Brett shook his head and resumed his task, hoisting the first set of plates into the sink and twisting the faucet. Serena decided to ignore him. She crammed torn decorations into plastic trash bags, and made a lot of noise doing it.

Brett peered up from the sink and secreted his grin, but Serena caught it. It aggravated her all the more. Hauling the bags behind the bar, she backed into the swivel door and used a free elbow to jar it open. When she returned, she paused in the doorway, inadvertently taking in the width of Brett's shoulders as he washed the plates in silence.

"I'll do that." Her voice was harsher than intended.

With a shake of the head, Brett kept washing.

"Brett, did you hear me, I said I would take care of it. Why don't you go upstairs? You're not supposed to be here anyway."

Brett set a saucer back into the milky suds and turned around, rubbing his hands with a dishtowel. His eyes roved over her.

"Do you want to tell me what's wrong?" he asked softly.

The calming pitch to his voice aggravated her. His smug expression provoked her. And the fact that he looked so damn good in black dress slacks and a crisp white shirt, with the sleeves rolled up only goaded her even more.

"There is nothing wrong." *Did she really sound that loud?* "I'm just very busy."

"Exactly why I'm helping."

Why was he so notably calm while she felt like a raving maniac? *And why was the heat turned up so high?*

Serena moved towards the thermostat and spun the dial down to sixty.

"Well, go help someone else."

Brett dropped the towel on the rim of the sink and advanced towards her. The move was slow. Deliberate.

She instinctively backed up, and made a sound of frustration when she was immobilized by the counter behind her. Her heart hammered as Brett closed in. In his eyes, a storm brewed, and she had nothing to protect her from the raw elements.

She searched for a route of escape, but it was too late. Brett stood before her, his hands on either side of her hips, locking her in place. Her chest pounded in agitation, but she lifted her chin defiantly, recalling just how angry she was.

"You know what, Serena?" He murmured lazily. "You're jealous."

"What?" She barked, now trying to push him away, but finding that his arms were like steel, fencing her in. "That's ridiculous, and do you mind please?"

"I liked it." he continued quietly. "I liked seeing you jealous. I liked seeing fire in those beautiful eyes and knowing it was because of me."

"Why, of all the arrogant—I *am not* jealous, Brett. Maybe I was angry," she stammered. "Sure I was angry, my God that woman—" Serena swept back her bangs because now even her forehead felt hot. Maybe she was coming down with something.

Brett lifted one arm, and when she thought she could make good on her escape, he caressed her cheek and rendered her paralyzed.

"Do you have any idea how much I want you right now?"

Serena's throat went dry at the huskiness of his voice. She opened her mouth, wondering where the bravado of her anger suddenly fled.

"You—you don't want me. You heard what they said about me. It's true."

"Let me be the judge of that."

"But, you're not supposed to be here," she whispered. "Somebody could be watching. Remember the act?"

"Screw the act." Brett's mouth was on hers, and Serena whimpered with a combination of need and pleasure.

It was no longer possible to delve for reasons against this. The fact was that she wanted Brett just as bad. In discovering this liberation, she responded to his kiss with a jolt of lust.

Drawing her hands up behind his neck, Serena sank her fingers into his hair and parted her lips to feel his soft warmth possess her. It was like sinking into a pool and being caressed over every inch of her body with liquid heat. But she never wanted to come up for air. She never wanted this kiss to end.

Brett cautioned himself to go slow. His hands still clutched the counter, though now with a feral grip as his mouth swept across Serena's, evading her demand for a deeper union. He heard her silent plea, a choked sob which he cut off with another kiss. Every hidden nuance of Serena's body begged for more—and God help him, he was going to deliver.

Forehead to forehead, the tip of his nose touched hers.

"Serena," His voice was rough. In one word, he warned her of what was to come.

Ever so slightly, Brett angled his head and touched Serena's lips. In tracing them, he knew he had lost all control. His hands released the counter to grab her hips. With a motion that stemmed from sheer need, Brett rocked into her. The cabinet held her in place, making his friction even more apparent. Serena clutched his shoulders and held on as if her very life depended on it, her quick gasp dusting across his throat.

"*Brett*?" It was another plea.

"I'm here, honey." he whispered, roving her neck with his mouth. If he dared return to her lips he wasn't sure he could stop there.

Serena didn't help matters as her inquisitive fingers grazed his chest and toyed with the buttons on his shirt. Her feathery lashes lowered and Brett nearly growled when he saw the possessive way she looked at him, like he belonged to her, and she was going to taste every inch of him to prove it. Those languid eyes and the broadening span of her fingers nearly undid him. He reached up and captured her face, forcing her to focus on him.

"Now do you know how much I want you?"

To Brett's surprise, a wicked grin crept over soft, swollen lips as Serena instinctively rocked against the part of him that ached with need. He had never seen anything sexier in his life than that sinful smirk.

Serena cocked an eyebrow. "I've pretty much got an idea."

A growl tore from his throat. He kissed her.

"Pretty much?" He kissed her again. "Let me convince you then."

This time his mouth opened and Serena groaned into it.

His determined hand climbed up her shirt until it was splayed across her breast, the tip of his thumb drawing constant circles that made her arch into his touch. In response, his hips ground into Serena, feeling every hidden tremor in her body and stoking the inferno he detected building inside her.

White hands fisted into the crisp fabric of his shirt as Serena's head lolled back. Brett seized the opportunity and lavished the pulse at the base of her throat. In a hedonistic pattern, his tongue scored the slim cord of her neck as he climbed up to re-claim her mouth.

Irrationally, Serena wanted to plead with Brett to stop the maddening friction, sensing that if he didn't, she would lose control—and she *needed* control. Her body betrayed her, though, and she met the motion—thrust for thrust. She was lost in undulating waves, looking for something, looking—

Suddenly, she grew taut. Her head dropped back and she let loose a moan that hitched in her throat. It turned into a startled gasp as her body trembled and fell immediately slack, her head nudging forward onto Brett's chest. She held on desperately and breathed, aware of the private throbs of pleasure that pulsed inside her—little heartbeat reminders that she was alive.

Not daring to look up, she whispered, "I—I—that—"

"You are beautiful." Brett murmured into her hair.

"Brett, I—"

"You what? You're certainly not going to try and tell me you're frigid are you?"

Serena didn't think her cheeks could possibly feel any more flushed. And resting against Brett's chest, listening to the racing beat of his heart, only intensified the heat in her face.

"I've never reacted like that," she whispered. "I've got to tell you, I'm a little embarrassed."

Clutching Serena beneath the chin, Brett tipped her head back so he could search her eyes. "Don't say that. Do you have any idea how crazy you make me? How perfect you fit in my arms?" His gaze dipped. "And how *hot* it is to feel you lose control?"

Serena nearly caught herself purring.

"Sshh." She touched his lips with the tip of her finger, but lost her train of thought at the sight of them and the images they evoked.

"Oh, Brett." Mortification closed in again. "You, you didn't—" she faltered, "I feel so selfish."

The soft masculine chuckle was alluring. "Selfish? Why, because you feel good?" His head shook slowly. "No baby, don't feel selfish about that. Selfish, is me wanting to be inside you, right now."

That husky declaration made Serena shiver. It made her throb. Her stroke slid down Brett's arm till her fingers laced with his. She stared at his chest, the rise and fall of his erratic breath, and the temptation of the warm flesh at his unbuttoned collar.

"Brett, I want that too."

Want that. Hell, Serena thought, she wanted Brett to take her right here on the bar.

Brett must have read the blatant desire in her eyes. He wrapped his arms around her, hauling her an inch off the floor so that she was splayed intimately against him. When she connected with the effects of his desire, her breath hitched. He let her slide back to the ground, and when her feet finally touched, he caught her mouth in a rough kiss.

"Come on," he growled. "We're going upstairs."

Serena relied heavily on his support as she scanned the chaos of her restaurant.

"I guess the mess can wait till tomorrow." She reached for the panel of light switches and hastily flicked them off, flashing him a look out of the corner of her eye. "*Everything* can wait till tomorrow."

It took a few moments to get through the door.

While she fumbled with the lock, Brett nuzzled her neck. Somewhere in there, a determined hand dipped beneath her jacket, against her skin.

"How am I ever going to concentrate with you groping me like that?" She pleaded with mock exasperation.

"I intend to make you concentrate on me, not the lock."

"Well, you've succeeded, but we're never going to get upstairs at this rate."

Brett reached down to twist the lever that had grown obstinate with age.

"This damn lock is too old," he remarked. "I'll replace it."

In the same breath as his observation about the lock, Brett swooped and touched his lips to the skin exposed above her collar. He groaned and drew her out into the night.

Hand in hand, they mounted the first step, but the muffled sound of a phone ringing made Serena tense.

"Was that upstairs or downstairs?" Brett hesitated.

"Upstairs." Serena hastened a step ahead of him.

"Let it go." His hand tugged on hers.

Serena stopped and looked down at Brett. His eyes reflected the moon, still smoldering with promises that made her feel weak.

"It could be the police." Reluctantly, she climbed another step.

"At this hour?"

At the door, Serena halted and Brett moved in behind her. In a haven of male musk, his body gloved hers as he dipped and whispered in her ear. "Whoever it is, get rid of them."

That soft voice made her shiver. The swathe of his body made her hot.

Inside the apartment, the phone continued to ring, the party on the other end persistent. It took all the willpower in the world, but Serena wrenched from Brett's warm shelter.

The phone sustained its shrill assault, and at this point Serena was tempted to just lift the receiver and drop it back in its cradle. Instead, she pressed it to her ear.

"Hello?"

CHAPTER XXI

Brett watched Serena. The healthy blush in her cheeks, the sparkle in her eyes, the swollen lips. His fists clenched to keep from touching her.

If this was wrong—if God looked down on him with censure—then he would willingly accept Hell.

"Brett?"

The blush had gone pale. The sparkle dulled, and her lips thinned in apprehension.

"What's wrong," he stepped towards her, "who is it?"

"Your Mother."

Brett reluctantly accepted the receiver, but wouldn't release her eyes. He locked Serena to him with that simple connection.

Distantly, he heard it all. Ethel Murphy's stern berating that she had to discover her son's death via a voice message. He listened to her admonishment that Alan was neglected by Serena all these years, and he listened to her distinct disapproval of Brett answering Serena's phone at nearly midnight. Ethel would have gone on were it not for his gravelly injection.

"Are you done?" He didn't wait for a response. "Firstly, Serena told me that she had tried to reach you, but you were off in Europe with no word left behind as to where you were staying. She had no choice. And as for Alan," Brett rubbed a hand over his face and suddenly felt deflated.

Jealousy could have made him point out all of Alan's faults. He could have hoped for once to disillusion his parents about their prized son, but instead he said, "Don't worry, I'll bring him home."

Serena saw the pain in Brett's eyes and longed to go to him, but something in his stance dissuaded her. In fact, she felt that she was intruding on his privacy. She retreated, but Brett seemed not to notice. He seemed tormented and continued speaking into the receiver.

"And as for me being here at this hour," he took a deep breath, "you are not the *only* one to grieve, Mother."

With a click, her bedroom door closed behind her. Serena rested against it, her palms touching the wood. It was a marvel that she could stand in this dark room and not rush towards the lamp. Instead, she focused on the trail of moonlight slicing through the window, sketching a path to her bed. Outside, she heard the soft murmur of Brett's voice on the phone and her heart went out to him.

It still amazed her how two families could be so different. The O'Flanagans knew nothing but love, while the Murphy's seemed cold and aloof. Right now they were probably telling their older son to keep away from her.

That was what truly hurt.

Because as immoral as it may be, she knew she wanted Brett more than anything.

A soft knock nearly made her claw her nails into the wood. Numb, she stepped away from the door and watched hypnotized as a pie of light pooled across the floor.

Brett filled that gap, his shadow obscuring the glow. "Serena?"

Serena moved to the dormer window. "Are they okay?"

"You worry if *they're* okay," he gritted, "when they've shown you nothing but disrespect?"

She shrugged. "They lost a son. I grieve for them for that."

Brett advanced a few steps, but hesitated at the foot of her bed. "Funny, but they don't seem to remember that they still have one son left."

Serena turned. "That's not funny at all. It's sad. What magic spell did Alan weave that he had everyone under such influence?"

Brett shook his head. "I wish I knew."

Outside, a storm loomed. Victory Cove was still basked in moonlight, but the first howling protests of wind assaulted the old inn. A shutter clanged against the façade. Serena jumped and Brett tensed, primed to charge after their nighttime assailant, but Serena's voice stopped him.

"Don't worry," she assured, "it always does that. Believe me I'd be able to identify an artificial noise from anything this old house can muster."

In the blue glow of the moon, Brett arched an eyebrow.

"Oh really?" he grinned.

Serena's own lips lifted as she realized that he was referring to her inability to distinguish her ghosts for what they really were. The fact that the insinuation was done so with a smile warmed her heart.

"Okay, maybe not always."

"I searched the loft," he said. "No sign of an intruder."

She nodded and silence descended between them. Brett's hand was propped up high on the doorjamb. He watched her in the dark.

"Look," he began. "I'm not going to stand here and deny how much I want you."

Serena trembled.

"But, I'm also not going to push you into something you're not ready for. Now is not the time for this to happen between us."

His hand slid down the jamb and in the dark their eyes met while O'Flanagans shook under the force of the wind. With a lingering glance that revealed all of his desires and trepidations, Brett nodded and left.

An arresting hand on his arm kept him from getting far.

"Now *is* the time for this to happen."

For a moment he stood perfectly still. Serena moved in behind him, slipping beneath his arm, her hands climbing up his chest.

"Now is the time, Brett."

She tilted her head back and caught the stark slash of his jaw in the moon's glow. That glow reflected off his eyes as she willed him to dip his mouth and take her—but he seemed adrift, lost in the tempest brewing over the Atlantic.

"*Brett*?"

It was a tangled cry of frustration and desire, and it succeeded in snapping his eyes to hers. That gaze dropped to her lips, lingered, and then with a low growl, he covered her mouth with his.

Brett's kiss was tender, yet it wholly enveloped her. Serena clung tight as her knees buckled when his tongue slipped into her.

Strong arms wrapped her tight, the impetus of the embrace making her bow backwards against the steel band of Brett's forearm. She was hauled close enough to feel the effect of his arousal, and she whimpered her need.

"Serena," Brett wrenched his mouth away and whispered hoarsely. "Are you sure? Baby, I don't want to hurt you in any way."

Rooted in his embrace, linked in a position that connected them intimately, Serena smiled. She felt intoxicated by the crisp, manly scent. Her fingers probed, sought, and demanded. She wanted him.

There was no doubt.

She wanted Brett Murphy.

"Oh yeah, I'm sure."

As if to prove it, she reached for the buttons on his shirt, baring his chest for her consumption. She felt the thunderous beat of his heart beneath a layer of muscle and the flesh was warm against her lips.

Heat.

Finally, there was something to warm the chill she thought she would die with.

"My God," Brett drove his hands into her hair, lifting her face. "I want to do that to you."

Perhaps it was the gravity in his eyes, or maybe the husky tone of his voice, or possibly just the fact that she was so damned turned on. Serena splayed her hands across Brett's chest and used the leverage to urge him towards the bed.

On the edge of the mattress, Brett submitted to the hands on his shoulders, but he could not stay idle with Serena close enough to taste. He reached out and slipped his hand under her blouse, climbing till he achieved his goal and watched her neck drop back and her mouth slacken. She felt perfect. Her breast filled his hand as his fingers toyed with her, masterfully arching Serena into his touch.

Locked between his thighs, she seemed to revive enough of her senses to coax him back onto the quilt. Using this leverage, she wrenched off his shirt and drew in a ragged breath, her eyes flaring. Brett nearly growled at the awe on her face. No one had ever looked at him like that before.

He reached for the bottom of Serena's blouse, and hoisted it over her head, watching her hair spill back onto her shoulders in a silken shower. In an equally swift gesture, he unfastened her white lace bra, and his eyes dipped to savor the view.

Bathed in the moon's radiance, the ethereal glow outlined Serena's body. Her arm reached up to brush back bangs from her face, the motion lifting the perfect curve of her breast.

"Serena." His voice was hoarse. "For ten years I've wanted you. I waited—watched, and all along I hoped—"

Sliding up her stomach, his palms sought that perfect curve and molded it with his hand, marveling at the immediate response.

"And now you're here, and the only thing in the world that can stop me from making love to you is if you say no."

Serena tugged her hair behind her ear, holding it in place as she bowed down to kiss him. Her breath whispered against his lips.

"Then I guess nothing will stop you."

With a growl, he hoisted her atop him. Outside, the Atlantic expressed itself with gale force winds picking up in strength, but he ignored its protest.

Clothes came off. Serena traced Brett's muscles, testing the resiliency of his thigh, playing with the course hair and nimbly climbing enough to elicit a strangled groan from him. Through a haze of arousal he noticed her slight hesitation and hitched his index finger beneath her chin so that he could look into her eyes.

"What is it, honey?"

"Is this wrong, Brett?"

Brett looked away, solemn. "Does it feel wrong?"

"No." She wrapped her arms tighter. "No, it doesn't."

Serena pulled Brett's mouth down to hers. He hesitated and then returned her kiss. When she tried to speak, compelled with the need to say what was on her mind, his gentle lips would not stop. Using her palms, she was able to push off and lay beside him, face to face. Her fingers reached for his black hair, loving the glossy sensation.

She searched Brett's eyes in the dim light and found the truth. Swallowing against the constriction in her throat, she whispered, "Brett, I love you."

Something kindled in Brett's eyes. "I know that."

"You know that?" Her tone rose just before he squelched it with a kiss.

Taking his time, Brett drew back from Serena's mouth with a soft smile. Tension eased from his expression as he caressed her breast.

"I know," his tone lost its levity, "because I love you too."

Before she could inject, he continued. "I wanted you, Serena. The first day I saw you—I wanted you." He touched her lips. "*I'll always want you.*"

On instinct, Serena's hand fisted over her heart. She had to put pressure against the alien sensation. Brett reached for that hand and gently pushed it aside, dropping his head down to skim her fevered flesh. His mouth trailed up the arch of her throat before he suspended himself atop her by his elbows. He looked down, and she was lost in his eyes, ready for the storm to take her.

The words were unsaid, but Brett waited for Serena—the decision was hers to make. Her kiss of assurance was blatant enough to make him even harder. With the flick of her tongue, Serena conveyed what she wanted, and Brett's answering volley said he would provide.

After ten years of marriage, Serena finally realized what it was like to make love. Her body hummed under Brett's mouth. It was first tender, then patient, and ultimately so hot, he made her feel molten.

When her caresses grew emboldened, when her kisses grew desperate, when she cried Brett's name against his shoulder—he took her.

And they found peace.

CHAPTER XXII

"Oh my God, I probably woke up the neighborhood."

Serena's arm was flung over her head, her mussed hair cloaking an eye. With her free eye, she studied the man stenciling innocuous patterns on her stomach with his finger.

"Which time?" Brett teased as his finger dipped lower, only to be halted by her emphatic grip.

"I'm being serious—I—I never—" Serena floundered for a way to describe her total abandon, the way she cried out when Brett drove her to yet another trembling climax.

How could she explain all that he had done for her tonight? His actions, let alone the quiet declarations he whispered in her ear had ebbed the pain of years of rejection and cold treatment. In his embrace there was an overwhelming feeling of devotion—alien—yet suddenly everything she ever wanted.

"I never made so much noise."

Brett snorted against her breast and looked up. "Honey, you can go on making all the noise you want, the rest of the world be damned."

Serena ruffled his hair.

"What's wrong?" he asked, so easily able to read her.

Continuing to toy with his hair, Serena evaded his glance.

"Do you think less of me?" she asked. "I just found my husband's body yesterday, and not even twenty-four hours later I'm in bed with you—his *brother* nonetheless."

Brett sat up against the carved wooden headboard. The sheet dropped to his waist. "Come here," he whispered. "Keep me warm."

Serena slid under his arm, resting her head against his chest.

"He was my brother, yes." Brett's voice was grave. "But you are the woman I want. The woman I love. Nothing else matters to me, do you understand?"

"But—"

Brett tipped Serena's head back and kissed her forehead. "Shh. Listen to me. We both tried to save Alan. During the course of his troubled life, we both battled a fight we could not win, and during that battle we were both duped by him."

Pain clouded Brett's eyes. "I believed many of his tales—particularly one he told me about you. Maybe I wanted so badly to accept what he accused you of. Maybe I wanted to convince myself that you weren't the beautiful, perfect woman I wanted to make my own, because I knew it was wrong at the time."

Brett shook his head. "For a moment, I allowed myself to think less of you." His fingers clenched. "And I was wrong."

Sensing Serena's protest, Brett silenced it by touching her lips before he continued. "What happened tonight was not solely your doing, Serena. I'd like to think I played a part in it."

"*A damned good one,*" she muttered before his finger hushed her again.

"When you think about it," Brett continued, "this should have happened ten years ago. So, no, I don't think any less of you. I think—" he grinned, "what took you so long?"

Lulled by the beat of his heart, the deep timbre of his voice, and the security of his arms, Serena whispered. "I love you."

"I love you too."

She bleated a protest as Brett hauled her away. He set her back so he could pierce her eyes, his tone serious. "And I'm not going to let anything happen to you. There's a killer out there—and we're on our own to find him."

"He almost took you away from me," she cried.

"I've got a hard head." Glancing at the clock, Brett turned back to her.

"As much as I'm dying to make love to you again—" he groaned when he noticed the sheet drop across her hips, "—it's almost four o'clock and you need rest."

Serena shook her head. "I need the terror to go away." She touched his mouth. "I *need* you."

Brett listened to the sound of the shower and smiled. Sleep was something Serena and he had evaded, and though they may regret it later in the day, it was worth every damn hot moment.

Hauling on his jeans and treading barefoot into the kitchen to start coffee, he was surprised to see the sun rising over a clear skyline. Entranced by the dusky rose eclipse on the dark horizon, Brett watched the stars fade and thought about the future.

"Are you okay?"

Serena stood in the kitchen entryway, her hair dark sable, still damp from the shower. Dressed in jeans, a white tank top and a red flannel shirt, she appeared wholesome, but her eyes were anxious as they followed him.

He nodded. "Yeah." Then with conviction, he added, "yeah, I am."

Brett crossed the kitchen floor and hooked his arm around her waist.

"And how about you, Miss Serena," he asked. "Are you okay?"

Resting her hands on Brett's shoulders for leverage, Serena thrust herself on the tips of her socked toes and kissed his cheek. "Are you asking if I have regrets?

She reached up and administered a kiss to the opposite cheek. "No, Brett. No regrets."

She felt the grip around her waist tighten as she extended one last time to touch his lips and groaned when Brett's mouth opened under hers.

Standing forehead to forehead, grinning like teenagers in love, Serena worried that this happiness could not last. She was convinced on some inherent level that she did not deserve it. But then again, that was the seed of insecurity Alan had so successfully rooted.

"Stop it," Brett murmured into her hair.

"Stop what?"

"You're tensing up on me—withdrawing. Don't, Serena."

"It's hard." Her hands curled against his chest.

"It's gonna be if you keep touching me like that."

For a moment Serena was speechless, then her head pitched forward and she laughed into his shoulder. The gesture felt so carefree and perfect. Dusting his throat with her lips, Serena dodged out of Brett's grasp when she heard him growl.

"Oh no you don't," she waggled her finger at him. "I've got to get downstairs and start cleaning up. If you'll recall, you kept me from that task last night."

"Oh, I recall alright." Brett grinned. "Give me a few minutes to shower and I'll come down with you."

Serena ducked into her room and talked loud enough for her voice to carry.

"Take your shower. I'll meet you down there." She reemerged with sneakers on, her eyebrow arched in confrontation should he pursue a debate.

Brett raised his hands and muttered, "Okay, okay."

Pretending to shrug, he ambled past her, but at the last second reached for her arm, and tried for an impish grin. "A parting kiss perhaps?"

Serena's frown deepened, but a chuckle erupted from her throat before she leaned into his embrace. She was staggered by the sweep of Brett's mouth and the texture of his naked flesh. *Hot flesh. Hot man.*

It was impossible to draw away. Brett's teeth were teasing her bottom lip and his hands were under her flannel shirt, touching her through the thin cotton tank top. Brett caressed the lace rim of her bra and then growled and hauled her against him.

"I'm too old to react like this," he murmured. "What are you doing to me, woman?"

Eyelashes fluttered coyly, though Serena's slight pant betrayed the act. She traced her finger down his collarbone.

"Mmmm, I have plenty of things in mind," she wrenched from Brett's grip and gasped from withdrawal, "which I will do *after* I have cleaned up downstairs and started serving the lunch crowd."

Before Brett could stop her, Serena made for the door. Her hand was on the knob.

"Serena,"

Something in his tone halted her as she peered over her shoulder and met those eyes—turbulent and alluring. She stood rooted by that gaze, aware that her knees trembled.

"Last night," A haunting quality mixed with the deep timbre of Brett's voice. "We didn't use anything. I could have gotten you pregnant."

Serena's knees threatened to give way completely, her stomach prepared to stage a mutiny. Condemning herself for being so reckless, she was ready to assure Brett that she would not hold him responsible for—

"If that happened," he whispered hoarsely, "I would be so damned happy."

A sob wrenched from her throat. Her eyes watered, although she was oblivious. Holding his gaze for a second, or an eternity, she yanked the door open and launched into the raw Maine sunrise.

Brett started to go after her, but drew up. Instead, he leaned against the kitchen counter, glaring into his coffee, recalling Serena's agonizing wince as he wished desperately he could take the moment back. Of course she would be appalled. She had just lost her child less than a year ago.

He would give her some time alone downstairs. Until Serena's ghosts were finally put to rest, he could only stand by and do his best to help her withstand the storm. And if his best was to silently love her, well, he'd been doing that since the moment he got here.

He wasn't about to stop.

Serena slammed the tavern door and leaned her forehead against the frosted pane, unsure which was colder, the glass surface, or her own skin. Her breath clouded the window as she reached up and traced a finger through the mist—a single line spiraling slowly downward until it landed on the splintered frame. With a sigh, she retreated.

Serena surveyed the murky interior of O'Flanagans and grabbed the remote, aiming it at the television. A winter storm warning flashed across the bottom of the screen. It cautioned that gusting winds could cause coastal flooding and near blizzard conditions. Distracted, she stared at the blue glow from the television reflecting off the lacquered counter, and rolled her head atop her shoulders to loosen tensed muscles.

Later. She had to force herself to think about Brett later. Right now she had to concentrate on work.

Serena cast a glare at the residual mess from yesterday's festivities.

No, dammit, don't think about Brett cornering you behind the bar. Don't think about his hot kisses. *Dammit, Serena.*

Shuddering as she heard the door open behind her, Serena spun around and choked back a gasp. "Oh—Simon." Her hand settled on her heart, but the beat was uneven.

"Mornin'." Simon un-wrapped an ivory scarf from around his neck. He glanced around the establishment, whistling softly. "Well, it looks like you didn't stick around much longer after I left."

"I was tired."

"Quite an evening, wasn't it? I spoke to Rebecca. She's stopping by to pick up some stuff."

"Money?"

"There's that I imagine, but she made it sound like she had some personal items lying around here."

Kneeling into one of the booths, Serena yanked out a pile of torn streamers and stooped completely under the table to reach a gravy-stained napkin lying on the floor. When she emerged her cheeks were flushed.

"There might still be some of her clothes in the kitchen closet." *Now* that quick change of clothes Rebecca left here made more sense.

Disgusted by the thought, Serena ignored Simon and slammed through the oscillating kitchen door. Determined to make Rebecca's visit as brief as possible, she delved through the metal utility closet and systematically pitched the woman's eclectic wardrobe into a potato sack. Careful not to draw in the scent of perfume as she touched the diverse material, Serena exhausted the closet as a source and moved on to the shelves that lined the wall.

Combing ledges lined by contact paper, she eyed the cupboards that were tucked inaccessibly behind a squat metal boiler. Serena considered these as potential hiding spots for more of Rebecca's diverse wardrobe and pried herself into the confined space.

Brett stepped into the tavern, his glance seeking, but not finding what he wanted. His first instinctive thought was that Serena was in danger. He started towards the kitchen, but was drawn up short as Simon rose from behind the bar, mechanically patting down a swath of blond hair. The maitre de stared at him, his long fingers splayed across the counter, tapping listlessly.

"Well, well, and how was *your* evening?"

Uncomfortable under the amused scrutiny, Brett managed a grim smirk. "Unique."

"I bet. Rebecca said she'd be in around ten." Simon peered over his shoulder at both the clock, which read ten minutes before the hour, and at the door to the kitchen where Serena could be heard rummaging. He cocked an eyebrow. "But I bet you knew that already. I bet that's why you're here."

Not in the mood for Simon's coy games, needing to find Serena, Brett moved towards the kitchen. Again the maitre de's voice arrested him.

"I wouldn't go in there if I were you. She's in quite a mood."

Convinced her mood was his own doing; Brett ran a frustrated hand behind his neck. He hesitated at the juncture of the bar, and listened to Serena's movements. The obvious slam of a cabinet door, even at this distance, made his head throb.

"Perhaps you should have a seat and wait this one out." Simon suggested.

Brett slanted a glare at the sneering maitre de and grudgingly agreed. He hooked his heel onto the brass rail and rested his elbow on the counter in an outward display of indifference. But his gaze kept drifting towards the kitchen.

Already unnerved, Brett muttered an oath as the front door banged open and Rebecca entered in a flourish of scarlet hair and winding hands.

"My God, that's one hell of a storm brewing out there!"

Rebecca flounced down on a stool near Brett and eyed him sulkily. "I don't appreciate being stood up."

Glancing at Rebecca first in the mirror, Brett then shifted idly to meet her pouting gaze. "I don't recall making any promises."

"Typical Murphy," she huffed. "Promises aren't big on their list."

Brett's hand clenched around the mug, oblivious to the scalding surface. He would have relished some deprecating reply, but in watching the small whirlwind of provocation, he was reminded that Rebecca was out of a job and most likely pining away over his two-timing brother.

Simon's hand thudded on the lacquered counter, drawing both sets of eyes his way. "I hate to break up Breakfast at Tiffany's here, but I've got to get going."

Addressing Rebecca, he said. "Look, I need to get my gym bag from the kitchen so I'll probably slip out the back door, but if you want me to grab your stuff out of there for you—"

"Is *she* back there?" Rebecca sulked.

"Umm hmm, it's why I offered."

"And why are you suddenly so chummy with me?" Her cool voice drawled. "Last night I was no better than a two-bit whore."

"Becky, honey, I would never consider you a two bit whore—" Pale eyes rolled in dramatic innocence. "I know you're raking in at least ten bucks a pop these days."

"Ugggg!" Rebecca would have launched over the bar, her red nails extended like talons, but Brett's hand restrained her.

"Let go of me, goddamnit."

"Cool down." Brett waited until Simon disappeared behind the swivel door and the tension poured out of Rebecca before he released her.

Rebecca sighed in frustration and laid her head on the bar, atop her crooked arms.

The zeal of anger fled as Serena sagged against the wall and blew her bangs out of her eyes. Her crazed search produced two fake cashmere sweaters, a pair of jeans, several lipstick containers and a silk negligee, which she disdainfully dunked into the potato sack. Along with these feminine items, she was surprised to locate one of Alan's college yearbooks, and even more astonished to discover it stuffed with bank statements between the rigid pages. Recognizing their account number, and cringing at the withdrawal figures, she was reminded how close he could have come to putting her into bankruptcy. Through the years, her focus had been on the O'Flanagans account, which fortunately Alan couldn't touch. But damn, she should have paid more attention.

Just another slap of reality.

Serena lifted her hair off her shoulders, feeling the heat emanating from the boiler as she eyed the last cabinet tucked deep in the corner. She glanced behind her and tried to listen over the low drone of the furnace. Should she forego this remaining cupboard for another day when there wasn't so much to attend to out in the dining room? Mulling over the small panel, she speculated that it held more clues to Alan's treachery.

In order to reach into the tight space, she squatted on her knees and yanked open the cabinet door. At first she was disappointed to discover it empty. Determined, Serena thrust her hand inside the dark confines and rummaged to the back end, her fingers seizing around a hefty envelope standing on its side. Drawing it out, while sweeping her fingers one last time for any remaining objects, she stood up and back-stepped hastily to get away from the furnace that now made her skin glisten.

Serena turned over the slim unmarked canary envelope and unwound the string, drawing out a stack of official documents stamped with the State of Maine insignia. Initially she was baffled as to what she was even looking at. Knowing Alan, she expected it was some deed to land that he did not own. She read on and discovered a government contract approving Class III gaming for the county adjacent to theirs. Puzzled, she read more, learning that the National Indian Gaming Commission had petitioned to engage in Class III gaming, a category that allowed all forms of gambling, including slot machines and table games. As she continued to scour the legal jargon, she realized that they had consistently been rejected. Flipping the stapled page over, Serena discovered a signed testimony from the District Court permitting the Class III status. The third page was a duplicate of the second, yet the signature of the judge was left blank, making page two extremely suspect.

Hah. If she were a gambling woman, she would bet the signature was a fraud.

"Oh, Alan, what did you get yourself into this time?"

Had he played with fire—been burned?

Folding the letters back up, Serena tucked them into the envelope and planned to review them later with Brett.

Thinking about Brett set her heart racing again as she reached out to grab the counter, suddenly feeling lightheaded. For a moment she had panicked when he pointed out their lack of discretion. If she were to become pregnant, she would do everything possible to protect the infant, no matter how wrong the circumstances of its creation.

But when Brett opened his mouth, it was not condemnation that he expressed; it was a heartfelt need to share with her. The pain and love in his eyes had overwhelmed Serena to the point that she needed to run.

Perhaps too many years with Alan had made her a masochist.

Brett made her believe in the impossible, but Alan's ghost made her believe she wasn't worth it.

Serena scowled at the papers in her hand, and the potato sack of clothes on the tiled floor.

She *was* worth it. And she was going to prove it to Brett.

Lodging the envelope under her arm, she nudged the sack with the tip of her boot.

Serena's deliberation was interrupted.

Pain, fast and intense at the base of her skull launched her into a bleak world where ghosts reigned.

CHAPTER XXIII

The ornate hand of the cuckoo clock crept towards its apex as Brett shifted his foot off the pedestal. Anxious, he eyed the kitchen door. Rebecca was immersed in her depression, be it theatrical or real, and he figured at this juncture she was inconsolable.

Determined to have it out with Serena and eliminate the anguish in her eyes, Brett launched towards the kitchen, but a billow of wind from the main entrance made him waver.

As murky as the light was outside, it was bright enough to eclipse the figure in the open doorway. The door slammed shut and John Morse's lanky form sauntered forward.

Morse's loose ponytail released errant locks of black hair that trickled down his brooding face. He glanced indifferently at the glum female who barely lifted her head to acknowledge him, and then he advanced, heedless of the challenge in Brett's glare.

"What the hell are you doing here?" Brett asked roughly.

"It's a bar. I want a drink."

"The bar is closed." Brett challenged as Morse settled down on a stool at the far end.

Morse extracted five singles from the back pocket of grease-stained jeans and thrust the money towards Rebecca's outstretched hand. "Get me some whisky."

An amber eye squinted open, peering at the money. She grabbed it with a vindictive "hmmmph" and rounded the bar to pour his shot.

"He's not staying." Brett threatened, pressing in on the man.

Morse skewed him a spiteful glance. With a shrug, Morse tossed back the shot glass and slammed down the tumbler, nodding at Rebecca. "Another."

"You better start talking, Morse."

Something in the undercurrent of Brett's voice seemed to rouse Morse from his indifference. He swiveled in his seat.

"*Ms*. Murphy has something that belongs to me."

Muscles tensed in rage as Brett barely resisted the urge to attack the man that was stalking Serena. He had to keep Morse talking, if only to find the rationale behind the man's actions.

"And what might that be? An unlimited supply of Ole Grand Dad?"

"Cute." Morse snorted into the bottom of his shot glass. "Seeing as you have spent so much time with your grieving sister in-law, you might have come across some paperwork her husband has for me."

Unable to feign composure any longer, Brett stepped away from the bar, bearing down on Morse.

"Sorry, can't help you. For that fact, neither can Serena, but if you want to let me know what it is you're looking for, I'll be sure to keep my eyes open."

"Yeah, right." Morse's pockmarked face stared disdainfully at Brett's reflection in the mirror.

"Were you into a little extortion maybe?" Brett goaded, dimly aware that this man was responsible for his throbbing headache.

"Hah, that's funny coming from a Murphy."

Impatient and angered to the point of losing his cool, Brett grabbed the collar of the man's denim jacket and hauled him off the barstool.

"Don't confuse me with my brother," he paused, but his grip did not relent. "Now let me ask you again, what is it that you think Mrs. Murphy has in her possession? What gives you the right to torment her every night?"

Wrenching out of the vise-like grip, Morse muttered some healthy oaths and sailed the shot glass down the bar. He growled at Rebecca who was watching with unabashed curiosity.

"That damn well better be on the house." He shifted his attention back to Brett.

"I don't know what the hell you're talking about," he continued, "but you're goddamn brother has caused enough damage between the Pasamaquoddy and the Penobscot, that if I don't get that doctored up document before it falls into the wrong hands—there could very well be bloodshed over this."

"It seems to me there already has been." Brett's voice was ice. "If you hadn't of killed him, maybe you could just ask *Alan* for the damn thing." His eyes narrowed. "Or was it that he didn't cooperate?"

"Jesus Christ." Morse swiped a hand over his face, perspiration glossing his wide forehead. "You got it all wrong. But hey, I don't have to defend myself with *you*."

"There you would be wrong."

Hanging on their every word, Rebecca moved a step closer to the phone mounted on the wall. The motion drew Brett's attention, concerned that Serena picked this moment to emerge from the kitchen.

Preoccupied, he followed Rebecca's red nails to the receiver. The piece of paper taped to the wall beside the handset was the focus of Brett's attention. Staring at it, he felt a lick of the Atlantic breeze invade the Inn.

"Go to hell, Murphy." Morse challenged.

Distracted enough to ignore the man, yet aware enough to be primed should he attack, Brett strained to see across the bar. Reading what seemed to be a grocery list, he grimly realized that the writing was an exact replica of the love note in Alan's desk.

"Rebecca," Brett's voice was hoarse, "is that your list?"

Puzzled that he was not concentrating on the imminent battle, Rebecca glanced at the sheet on the wall, and heaved a sigh.

"No, that's Simon's. He better friggin pick that stuff up today for the Black Friday rush." Shrugging her shoulders, Rebecca continued. "What the hell do I care anyway, I don't work here anymore."

Her words were lost to Brett as he felt the vise of panic cinch around his stomach. "Serena," he whispered in desperation.

Brett launched through the oscillating door, into the empty kitchen where he saw the back door banging restlessly in the wind. For a moment he stood rooted, captivated by sporadic glimpses of the frigid hell outside.

Gray—black—gray—black, the door swung back and forth, mocking him. *Too late. Too late.*

A footfall behind him caused Brett to whirl and discover John Morse at his heel. The man peered over his shoulder into the fog bank beyond the gaping door.

"Let me guess," Morse said, "she's gone? And you know who took her, don't you? It's time to start redirecting your anger, Murphy. There were several people that had issues with your brother," he nodded outside, "and that Turner was one of them."

Frantic with the need to burst into the storm and find Serena, Brett managed enough restraint to determine the source of Simon's madness before pursuing him.

"What!" Brett's voice pitched. "*Goddamnit*, what issues?"

"You're not too observant, are you? I haven't even been around here much, but I heard your brother bitch about it enough. Simon had it bad for him. Puppy dog eyes. The whole nine yards." Morse shook his head as the wind caught a lock of his hair. "Of course, you know Alan—it was an angle he could play. And use him, he did."

Brett clutched the doorframe and leaned out into the nor'easter, watching it swarm funnel clouds up the cliffs. Violent wind fueled by saltwater struck him in the face. Desperate, he shouted Serena's name, but the sound lashed hollowly back at him.

His sweeping gaze confirmed two things. One, they had not left the establishment by vehicle, and two, the untouched umbrella jimmied against the loft door revealed no one had tampered with Serena's apartment.

Where was she?

"If you've got something more to add," Brett growled, "explain it along the way. I'm going after them."

"You've got no clue where he took her." Morse cursed and hastened after Brett, adding in vain, "*or if she's still alive.*"

It was impossible to discern any movement within the milky realm of wet snow. Brett stumbled blindly, instinct drawing him up the precipitous knolls towards the lighthouse that remained invisible within the storm's cloak. Slipping on the slick surface, he sought in vain for signs of the trail. Even now, glancing behind him, his own steps were quickly obscured by snowfall.

Bleakly aware that Morse pursued him, Brett paid no heed to the man. He thought only of Serena. He exposed the cellar entrance by literally tripping on it. Wrenching the door open, the wind nearly tore the panel from its moorings. Into the dark prison he lunged. The sudden cessation of wind made the sound of his heart even more prevalent. He cursed as Morse's frame depleted what little light was left. The local ambled down the stairs, the relentless patter of sleet echoing his lumbering footsteps.

"How'd you know about this place?" Morse shouted at first, and then jerked at the resonance. Lowering his voice, he added, "and what the hell made you decide to come here?"

"Simon's car was still parked out back." Brett's hands scoured the far wall, working off of memory to locate the secret doorway. Stumbling over a stack of rusted pails, he kicked them out of the way. "And what the hell are you doing here, Morse? Scavenging for the few remaining morsels?"

"I've got an investment to protect." Morse joined in the search, kicking the same pile of tumbled buckets out of his own path. "Believe it or not, I had or have no intention of harming your precious little Serena. Heck, I don't really give a damn about her one way or the other. I guess as a resident of Victory Cove I wouldn't want to see O'Flanagans fall in a bad way, but—"

Brett yanked his hand back, cursing the splinter that pierced his flesh. "I found it."

Prepared to launch, Brett crouched as he entered the light keeper's house, but the room was empty. Drawn to the bank of windows, there was only a thin pane of glass and a sheer plunge of bedrock to separate him from the violent gale. Brett stared into its fury—a tempest with surging white arms, seeking to claim the forsaken head light in its deadly embrace.

With a roar aimed at the squall, he slammed his fist down on the roll top desk. Under the red veil of anger, the door to the tower beckoned as Brett charged into the chamber. His shout reverberated in the lofted cylinder, echoing back unanswered.

"Where did he take her?" Brett paced crazily, his hands plunging into his hair, ignorant of the throbbing pain or the faint trickle of blood the gesture incurred.

Morse watched him. "I know how this Simon feels. I was him for awhile—used, duped, deserving of what should rightfully be mine—waiting for Alan's promises to become reality."

"Christ, Morse," Brett shot back, "are you going to tell me you were in love with my brother too?"

"Hell no!" Morse's face pinched in aversion. "He just had a way of roping you in, making you believe in his schemes, only this time he—"

Brett crossed the earthen floor in two strides, seizing Morse by the collar. He tugged the man closer.

"Please," Brett's voice was lethal. "Don't stop now."

Morse swallowed, but the scowl remained fixed on his face.

"He was trying to get the approval for a casino to be built in Harris County. Not just some damn Bingo parlor, but a full blown Class III status," he explained. "Craps, Blackjack, slots, everything. Alan rallied the local Pasamaquoddy into a frenzy, which in turn drew the interest of the Penobscot. Everyone thought Alan had legitimate connections. He trusted me enough to admit that he was doctoring up paperwork to advance to the next higher level in the government."

Waves crashed against the cliffs with such ferocious recurrence there grew a constant trembling of the ground they stood on. Morse glanced down as if he expected the earthen floor to gape open at any second.

"I've got to get a hold of that documentation before it falls into the wrong hands and sets back our efforts another ten years. I can hear it all now," he said, "their government is filled with nothing but snakes—" Morse cut himself off before he digressed to issues they had no time for. "You got to understand, the way Alan presented it, I believed it was all going to work out. I thought he could pull it off, but then he started losing it, growing so greedy he was careless. Opening his mouth to everyone with promises of a piece of the pie."

Morse paused. "And a lot of those promises were directed at Simon Turner. He was milking Simon for money as an *investment* towards their future," his eyebrow hefted, "implying together of course."

"So Simon thinks that this—this documentation rightfully belongs to him? What the hell would he do with it? He's as white as they come. He can't just walk in there and represent the local tribes."

Morse smirked at the analogy. "There are any number of Pasamaquoddy or Penscobats that would go forward with the motion—press the government for their claim. And I imagine by Simon supplying them with this so-called legitimate contract, he would demand a percent of the action."

With no time to contemplate Morse's tale, Brett ducked back into the house. Straining to see through glass coated with streams of ice and snow, despair seeped through Brett as he clutched a splintered window-frame and closed his mind off to everything but a vision of Serena, imploring the image,

"Tell me where you are, baby. Please tell me."

Serena woke violently.

Pitched against a barrel, she strove for equilibrium. Her hands flew to seek hold of something stable, though the drum by her side rolled as unsteadily as she. Fighting pain, she tried to open her eyes and blinked when a stream of saltwater poured into them.

Drenched in seawater, resting on all fours, Serena cried out and thrust open her gaze. Waves crashed into her, and were it not for the rope fashioned securely about her waist she would have lurched off the deck into the black sea.

Identifying her situation as incomprehensive and grave, Serena reacted by gripping the rope and yanking it till she could locate its origin. A lantern swung inside the pilot house. It framed a murky silhouette hunched over the controls, fighting for balance. Around her, the boat groaned against undue treatment, each thrust of the hull into the blockade of waves, potentially its last.

Even in the throngs of the gale, where visibility was nil, Serena recognized this trawler as being one of Harriet's rentals. Unable to stand against the force of the wind, she squatted down on her knees, immersing her hands in the swirling water trapped several inches deep on the deck. Lurching across the slick surface, Serena cried out in frustration when a rebellious wave crashed across the deck to flush her back against the wall. Desperately, she sought for a handhold, and tasted brine behind her clenched teeth. She trembled against the debilitating memory of being held beneath the surface.

Convinced she had finally succumbed to one of her nightmares, trapped for eternity where ghosts and death roamed the night, Serena folded into a catatonic refuge.

Another surge of the ocean poured over her, jolting her from the spell. She dredged in a deep, sodden breath and regrouped her efforts by crawling closer to the cabin door. Frustration and anger proved persuasive incentives as she slipped and lurched one last time to reach the door handle.

Serena yanked it open, and from her crouched perspective, Simon seemed taller than ever. Within the diminutive cabin, his soaked features depicted him as a creature of the sea, a monster come to claim her for his subterranean world.

Releasing the wheel, two large hands grabbed for the slack on the rope and jerked her body inside the cabin, grunting with effort as he hauled the door shut. Using the tip of his boot, Simon pushed her into a corner and grimaced when he noticed the wheel begin to spiral out of control. He lunged at it, his muscles tense until the boat fell under what little control was manageable in these conditions.

"Well, one thing's for sure," Simon grinned maniacally. "They damn well won't find you out here for awhile."

Without the steady mixture of rain, snow, and the sea dousing her, Serena became aware of a deathly chill stealing over her body. She had on only the flannel shirt and jeans, and felt the beginning stages of hypothermia kicking in as she tried to quell her trembling lips long enough to speak.

"Y-y-you th-think they won't know it's y-you?"

Simon's pale hair was pasted to his head, blue veins visible around his temples. They meandered down his cheek and curved into his crazed smile.

"My dear, with the paper you were nice enough to locate for me, I can secure enough support that if anyone even suspected me, they would see to it that it's covered up."

"Th-they?"

Affording a glance away from the bleak windshield, Simon cast a revolted look at her.

"Never mind," he snarled. "You know, Serena, Alan wasn't too happy with you. He didn't like the fact that he couldn't get his hands on the tavern's money."

Serena felt surreal in the musty cabin and blinked against the flash of the swinging lantern. A wave threatened to pitch the trawler on its side until it stubbornly righted itself. "Th-that's t-t-too bad."

Hugging her arms about her, Serena realized she barely felt cold anymore. There was no sensation in her fingers as they fell helplessly onto her lap. "Th-this is insane, Simon. You know y-you won't survive out here. How the hell do you even know how to h-handle this thing? I've never seen you in a boat before."

Simon slammed his foot down and caught his balance as the hull hurdled over another wave. The surf broke atop the vessel in a cascade that poured under the door, swirling around the cabin floor. Engulfed in the frigid seawater, Serena barely shivered, and struggled to stay conscious. The allure of sleep became too tantalizing. It began to numb her mind, and only her struggle to hear Simon's words kept her awake.

"Alan taught me," he explained. "He used to take me out here all the time. You know, when you thought he was out of town, he'd be with me−" Simon's frown over the panel before him was fuzzy to Serena, but she heard him continue, "—or somewhere in town, working out this deal. We were out on the sea the day Alan told me that I had it all wrong, that he was not attracted to me, that he was cutting me out of the deal. He—he threatened me with this god-awful *hook*. He said if anything happened to me, it would look like an accident." Wild blue eyes implored her. "I had no choice, Serena."

Her hands useless to prop her up, Serena sagged against the wooden panels, struggling to comprehend what Simon was saying. Her brain felt anesthetized.

"Y-you killed him," she stuttered. "F-for God's sake, why?"

The lantern produced a strobe-like effect, flashing on and off Simon's sallow skin as he glanced down at her with tears in his eyes.

"He couldn't just turn me off—just pretend that I didn't exist. I really didn't mean to kill Alan, Serena. He just made me so angry, I shoved him, and next thing I knew he was overboard—and he never came up again." An eerie calmness overtook Simon. He shrugged.

"And now my sweet, I've finally got what was coming to me." He patted the bulge in the back pocket of his jeans. "And you are simply another casualty of Alan's mess."

Simon chuckled, a hollow sound swallowed by the waves. "Oh, Serena honey, you were so easy to play. Just a little rigged speaker system that my DJ friend loaned me, and you were a raving basket case. You thought you had ghosts, didn't you, sweetie? Alan. The baby." Simon laughed again. "I thought that was a particularly clever touch. Alan told me about how you lost it. I figured that it would put you over the edge. Get you out of the Inn so I could search upstairs without risking you coming home. But it didn't matter in the end. You found the paperwork for me."

It was too late.

Serena couldn't hear him anymore.

Darkness funneled around her, channeling into a passageway she tremulously followed. She listened to the sound of childish laughter and was drawn towards it, her hands extended, awaiting that soft touch.

CHAPTER XXIV

"Come on."

Brett set off. Snow fell steadily just inland, but intermittent surges of hail indicated that perhaps the storm took on a different caliber out at sea.

"Where are you going?" Morse hollered behind him.

"I think I know where they are."

Brett turned his head back into the gale, staggered by its force. A vicious veil of snow blinded him. He shouted over the wind. "How good are you with a boat?"

"What the *hell*!" The Indian's ponytail whipped from its confines, billowing ebony strands around his face in a spider-web effect. "You've got to be shitting me."

"Let's get down to Harriet's." Brett motioned incase his words were slurred by the weather. "She'll know if any of the cruisers are missing."

Harriet Morgan answered the emphatic pounding on the shop door. Pinpricks of ice cast a sheen to her puffy cheeks as she shifted back, watching the two men stumble past her. The CLOSED sign banged as she slammed the door shut.

"For Christ's sake, Murphy. Now is not the time to prove to me you want to be a fisherman."

Doubled over, hands on knees, Brett coughed before he could stand up and manage a single word. "*Serena*."

A steely look of alarm altered Harriet's expression.

"Where?" she choked.

Catching his breath, Brett shifted towards the window, barely distinguishing the bulky forms that bobbed erratically in the heaving surf. He nodded outside. "Can you tell if any of them are missing?"

Harriet pushed past him and cupped her hands around her face as she peered through the cold glass out into the void.

"Hard to tell without going out theah," she muttered.

"Wait—my trawlah, the rental, it was in the first slot just this afternoon. Dammit Murphy, what's going on?" The pitch of her voice rose.

Brett gripped her plump upper arms, delving into eyes that shifted from his, to the storm, to Morse, and back again. He strove for assurance he didn't feel. "Harriet. I need to go out there."

"What?" she cried. "Are you insane? You won't even make it out of the cove!"

Conviction stole over Brett as he turned towards Morse. "You don't have to do this. I'll go out on my own."

Morse snorted. "Don't be a fool. Even if they did head out to sea, you have no idea which way they went." He swiped back a lock of black hair and took a deep breath, "Let's just suppose that Simon can handle that trawler—even the most seasoned of sailors would be at the mercy of this squall. There's no navigating. No charting a route. You go where the ocean takes you."

"Maybe so," Brett turned away from them, watching a wave spill onto the pier, its sodden fingers fisting around the wooden planks. His voice was full of torment as he added, "But I can't stay here."

It was one thing to be in love with Serena. The inherent male drive to defend his mate was a strong enough motivation. But after last night, knowing that Serena loved him, that she could be carrying his child—Brett realized that he would challenge God himself to protect her.

This storm would not stop him.

"You'll need one of the newer Pilot House's, not the *Morgan*." Harriet started to dictate. "At least that'll protect you a bit. I've got another trawler; it's got a fancy chart plotter and GPS, so at least we'll be able to trace you."

Harriet left them to rummage behind the counter. The sound of her sifting through a conglomeration of keys was followed by a muffled grunt of triumph. "You may need this too."

Brett reached for the keys and then took the other offered item. A .22 caliber handgun. He smirked with forced amusement. "For the serious fisherman?"

"Damn straight, Murphy." Harriet's eyes were full of angst.

"Give me those damn keys." Morse swiped the ring from Brett's hand and started toward the door.

Brett slammed his fist against the panel at the same instant Morse's hand landed on the knob.

"I don't get it," Brett uttered tightly. "Why would you risk your life out there to help me?"

Morse skewed a glance at Brett. He exhaled an expletive. "Don't flatter yourself, Murphy. I told you I don't want that paper getting into the wrong hands."

Brett dropped his fist and nodded in reflex.

Harriet's anxious voice interrupted them. "Oh God, this is insane. If I didn't love that girl like a daughtah, I'd never let you do this." She stepped up to Brett and gripped the hand that held the gun. "Bring her back to me. You *all* come back to me."

Nodding, Brett hauled open the door and stepped out into the storm's wrath.

The tempest raged at him.

He raged back.

"Serena!"
Echoes.
Bantam sounds lulled Serena from the ecstasy of sleep.

"Serena, dammit, I'm talking to you." Simon roared as the ocean poured over the helm.

It crashed through the windshield and pooled inside the cabin to wrench Serena from her stupor with a jolting chill that she was still capable of feeling. She swiped her soaked hair back from her face and instinctively looked towards the dim bulb.

"Go to hell," she choked.

The laugh was a sordid version of the throaty sound she recalled her maitre de make on hectic nights with a tavern full of boisterous patrons.

"Probably," he agreed. "Bitch!" Simon's expletive was aimed at the turbulent sea, tossing the trawler about till the solid wood frame groaned in protest. "Serena, the compass is worthless. These controls aren't the ones Alan taught me. Tell me which way leads back to shore."

Perhaps the hypothermia had placed her on the brink of madness, but Serena tilted her head back and laughed.

"Why should I help y-you? Y-you're just going to toss me into the ocean." Her voice took on a sing-song tease. "Don't y-you want to j-join me, Simon?"

Yanking the nine-millimeter from its secure position beneath his belt buckle, Simon jabbed the barrel at her face.

Serena snorted. "That's supposed to be a th-threat? You're going to kill me anyway—actually I'd prefer the gun."

It seemed like hours that the hull trembled and advanced unsteady through rupturing waves, the windshield useless against the pelt of snow and ice. Morse's face was cast in a scowl, made all the more daunting by the austere glow of the overhead light. He scanned the radar while Brett remained silent, divvying his anxious glance between the green LCD screen and the wintry void outside.

"There's something out there," Morse muttered, distracted.

"Where?" Brett reached for the door, ready to launch into Hell.

"Jesus, don't go out there. Wait, let me get a fix on this. Yeah, see that, it's about fifty meters away."

Brett traced the direction of Morse's finger and read the display, following the throbbing blip on the screen. It matched his pulse. "How long to get there?"

"It could be two minutes or two hours, depends if the waves cooperate or go against us."

Brett's hand cupped the Pasamaquoddy's shoulder as he uttered hoarsely, "Make it two minutes."

Simon yanked on the rope, jerking Serena's body towards him. He cursed and lodged the gun back against his waist so he could use two hands to haul her. "Stand up!"

On her knees, struggling for any form of sensation in the pads of her sneakered feet, Serena thought fleetingly, *don't you think I would if I could?*

Out of frustration, not by the context of Simon's command, Serena grabbed onto the polished wood rail. She used the strength in her arms to compensate for the frailty in her legs. It was a struggle, but she managed to prop herself against the helm, now able to glare in condemnation at her captor.

"You're going to die out here, Simon."

"I see it!" Brett was out the door before Morse could stop him.

The attack was like nothing Brett had ever experienced before. Tendrils of water licked his boots, trying to topple him. Unruly bursts of wind heaved with successive blows as he felt rooted in the center of a boxing ring rather than clutching the starboard rail of a boat.

What Brett *saw* was a bobbing light, first visible then gone behind a swollen wave. Numbed fingers wrapped around the balustrade as he stood his ground when the ocean loomed and scoured him with brackish water.

Morse urged the trawler forward and flicked on the external lights so that the horrifying pitch of the waves became visible in a frothing surge around them. Having lost sight of the other boat's lantern, Brett leaned over the rail and was nearly sucked off the deck. He shook his head, trying to clear his eyes of saltwater.

"*Serena.*" Brett shouted into the maelstrom.

Behind him, a persistent bang on the door drew Brett's attention. Focusing on the black sea, Brett clutched the rail and howled out his frustration before retreating into the cabin.

"Ten yards off the starboard side." Morse shouted over the din of the storm.

Brett acknowledged with a quick tip of his head and then surged back into the night. Progress was hindered by the water around his feet. Squinting against the siege of ice and rain, he finally located the dancing light only several yards away. The desire to dive off and swim the remaining distance nearly overcame him.

They were close enough now for Brett to distinguish shadowed silhouettes within the cabin. Simon's lanky profile was easily identifiable—the other wilting outline, a perhaps injured, but blessedly alive Serena. Insane with the need to reach her, Brett roared back at Morse.

"Get closer!"

Morse maneuvered the trawler with care. The ocean could easily ram them into the hull of the other boat, with no more care than a cow's tail swatting at a fly. Cursing in a tongue that would probably do his Father proud, Morse stalled the engine as the trawler rocked helplessly towards the shadow of Harriet's rental.

All they could do was wait.

Without the motor, a hollow silence made the storm resonate. Waves provided the crescendo, rain supplied the staccato, and percussion was injected with the loud bang of impact as they collided.

Brett moved fast, tossing the heavy rope onto the opposite deck. He timed the descent of a wave and launched across both railings. He tumbled onto the slick surface of the other trawler, sliding clear to the aft of the ship before gripping the rope, using it for leverage. Knocked down twice by sequential waves, he struggled upright. Brett then wrapped the slack of the rope around the balustrade, faltering as the two vessels bumped with each pitch of the sea.

"Great!" Simon lunged for the wheel, feeling the tug of the other boat root them in place. He screamed his frustration and smacked the helm. Relinquishing the rudder to the pull of the flanking trawler, he spun to face Serena. In a pale hand interweaved by indigo veins, he held the gun.

"Your boyfriend has arrived."

Simon appeared rabid. "Which means, my dear, it's time to cut you loose." Tapping his fingers along his jaw, he mused. "And I guess I'm going to have to kill him too," he chuckled. "But what's another Murphy in the water?"

Serena struggled back into the corner, searching in vain for an avenue of escape as Simon loomed with both knife and gun in hand. Numbed enough to merely yelp when his quick motion sliced the blade through the twisted fiber only inches from her fingers, Serena dimly realized she was no longer confined. Wishing that her limbs would be more cooperative, she struggled to crawl, but found that every avenue she pursued, Simon quickly blocked her.

"How pathetic." He stooped to hoist her up and stumbled unbalanced as a wave struck the vessel.

Brett hauled open the cabin door and clutched its frame with his free hand. He roared at the scene before him. Simon had an arm wrapped around Serena's waist, and the other possessed a handgun, which was aimed at her head to enforce compliance.

Looking at Serena, Brett realized that enforcement was not necessary. Her skin was the color of a frozen pond and her eyes seemed to roll with the pitch of the sea. She futilely struggled for freedom, barely conscious enough to realize he was even there.

"Serena," Brett called.

Her head snapped up. Her stare was blind.

"Brett?" She blinked.

"Hey, I hate to break up this emotional reunion," Simon injected, "but I've got to dispose of Mrs. Murphy here." He glanced at the gun aimed at him and responded by lifting his own weapon even with Brett's glare. "And I've got to do something about you."

"That's fine," Brett replied coolly. "So let her go and deal with me then."

"No." The gun wavered as the choppy surf pitched the trawler.

"Simon, you're rigged to our boat." Brett inclined his head to indicate the light outside the window. "You can't go anywhere. Back on shore, everyone knows what you've done—to Alan—so don't think you're going to escape from this."

Simon snarled and secured his hold of Serena as he inched towards the cabin door. "If I kill all of you, I don't see a problem with me escaping."

"And the paper that you've gone through so much trouble for," Brett pointed out, "what good is it going to do you? As soon as you produce it, you'll be arrested."

A flicker of doubt sliced through the cerulean eyes. "The tribal underground will hide me. They'll know how to handle it."

Brett shook his head. Outward, he appeared calm, though his eyes measured Serena, afraid that her condition was deteriorating. His gaze shifted to the automatic that wavered in Simon's white-knuckled grip.

"John Morse is in the trawler next to us."

Simon's brow jerked. "What the hell is *he* doing out here?"

"Protecting his investments. He speaks for both the Pasamaquoddy and the Penobscot when he says that they aren't interested in Alan's illicit schemes. If there is going to be a casino, it's not going to happen outside the law. They feel the repercussions are far too great."

"But Alan said the government would never approve it without a little intervention on his part. He said that the Indians are only a *front* anyway—that everything is really run by white businessmen." Simon whined and cursed irritably when Serena struggled against him.

Frustrated into violence, Simon hoisted the gun in the air intent on cracking it down on Serena's skull. He hesitated at the lethal chill of Brett's voice.

"*Don't do it.*"

Simon's eyes dropped to the weapon aimed at his brow. Staring each other down, Simon figured he had the upper hand, possessing both the gun and Serena.

"We're at an impasse here," he declared. "So I'm just going to scoot by you and take little Miss Rena out on deck."

Serena chose this moment to pool her last remaining strength as she jabbed her deadened foot on Simon's instep, and then thrust her free arms upwards, cracking them against his extended grip. She watched in satisfaction as the gun arced from his outstretched fingers.

"*No*," Simon howled.

Discarding her, he surged after the spiraling device.

Brett reacted instantly and would have reached the weapon were it not for the wave that crashed against the hull. It spilled into the open cabin and tossed all three parties off their feet as the trawler pitched onto its side.

In a whirlwind of limbs and brine, they tumbled in the tight confines, watching with horror as the cabin windows immersed under water. The keening groan of the flanking boat sounded hauntingly muffled in this bleak environment. As the wave continued its trek towards Victory Cove, the trawler rolled lazily upright.

Dazed, Brett shook his head and spat out saltwater. Wild with concern, he sought and found Serena on her knees, racked by an uncontrollable cough. He reached for her, his arm winding around a body that was deathly cold to the touch.

Water poured into the cabin from a fatal crack in the hull and the boat began to list astern. In his periphery, Brett noticed his own gun swirling in a whirlpool, and lunged for it.

Simon's boot beat him to it.

Simon loomed, his balding crown slashed with blood, the crimson liquid mingling with saltwater as it spilled in jagged treks down to his ear.

"New plan." Simon announced in a tremulous voice. "This ship isn't going to make it," he coughed. "So I'll just leave you two here and go deal with Morse."

In the glow of the flanking vessel, Simon must have caught Brett's condemning glare. "But I don't trust you," Simon added.

Using his automatic to keep Brett at bay; Simon reached for Serena's arm, startled by the tenacity left in her weak frame. She rooted in place, but lost her foothold on the slick surface, careening into his arms.

Simon clamped down on both the weapon and Serena. With his head cocked, he considered Brett.

"Sorry it had to end this way," he whispered. "She really wasn't too bad for a woman. She just made a poor choice in husbands. And as for you," he said, "well you showed promise, but you were just too damn nosy."

Brett shrugged. He leaned his shoulder against the doorway of the pilot house, dipping his freezing hands into his pockets.

"Your loss." Brett smiled.

In a fluid motion, Brett ripped the plastic eel from his pocket and propelled it with a snap of the wrist, straight at the laceration on the blonde man's head.

Simon recoiled, unsure what had launched at him. His hand soared to protect his face as Brett seized the opportunity and vaulted towards him. He caught Simon by the waist and launched them both out onto the sloping deck.

Simon screamed. Pitched backwards, his hand smacked the fiberglass frame, jolting the gun out of his grip and sweeping it out to sea. Splayed on his back, with Brett's steel-like arm bearing down on his throat, Simon searched the rigging for something to use as a bludgeon.

Listing even further now, the two men skated towards the aft of the ship as Serena struggled upright. The ocean swelled closer, inching further onto the deck as it sought to haul the ship down with its weight.

Inch by inch, the trawler began to wane.

"Serena!"

Serena heard her name and spun around. Bright lights pierced her eyes as a murky silhouette beckoned from the nearby trawler. Fearing this unknown entity and seeing Brett in a struggle for his life, Serena crept towards him, trying to avoid a headlong plunge into the rising water.

For a moment, time seemed suspended. Brett and Simon were lost in the shadows at the far end of the deck, and the ocean stopped its assault long enough to allow her to stand. There was a perverse sense of calm as the screeching gale winds grew faint.

Using the rail for leverage, Serena forced her numb feet to cooperate, and managed a few awkward steps.

Something made her stop. That prickly sensation at the back of her neck—the same paranormal sensation that occurred just before her ghosts arrived.

Under the beacon atop the bordering trawler, Serena traced the arc of light. In horror she watched the surging black wall of water that came straight at them.

Her scream was severed by its impact.

Launched from the deck into the frigid void–suspended in churning darkness for an eternity, Serena surfaced, choking. She squinted against the onslaught of the storm and located the shifting shadows of the trawlers several feet away. She struggled to kick her feet, and flailed her arms to keep above the waves.

Cruelly, Serena's mind flashed to the past. She felt the weight of Alan's hand on her head. Sputtering for breath, she tilted her neck back so that only her face reached the cold night.

Two kicks.

One.

Serena's legs stopped moving.

With a last twitch of strength, her arms fell still.

Giggles.

From the murky depths of the ocean, Serena heard a child laugh. With her limbs motionless, she began to sink and opened her eyes to the black world around her. Beneath the surface, the haunting sounds of merriment were distorted, chaotic, *evil*.

Conscious now only of the cold that stole the last bit of air from her lungs, Serena closed her eyes.

Dimly aware of the hand on her collar, Serena struggled against it, determined not to let Alan's hand be the instrument of her death. The grip was undeterred. It hauled her to the surface, yanking her from the ocean's frigid fist. Barely conscious of being sprawled out on deck, or the tender fingers on her chest, or the worried touch of lips on her mouth, Serena chose hibernation in the shadowed caverns of her mind.

"Breathe honey. You've got to breathe."

It was the voice that infiltrated. Strong. Full of love. A voice that could make the darkness retreat.

Straining, she waited for it to repeat.

"Come back to me," it urged, *"dammit Serena."*

Water shot from her lungs as Serena doubled over in a cough. She swayed onto her side to ease the pressure in her chest and groaned into the icy deck.

In a ragged voice, she managed, "Ss-since y-you asked so n-nice."

Morse struggled to aim the trawler into its slip, but shook his head to the man that stood behind him. Realizing the ocean was not going to cooperate, Brett grabbed the slack of the rope and gauged the distance to the pier. Impatient, he cursed and waited for the breakers to stabilize long enough to attempt a jump. As the boat dipped down, he leapt up, alighting on the frozen wood with a skid and a prayer of thanks.

Once the trawler was secured, Brett turned his attention back to the precious cargo Morse offered up to him.

Gas heating and ample lights increased the temperature inside Harriet's guest room. Brett removed Serena's clothing and took the white terry robe from the shop owner, securing it around Serena. He wrapped a towel about her hair, squeezing the moisture out of the locks.

Wary, Brett reached out and touched Serena's alabaster flesh.

So cold. So deathly cold.

Blue lips trembled, but her eyes remained closed, locking out the world. Locking him out.

Alone with Serena while Harriet searched for brandy and more blankets, Brett quickly shrugged out of his sodden jacket and shirt, and yanked off his frozen boots, impatiently tossing them into the corner. Discounting his soaked jeans, he leaned over Serena's inert profile and clutched her robe tighter. He stroked her cheek and brushed his fingers across the faint pulse in her throat. He felt a steady rhythm.

It was *his* heart that struggled to beat.

Don't take this woman from me.

"Here!" Harriet barked, tossing a pile of blankets at Brett.

Wrapping Serena in a cocoon of downy heat, Brett was troubled by her lack of response. He lifted her to him, tucking her into the shelter of his arms, where he could provide the only warmth he knew how.

"One of them is for you, Murphy." Harriet's face was red from exertion and anxiety. She stooped to drape a thermal cover across Brett's shoulders. "You're shaking too. Take some of this." She handed him a Bugs Bunny jelly glass filled halfway with amber liquid.

Brett reached behind Serena's head to elevate it and touched the rim of the glass to her cold lips, urging her to drink. Serena coughed, recoiled, and finally managed two sips before she choked in a raspy voice. "God that stuff is awful, Harriet."

Sagging against the doorframe, Harriet swiped back her drenched hair and snorted.

"Morse doesn't seem to have a problem with it." To confirm this, she peered around the corner into the living room, and snickered at the sight.

Dark eyes blinked several times and then grew more luminous as they anxiously sought out Brett. "Morse?" Serena mouthed.

"Like it or not, honey, he saved our lives."

"Why?" She struggled to sit up, but Brett's fingers gentled her back against him.

"It's a story we'll share later when you're up to it." His voice was rough. "But maybe the guy isn't so bad after all."

Serena dragged her hand out of its confines so she could touch Brett's chest.

Solid. Real.

A strobe-like image of him immersed beneath a wave made her shudder. Questions assaulted her with the same relentless precision as the rolling ocean.

Harriet slipped from the room, but her brash voice could be heard mingling with the low timbre of Morse's as they debated the scope of the nor'easter.

"Brett?"

Oh God, the pain she detected in Brett's eyes. She wanted to hold him. To reassure him.

Serena's arms dislodged from the blankets to encircle his neck, feeling the cool flesh grow warm beneath her touch.

Forget the blankets, she thought. This was what would thaw them. She hugged Brett even tighter, feeling his arms encircle her and his head dip into the crook of her shoulder.

"Oh, baby." His voice was husky. "I thought I was going to lose you. I didn't know where you were, or if I'd get to you in time," he growled into her neck. "When I went back to the kitchen and you were gone—I should have gone back there sooner. I wanted to. I wanted to say I was sorry—"

Cool lips touched Brett's. He responded more harshly than intended, but the need to feel Serena alive overwhelmed him. Brett took her mouth and infused it with heat, tasting the sea and the sultry tang of brandy. Gentling to a soft kiss, he drew back and brushed his lips against Serena's furrowed brow.

"Sorry?" she whispered. "For what?"

His forehead touched hers. He closed his eyes. "Sorry about the comment about you getting pregnant. I didn't mean to hurt you, I was being selfish. I don't know—" he hesitated, "somehow I thought—if that were the case, you'd stay with me."

Brett opened his eyes again and saw the moisture pooling in Serena's. Her hands reached up to cup his face as she pulled back to look at him in that wholly encompassing way that made him feel exposed to the core.

Then she smiled.

"How are you two doing? Oh, sorry." Cheeks flushed, Harriet bustled over to the nightstand and poured more brandy into the near empty glass.

"Please Harriet, no more." Serena pleaded with a laugh.

Glancing over Harriet's shoulder, Serena frowned and dug her fingers into Brett's arm. With a muffled gasp she acknowledged the brooding figure whose shoulder rested against the doorjamb.

Morse tipped his head. "Feeling better?"

Serena slanted a quick look at Brett and found assurance there. So much so, that she didn't want to leave his face. She wanted to trace the stark jaw, the shadow of his stubble…to bask in the warm eyes that made the winter recede. She wanted to touch his hair—the damp, dark ends that curled up above his ears.

Instead, Serena addressed Morse. "Yes. I—I understand I owe you my life. I-I don't know how to thank you for that."

Morse hefted off the doorframe and snorted, dismissing the gratitude with a wave of his hand. "Hey, I just drove the boat. This guy did all the dirty work. I thought you were both a goner personally, but he somehow managed to disarm Simon—"

Serena's gasp echoed in the tiny room. Recollection flooded as swift and devastating as the sea.

"Oh my God—*Simon*!"

It still staggered her—the look of hatred in the eyes of a man she had known for years. He was going to kill her. *He had killed Alan.* And the gun, it was aimed at Brett, only Brett and Simon both went overboard—

"W-what happened?" Disjointed images had her scrambling to touch Brett, ensuring he was alive.

No more ghosts.

"I saw you both go under," she choked.

"Morse dragged me out of the ocean. He had a handful because I wanted to go back in to find you." Brett cleared his throat. "I couldn't see you. You went under and I was scared to death, and then I saw your hand and I had a hold of your shirt—"

"Simon?" she trembled.

"We circled around, but never found him."

For some reason, Serena felt an overwhelming sense of loss. Simon had murdered her husband and attempted the same with Brett and yet she still mourned him.

Perhaps it was just like Alan, mourning the young man she once knew, and not the creature he had become.

Nodding in mortal acceptance, Serena smiled at the tall figure looming in the doorway. "Stop by O'Flanagans, Morse. The next drink is on me."

"I'll be sure to take you up on that." Morse tipped his head and retreated to the living room.

"You okay, Rena?" The gravity of the night settled on Harriet's face, making the deep laugh lines all the more prevalent.

"Yes. I'm feeling much better." As she said it, Serena truly believed the testimony. Her head rested against Brett's shoulder as his arm tightened around her.

"Umm, Ms. Morgan," Brett spoke, stirring Serena's hair, "I owe you some gratitude—I mean besides the obvious."

Harriet's gray eyebrow arched.

"The five dollar fish bait you sold me," Brett explained, "it came in real handy."

Perplexed, but caught up in his confident grin, Harriet cleared her throat. "That's good." She started to retreat from the room, but halted just outside the doorway.

"Oh, Murphy," she paused. "Call me Harriet."

Silence.

Listening to the groan of heaving boats against the pier it seemed the ferocity of the storm had died down. Serena rested against Brett's bare shoulder, tugging the blanket about him. She touched her lips to his throat and felt his pulse beat.

"When I was underwater," she whispered against that steady rhythm, "I heard a child crying."

A concerned protest sounded on Brett's lips, but she reached up and hushed it with her fingertips. "I realized something, and it's something I'm going to need your help with."

"Anything." His voice was hoarse.

"I want a baby, Brett." Serena lifted her head to meet his eyes. "I want your baby."

Aware of a flash of pain in Brett's eyes, she watched his meditative nod.

"I think I can try and help you with that," he said.

Just the thought warmed Serena from the inside out. *Brett's baby. Brett helping her to make the baby.* Love welled up so much inside her, it bubbled onto her cheeks in thick drops.

Quiet again; content to simply hold him, Serena stroked her fingers across his chest. There was such fascinating diversity between the muscular hills and well sculpted valleys. Brett was as rugged and strong as Victory Cove's mighty cliffs. But unlike those soaring precipices, he gave more than he took.

Glancing at her hand, a sad smile tugged on Serena's mouth. "I must have lost my ring out there."

Brett reached for Serena's fingers, dusting his lips over the knuckles. He took a deep breath and whispered, "I'll get you another one."

Maybe it was not how he had wanted to phrase it, but feeling Serena's body stiffen, Brett cursed his tactless proposal.

"Doesn't it bother you?" Serena looked up at him. "For the past ten years I've been married to your brother. Doesn't that upset you?"

Brett adjusted the mound of blankets so that Serena was securely sheltered. In doing so, he shifted from her side and sat hunched forward with his elbows on his knees, his head clutched in his hands.

Did it bother him?

Sure it did. He'd be inhuman if he admitted otherwise. But knowing Alan as he did enabled Brett to understand what

Serena had been going through for all those years. It gave him insight into her character, and offered a glimpse of what might have been if he had run away with her on that autumn day ten years ago. Yes, he would have loved her. But could he have possibly respected her as much as he did at this moment?

"I'm not going to tell you I want to make a habit of flipping through your wedding album." Sitting up, turning towards the elfin figure gathered in a cloak of cotton, Brett grinned.

"But," he sobered. "I'm not going to deny that I'm in love with you, Serena. Whatever the past was—it was the past."

Tremulous fingers grazed along his temple. They brushed phantomlike over the injury concealed beneath his hair. "I love you, Brett."

He looked at her a long time before he asked, "Is that enough? You sound so sad when you say it."

"It *is* sad how we came together."

When Brett tried to interrupt, Serena's finger swept down to his lips, silencing him.

"But it won't always be," she said. "And I know that I'm not going to bear my grief alone. I know that I have a shoulder to cry on, and I hope for the privilege to offer you that same compassion. So yes, maybe I was sad in the past, but—" she smiled with confidence, "all that matters to me is this moment, and all the millions of moments after it."

Brett's hand linked with Serena's as he brought it to his lips, closing his eyes to the poignant emotions she evoked.

He leaned forward and kissed the corner of her mouth. "Well, let's start with this moment," he murmured, "and make it memorable."

Brett's lips returned for a slow sweep, tasting the smooth trace of brandy on her smile. He cupped Serena's face in both hands and angled in for a deeper sip. He kissed her like he wanted to the first night he met her, and he kissed her with a hunger to make up for the decade they had missed. And only when Brett felt his name expelled from her lips did he draw back.

Somehow, when he listened to Serena say his name, with reverence and love in that brief oath, the rest of the world vanished.

"I love you so damn much," his voice was rough.

Her eyes welled with tears. "What one miraculous thing did I do to deserve you?"

Brett pulled back. Silent for a moment, he finally declared, "You smiled."

Serena's lips curled up in response. "Plenty of women smile at you, Brett."

Dipping down to touch his mouth to hers, Brett whispered, "None of them could ever paralyze me with their eyes."

"Your opinion sounds biased, but I like it."

Again Brett's mouth took Serena's, and again he raised from that kiss enough to declare, "None of them ever tasted like you."

"Do you know what you did to make me fall in love with you?" she asked quietly.

"No. Not in the least."

Earnest in what she wanted to convey, Serena's fingers bit into his forearm. "You chased my ghosts away."

"No, honey," A wrench in his chest nearly made Brett wince. "You did that yourself."

The glow of unshed tears sparkled in Serena's eyes. "Okay," she yielded, "you washed dishes."

Brett laughed.

Serena's smile fell. When she spoke, it was so quiet he had to strain to hear her.

"You kissed me." There was no levity to Serena's tone.

"That night when I heard the baby laughing. When I thought I had finally gone completely mad—" Serena hesitated. "You kissed me. And you didn't stop. You thought I didn't know what was happening. You thought I couldn't feel that." Serena shook her head. "You kissed me until there were no ghosts—" a tear started to slip onto her cheek, "—just you."

Brett drew Serena tighter into his embrace, and dipped his head into her hair, smelling the sea.

"Serena," he choked. "Oh God, what you've been through."

Serena rested her cheek against the warm skin at the curve of Brett's throat. She felt safe. The steady beat of his heart was stabilizing–a constant rhythm that communicated his love for her. Her fingers curled beneath the blanket to touch the sustaining cadence.

"Kiss me again, Brett," she whispered.

Serena tipped her head back to look up at Brett and met those steady gray eyes.

Once she had thought she saw storm clouds churning there.

Now, when Brett smiled, Serena saw the sun rise.

ABOUT THE AUTHOR

Maureen A. Miller is the author of several romantic suspense novels, JUNGLE OF DECEIT, ENDLESS NIGHT and WIDOW'S TALE.

WIDOW'S TALE was nominated by the Romance Writers of America for a Golden Heart Award in the Romantic Suspense category.

Working in the software industry for fifteen years, in a job that required extensive travel. Instead of reading during all those lengthy airport layovers, Maureen chose to write. Escapism at its best. Six novels were produced in those years of travel.

Currently, Maureen is hard at work on, another romantic thriller set in Maine.

For more information on Maureen A. Miller, please visit www.maureenamiller.com

13557223R00151

Made in the USA
Lexington, KY
07 February 2012